Also by Donald E. Carr

DEATH OF THE SWEET WATERS

THE BREATH OF LIFE

THE ETERNAL RETURN

THE SEXES

THE DEADLY FEAST OF LIFE

THE FORGOTTEN SENSES

ENERGY AND THE EARTH MACHINE

THE SKY
IS STILL
FALLING

THE SKY
IS STILL
FALLING

Donald E. Carr

W.W. NORTON & COMPANY • NEW YORK • LONDON

Library of Congress Cataloging in Publication Data

Carr, Donald Eaton, 1903–
   The sky is still falling.

   Includes index.
   1. Air—Pollution. I. Tile.
TD883.C36   1982   363.7'3922   81–14067
ISBN 0–393–01508–4   AACR2
W.W. Norton & Company, Inc. 500 Fifth Avenue, New York, N.Y. 10110
W.W. Norton & Company Ltd. 37 Great Russell Street, London WC1B 3NU

1 2 3 4 5 6 7 8 9 0

TO STEPHEN

Contents

THE SKY
IS STILL
FALLING

1

The Backlash

Man is certainly stark mad.
—Montaigne

If we could by some spiritual alchemy convert all the energy
that has gone into resisting and spitting on the regulations
that came out of the Clean Air Act of 1970, we would have
reinvented the automobile, restored mass transit, made the
United States an ecological paradise, and refined to ecstatic
perfection our sex lives.

It has always been American to gripe at authority—at any
authority. Now, however, we do more than gripe. Terrorism
is on the scene. In Los Angeles a popular pastime is to tear
off the catalytic mufflers designed to gentle the smog. When
the natives out there are not having fist fights and even
gunfights over minor freeway collisions, they are using crowbars to pry apart the gas tank openings of cars designed only
for unleaded gasoline, so they can fill up with fuel containing
lead, thus immediately ruining the exhaust catalysts and
spraying even the mountains with more poison than they can

take. It is impossible to estimate how much this sort of self-inflicted vandalism has damaged the pollution control programs of horribly smogged cities, such as Denver, Los Angeles, Cleveland, Phoenix, Washington, and, worst of all, New York. This thriving form of self-destruction was mostly responsible for the monstrous smog of 1979.

This activist form of backlash is in a sense mere childishness. It is based on the innocent notion (that certainly was once true and may be again) that the Puritans are out there to get us—and the Puritans have taken over the government: the Environmental Protection Agency, the Occupational Safety and Health Administration, the Department of Energy, the Department of Transportation, and all the state and local agencies. The Puritans are trying to get us to give up our cigarettes, as they once took away our beer. They don't want us to drive over fifty-five miles per hour, based on the screwball notion that there is an actual shortage of energy, while everybody knows the shortage is an invention of the oil companies, and of the Puritans (but only in the sense that these Puritans value money even more than austerity).

There have been so many warnings, so many laws, so many paper shufflings that the mass of people is shifting its hideous strength toward the idea of an uncontrolled atmosphere. This is the most dangerous shift of the century. Again it is a peculiarly American shift, because it is barbed with humor, sometimes very irresistibly. Let me give an example penned by the Honorable Andrew Hinshaw (R, California) which appeared in the Congressional Record, October 10, 1974:

GOD & EPA

In the beginning God created Heaven and Earth.

He was then faced with a class action lawsuit for failing to file an Environmental Impact Statement with HEPA (Heavenly Environmental Protective Agency), an angelically staffed agency dedicated to keeping the Universe pollution free.

God was granted a temporary permit for the heavenly portion of the project but was issued a Cease and Desist Order on the earthly part, pending further investigation by HEPA.

Upon completion of the Construction Permit Application and Environmental Impact Statement, God appeared before the HEPA Council to answer questions.

When asked why he began these projects in the first place, he simply replied that he liked to be creative.

This was not considered adequate reasoning and he would be required to substantiate this further.

HEPA was unable to see any practical use for earth since "The earth was void and empty and darkness was upon the face of the deep."

Then God said: "Let there be light."

He should never have brought up this point since one member of the Council was active in the Sierrangel Club and immediately protested, asking "How was the light to be made? Would there be strip mining? What about thermal pollution? Air pollution?" God explained the light would come from a huge ball of fire.

Nobody in the Council really understood this, but it was provisionally accepted assuming (1) There would be no smog or smoke resulting from the ball of fire, (2) A separate burning permit would be required, and (3) Since continuous light would be a waste of energy, it should be dark at least one half of the time.

So God agreed to divide light and darkness and he would call the light Day, and the darkness Night. (The Council expressed no interest with inhouse semantics.)

When asked how the earth would be covered, God said, "Let there be firmament made amidst the waters; and let it divide the waters from the waters."

The ecologically radical Council member accused him of double talk, but the Council tabled action since God would be required first to file for a permit from the ABLM (Angelic Bureau of Management) and further would be required to obtain water permits from appropriate agencies involved.

The Council asked if there would be only water and firmament and God said, "Let the earth bring forth the green herb, and such as may see, and the fruit tree yielding fruit after its kind which may have seen itself upon the earth."

The Council agreed as long as native seed would be used.

About future development God also said: "Let the waters bring forth the creeping creatures having life, and the fowl that may fly over the earth."

Here again the Council took no formal action since this would require approval of the Game and Fish Commission coordinated with the Heavenly Wildlife Federation and Audubongelic Society.

It appeared everything was in order until God stated he wanted to complete the project in six days.

At this time he was advised by the Council that his timing was completely out of the question . . . HEPA would require a minimum of 180 days to review the application and environmental impact statement, then there would be the public hearings.

It would take ten to twelve months before a permit could be granted.

God said, "To Hell with it!"

The Honorable Andrew Hinshaw should have stuck with his antic pen. He was among the Rogues Gallery of congressmen convicted of soliciting bribes during his 1972 election campaign and was sentenced to one to fourteen years in jail. It is really too bad that so many gifted humorists regard even criminal law as a pietistic repression of their rights to the life of an unfettered faun.

Congress theoretically follows, at an elephantine pace, the heavy thunderstorms of public displeasure. The tides and vortices of public sentiment have been immensely magnified and often dictated by television, which indeed is a form of media which *produces* the tides and vortices. Whether the catchwords or the fake ideas come out of Milwaukee bars, Wall Street liquid lunches, or columnists torturing a phrase from a grimacing typewriter, they are potent, mean, and foxy. Some examples:

• Which is dirtier: environmental pollution or vast unemployment? Do you want clean air or a job?

• President Reagan justified the federal bailout of Chrysler on the grounds that it was the federal government that created the problem for Chrysler. "Political pollution" was the trouble. The filthy bureaucrats gave us the seat-belt interlock system, the heavy bumper, and "patchwork pollution-control plumbing." (There is a hopeless confusion of ideas here, unclear to start with. Who was responsible for the patchwork? I know of no case where the EPA or Department of Transportation gave blueprints on an exhaust catalytic converter to Chrysler or to anybody else. As a matter of fact, harmful exhaust gases, such as hydrocarbons and carbon monoxide, were removed, unsuccessfully, by simply adding additional air to the exhaust system. The government, state and federal, set standards of purity; they recommended no plumbing, and actually it is possible to meet the standards by redesigning the engine, not the plumbing.)

• "Let's return to good old Yankee ingenuity." (What is implied is that by getting rid of all the regulations on safety and pollution, the free ozone of creativity would descend upon Detroit and Dearborn and allow them to solve everything. Among the burdens that the automakers especially complain of is the mandated choice between the automatic seat belt and the anticollision air bag. But the air bag is peculiarly an example of "good old Yankee ingenuity." Indeed foreign carmakers, notably Daimler Benz, continue to show interest in the American invention. A 1982 model Mercedes equipped with air bags will be sold in the United States.

• Antienvironmentalists promise a night of the long knives

7

when the Clean Air Act expires in 1981. Muskie had been relied upon to improve the act without spilling blood all over the place. But so fearsome are the growls from the wolves on the Capitol steps that the ordinarily mild Douglas Costle, Administrator of EPA, was inspired to remark: "What they (the industry lobbyists) cannot hope to get at the ballot box, they plan to obtain through judicious use of the check book . . . A gutting of the Clean Air Act is possible . . . Probably at no time since the era of trusts, of watered stock, of 'anything-goes' profiteering, have private interests had such influence in Congress as they do today."

• In the budget what is untouchable? The pork-barrel water projects. What is most expendable? The environmental program. Congress has not been alone. Carter proposed a meat-ax reduction in the Land and Water Conservation Fund used by federal and state resource agencies to acquire parks, forests, wildlife refuges, and recreation lands. With terrifying euphemism Carter proposed "more flexibility" in the federal regulatory approach. All agencies were to use great delicacy, as modeled by the demure minuet of the two-year-old United States Regulatory Council. For example:

1. *Create government-conferred rights that can be traded.*

This is federalese for the damnedest mess imaginable. When you get to "trading rights," you have started a sort of Chinese revolution or Chicago futures exchange run wild.

2. *Make business costs more consistent with social goals.*

If this has any meaning at all, it is a flowery way of recommending that pollution standards be lowered so the manufacturer won't suffer loss of profits.*

---

*The United States steel industry is a notable example of wolverine savagery, although its stupidity insults the animal in the comparison. Steel in its hoarse arguments against environmental control forgot to mention that these laws were turning out to be costly because it refused to comply with them. Nor did it mention that the Japanese steel companies, which have outhustled American firms every-

3. *Replace detailed compliance standards with general performance standards.*

This works into the dangerously popular modern custom of "upgrading"—giving a student a B— for an F performance.

4. *Replace or supplement government compliance and monetary activities with other mechanisms and as supervised self-certification.*

The honor system doesn't work at West Point. Why should it work with a private organization with no incentive for honesty?

5. *Reduce barriers to competition.*

This is theoretically very nice. What actually happens, however, is that you reduce the viability of the small industry. Without antitrust (the most expensive failure in United States history), you have left only one automaker and one airline. The antitrust monkeyshines simply provide a living for thousands of lawyers.

6. *Ensure informed consumer choice.*

What are consumer choices? An immense majority of choices are made through advertising. Does this sentence mean cutting off the head of advertising? This is an absurd idea, since it would simultaneously reduce TV to a home theater priced at the now intolerable level of movies. It would eliminate two gigantic businesses adding up to perhaps a trillion dollars a year. But whatever *choice* is, it is politically holy in another sense. The guys at the Milwaukee bar are vaguely conscious that the government is taking their choice away. As Gus Peth, chairman of the Council on Environmental Quality has warned, what we as environmentalists have most to fear is "the cold-blooded exploitation of such

---

where on the globe (including the United States), are subject to much more stringent pollution restrictions.

fundamental education traits as suspicion of government interference with private choice."

7 *Rely on voluntary standards developed by groups outside government.*

I guess to refute such romantic nonsense we need the cold shower of a powerful woman's words. Eula Bingham, former Chief of the Occupational Health and Safety Administration (OSHA) states that "voluntary compliance is a myth."

8 *Tier or differentiate standards, according to type of firm or product being made.*

This makes sense, if the differential is big enough. Certainly we would not impose the same standards on a diamond-cutting shop as on a coal mine. The trouble with such concepts is that they tend to get gringy as the firms approach in size and function and start to flirt or fight with each other. Does one apply the same standards to oil shale recovery as to the strip mining of coal? This is setting up to be one of the biggest slugfests of the 1980s.

• Senators are on the whole more dangerous to environmentalism than congressmen. A typical opinion is that of Utah's Orrin G. Hatch: "Environmentalists are against everything—period" and the term "safety and health fascists" is popular in his office. A real backlash has emerged in the form of a Senate crunch to water down the strip-mining laws. The Senate of the ninety-sixth Congress has seen environmentalism cease to be a popular crusade and become instead a grim holding action. The more ferocious senators attach their bayonets for the final kill.

• In the House the most ominous trend is to weaken pesticide controls. One could expect the whole country eventually to be a sort of extended Love Canal.

• In the West the antiecology-freak ferocity has surfaced in the Sagebrush Rebellion, a move to switch control of federal land (chunks of immense acreage) to the states and therefore, ultimately, to the logging and mining companies.

• Environmentalists of the more theologically minded sort have made themselves ridiculous, it is true, by insisting on havens for endangered species like the snail-darter fish, the Illinois mud turtle, or the Colorado squawfish. It is true that we are our brothers' keeper, but where does the extrapolation end? Albert Schweitzer refused to stamp on a poisonous ant. Will his followers campaign for the protection not only of the tiger snake and the black widow spider but of the typhus germ? Maybe it's because I'm no longer young, but the spectacle in Boston on Earth Day no longer pleases me—young eco-freaks offering very expensive natural foods and lectures on Tibetan relaxation techniques. And it is plain damn foolishness for the Wyoming Environmental Quality Department to request that a coal company go to the bother of planting sagebrush on the top of a worked-out strip mine even as federal authorities are spraying large areas of the West to eradicate sagebrush.

• Yes, there are fools among us, but wisdom outraces asininity. Marshall McClosky, executive director of the Sierra Club, has shrewdly suggested that the true obstructionists to various projects are not environmentalists but companies that seek to delay or avoid compliance with the law—and are thus responsible themselves for much of the regulatory confusion they complain about.

• The EPA's glowing plans upon its day of creation in 1970 have flickered low indeed, and some mighty stout breaths are needed to brighten the coals. One of the worst defeats has been the defection of once-trusted politicians. Governor Richard D. Lamm of Colorado, formerly an ardent environmentalist, has been devastatingly frank about his own case. Claiming that the environmental movement cannot look to him or other politicians for leadership, he pointed out "Politicians fear impotence even more than defeat." Early in his first term, Lamm recalled, he tried vainly to stop construction of twelve miles of interstate highway in metropolitan Denver—a region with perhaps the third worst air pollution problem in the country. He wanted to shift the funds to mass transit. At this the public outrage was such that government practically came to a standstill. "People were giving me the victory sign—one finger at a time. . . . The civil rights movement, the women's movement, the environmental movement—all these were initiated and led by people outside the political system."

• The EPA accomplishments are so pitifully meager that a sort of wake was held in April 1980 in Estes Park, Colorado, at which it was hoped that some shafts of inspiration would pierce the smog. John Quarles, a friendly retiree from EPA, claimed that the agency was severely overloaded. In nine years of EPA its manpower had doubled while its program responsibilities have multiplied by a factor of twenty. Quarles recited a litany of missed goals:

State Implementation Plans (SIPs), established under the Clean Air Act and representing, so to speak, the registry of action. The EPA works almost entirely through these documents. Revised SIPs, supposed to have been completed in mid-1979, are far from finished.

Pesticide Registration, supposed to have been completed by 1975. That effort has ground to a halt. After eight years only ten active ingredients have been registered.

Toxic Substance Control Act of 1976. After about four years EPA's plans are in a state one could confuse with a drunken kindergarten. The agency has been absolutely overwhelmed by the difficulties of establishing an inventory of existing chemicals. They don't even know how to spell some of them.

Resource Conservation and Recovery Act of 1976, which is supposed to prevent more Love Canals. The EPA is three years behind in activating the necessary regulations. A thousand Love Canals spring up for every one documented in the media.

Thomas Jorly, former assistant administrator, believes the problem is not really one of overload. It has to do with a tendency of polluters to try, through the legal system, to avoid complaince with the law. Again the country's infestation with swarms of lawyers is bringing about a series of crises.*

• Antienvironmentalism can emerge from the ivied walls of academia. Old, bald, and ferocious professors, sure of their tenure, can dismiss the modern environmentalists with unexampled scorn. In his book *Environment, Technology and Health,* Merrill Eisenbud of New York University, sneers at the mere idea of chemical environment as a cause of cancer. The professor's idea of environmental problems are rickety home ladders, improperly maintained autos, and slippery bathtubs. "They may be less exciting scientifically" (falling off a rickety ladder is exciting enough for my taste) "than the presence of DDT in mother's milk or benzopyrene in city air. However, the former are hurting and killing people in great numbers, whereas the hazards of the latter are far less, if they exist at all."

This is the ancient fallacy of antigerm theorists. "What you can't see can't hurt you."

• Of all the antienvironmentalist backlashes the most virulent has been carried out by the coal strip miners, led by the incongruous figure of Governor Jay Rockefeller of West Virginia. The basic thrust of the 1977 strip-mining law is to give the state governments primary responsibility for mining operations *after* their proposed program has been accepted by the Interior Department's Office of Surface Mining (OSM).

---

*Jorly is rather sociological about this. He believes the tendency to search for loopholes is traceable to the Internal Revenue Amendment of 1913. This led to a proliferation of lawyers, trained as "clever semanticists," who interpret the law in such a way to wring from it every advantage for the taxpayer.

Wyoming, Montana, and Texas have had most of their programs approved. The large coal companies are making token gestures to comply with the law even while fighting it in the courts and in Congress.

An industry-supported bill, heavily lobbied by Governor Jay Rockefeller, seeks to further delay compliance and to allow states to comply only with the "intent" of the law and not with the stricter state regulations. The bill (S 1403) passed the Senate in September 1979 but has been effectively blocked in the House by the Interior and Insular Affairs Committee chairman, Morris Udall. The impact of the strip-mining law is being partly offset in Virginia, West Virginia, Kentucky, and Tennessee through the efforts of small mining companies and wildcatters to get state and county governments to provide loopholes and exemptions. West Virginia is allowing operators to scratch off the tops of mountains without any guarantee that the land will be returned to grazing, as the law requires. Virginia is getting around the law (which exempts two-acre plots from red tape) by allowing operators to designate their hauling roads as "public highways" and thus not included in the two-acre rule.

If everybody regards the federals the way the moonshiners of the Sun Belt regarded the "revenooers," there is no hope for stopping the cold arrogance of steel cutting up the fat, pretty land into moonscapes. Jay Rockefeller will continue to get his soiled votes.

In the West the situation is even worse. The coal land is not regarded as pretty. There are no Blue Ridge Mountains. Because of budget shrinkage the Department of Interior plans to cut to the bone the number of OSM inspectors. In Region Five, which covers the entire western United States, the 1982 budget will allow only one OSM inspector. He may disappear some dark night, and then there will be none.

For every Senator like Gary Hart, the Colorado Galahad and defender of pollution control, there are many senators like Hatch, Jackson, and Long, who would obviously like to pin EPA to a pine board and hang it out to dry. And in the more unruly lower body there are men, young and old, who spend an incredible proportion of their time inventing new cusswords for environmentalists.*

There is strong pressure on Congress to castrate the present controls on exhaust poisons, not only from gasoline but from diesel engines, on the grounds that otherwise we cannot compete with the Japanese. There is real irony here. The Japanese have no restrictions on the importation of American cars as such. The only thing they insist upon is that the imported American cars live up to the strict Japanese air pollution standards. Squawking on the part of General Motors and others was so hysterical that one would think Pearl Harbor had happened again. Actually this squawk was more theatrical than realistic, since the California standards (which always had been met) are similar to the Japanese; and at any rate, for price reasons American cars could hardly expect to compete with the Japanese on their home grounds, while losing the same competition at home.

More will be said about the automobile and its reinvention in a later chapter, but there is one aspect of this immense and irrational focus of public demand that deserves to be noted now, since it may take some of the curse off what has been said and will be said here about the barons of industry.

The rush to make small, gas-sipping cars as the result of the OPEC extortions was going ahead at a frantic pace through 1977 and 1978. In the winter and early spring of 1979 acres of small cars were available *but no one was buying them.* Detroit evidently had guessed wrong again. What the public wanted was intermediate and even big cars. The

*Fifteen years ago, after my book *The Breath of Life* came out, I had the honor of being coupled by an oil company public relations executive with the late, great Rachel Carson. Oilmen are not very original or grammatical. He called us both "sons of bitches."

manufacturers went into reverse and started producing again the big Chevrolets, Pontiacs, LTD's, Oldsmobiles, etc. Then suddenly came the complete collapse. A year later you couldn't give away the big cars. Mr. Lee Iacocca, a big-car man—responsible, along with his boss for Ford's falling behind on compacts and subcompacts—was in the depths of a well-paid despair. Immense and unpredictable stampedes like the big-car rush of early 1979 are what give planning committees cerebral hemorrhages.* (The movie and TV industries are built upon gambling on such unpredictable stampedes. Who could guess that an absolute stinker such as *Star Wars* would be the biggest hit of all time? Who could guess that the modest van, looking like a milk delivery truck, would be for the young the most popular car body in the West, if not the entire country?)

So much for the natural American. Much is made of the "good sense" of the public. I confess myself confused. I can only fall back on the conviction that the public has good sense when it agrees with me; otherwise it has no more sense than a school of drunken mackerel.

Pollution is Good for You and the Vegetables Too

Nearly as much money has been spent on fake proofs of the harmlessness of pollutants as on attempts to eliminate them. The big guys don't rely entirely on their own laboratories (although some mysterious giants such as Dow Chemical are exceptions, and strange chemical heresies drift out of its installation in Midland, Michigan, as often as toxic vapors).

---

*As John DeLorean has pointed out in *On a Clear Day You Can See General Motors,* the famous "14th floor" of General Motors didn't have a planning committee. They had daily executive meetings at which nearly everybody enjoyed a good nap, after the morning's arduous paper shuffling. The worst faux pas in these august sessions was to show up in a brown suit. The next worst was to propose some wild idea, like putting out a four-cylinder engine.

Grants, for example, will be given to a professor to test the toxicity of nitrogen oxides on his pupils. Since they do not fall dead on the floor in a semester, the professor's conclusion is that nitrogen oxides are harmless. As we shall show later, this is equivalent to concluding that nerve gas is innocuous because it takes more than ten seconds to kill a human being with a drop of it.

The Argonne National Laboratory and the Tennessee Valley Authority have stoutly maintained that sulfur oxides and nitrogen oxides produced in coal-burning power plants are good for human beings in a very peculiar way. Both the sulfur oxides and the nitrogen oxides act as fertilizer for downwind farmland. They are especially good for soy beans and cotton. This would be fine if farms were run by lungless robots, but the ingredients of what has become known as "acid rain" may shorten the life of human beings. They may not retire to Florida to enjoy the rewards of more bounteous crops. Furthermore, as we shall see in chapter 7, the detrimental effects of wind-carried pollutants are devastating to more important plant organisms than soy beans and cotton.

TVA burns more steam coal than any other organization. And in spite of its federal geneology it has taken to emitting all the snorts and harrumphs that one would expect to hear in the boardroom of a private utility.

In the backlash campaign most big operators don't go so far as to insist that their pollutants increase the health and vigor of people, or animals, or even flowers. They simply deny that they have any effect at all, except perhaps a ghostly and contingent benefit which is the sweetish odor of money. Within the past two decades absolutely irrefutable evidence is at hand to show that, except certain types of smokes, asbestos dust is perhaps the most insidious cause of lung disease known. A most treacherous source of lung cancer was the asbestos sprayed in schoolrooms almost universally from 1946 to 1973, when the federal government barred it.

Up to this time many local building codes *specified* the use of asbestos to protect against school fires. Johns-Manville, the largest asbestos producer, still maintains there is no evidence that sprayed-on asbestos "poses a health hazard to anyone." Even if it did, they intimate, would you rather your child died of cancer twenty years from now or next week from a holocaust?

The Houston Hassle

Houston, a very big city full of money and Texas piss-and-vinegar, has been the site of one of the most elegant and expensive backlash campaigns ever staged. With contributions from some two hundred chemical and oil firms (including Dow, Monsanto, Shell, Du Pont, Celanese, and Gulf*) a multimillion dollar "Houston Area Oxidant Study" was prepared over the course of three years and came out in all glossy glory in August 1979. This is the largest privately financed air pollution survey ever undertaken and was supposed to knock EPA flat as a dime.

The study concludes that the air quality in Houston is good and that the EPA's plans to reduce ozone by controlling the innumerable hydrocarbon emissions from the factories and cars are not relevant to the Houston situation. Houston, it seems, has received a peculiar blessing from God—or perhaps from Oral Roberts. *Its people are immune to ozone.* There are no adverse health effects even at ozone concentrations as high as 0.20 parts per million. (The EPA maximum is 0.12 parts per million.) Where the natives of Denver, Phoenix, or New York are afraid to go out on a high ozone day, the Houstonians are impregnable. They may stagger but they remain reasonably erect while getting their car doors open.

If EPA is villainous and stupid enough to go ahead and

*Chemical Week, August 15, 1979

apply control strategems for nitrogen oxides and hydrocarbons, Houston has a story so pitiful it would melt the heart of even a native of Dallas. EPA's controls would reduce both the 1995 projected output and employment in Houston's chemical industry by 26 percent.

The report recommends that pollution control strategies for Houston and the Texas Gulf Coast be based on predictions from "models developed specifically from this region." These models, presumably, would delineate the great, strapping, smelly metropolis as a sort of Honolulu cleansed by winds through frangipani trees.

All the standardized backlash columnists and media are heartily rooting for Houston in this row, and there seems very little chance of EPA standing firm. James Fitzpatrick refers* to the "latest *mind-boggling* demands that the EPA will place on chemical manufacturers." (This columnist's mind is easily boggled. EPA's very modest attempts to prevent a continuous series of Love Canals would make unnecessary the building of two dozen special lung hospitals.)

"Environmentalist" in many politicians' eyes and in the eyes of their masters has become not only a pejorative but a positively dirty word.

When You're Rich, You're Clean

I am not going to refer in this chapter to the backlash against environmentalism in Europe or South America. One can hardly speak of a backlash when there wasn't a lash in the first place. Save for Japan, very few industrial countries adopted the environmental ethic. Great Britain, though, is perhaps another exception; a good deal of powerful sentimentality has always existed for the plight of animals and London's legendary smog became so intolerable that heroic

*Tulsa Tribune, March 8, 1980

measures were taken to alleviate it.) But I cannot resist the temptation of telling a Canadian story.

International Nickel (Inco) at Sudbury, Ontario, has an enormous smelter with perhaps the highest smokestack (400 meters) in the world. It manages to spread sulfur dioxide and various other goodies not only over all of eastern Canada and northern New England but as far as Iceland and even Scandinavia.

When Inco was asked to cut sulfur dioxide emissions in 1976 it icily informed the government that the cost estimates for installing the necessary equipment had increased from $200 million to $300 million and as a result the project would be dropped, since "a program which is not economically and commercially feasible is not in fact technically feasible."

The meekness with which the provincial government accepted this snooty and disingenuous argument (which later attained international fame and praise through such organs as *Barrons*) can be ascribed to one brutal fact. Inco had a site in Indonesia, where the authorities had never heard of sulfur dioxide. During the time the company was supposed to be installing antipollution devices, Inco enjoyed profits of $1.4 billion. It could have easily afforded the equipment. But that is not the way multinational companies operate.*

When Congress Screws It Up

It is now legally almost impossible to burn coal in power plants in this country without going broke. This is not due to the high cost of meeting EPA's emission standards but to

---

*Since this was written, Inco has seemingly gone through a born-again redemptive process—or the province of Ontario has suddenly become a wildcat. The province's Department of the Environment summarily ordered the company to reduce its 2,500 tons per day of sulfur-dioxide emission to 1,800 tons by 1983. In the meantime Inco's credit position has gone down. Standard and Poor lowered the rating of its commercial paper from A-1 to A-2, triggering an immediate 4 percent dip in stock price. I remember from my childhood: *Cheaters never prosper.*

a kind of war between the states. In the 1977 amendments to the Clean Air Act of 1970, Ohio and Kentucky lawmakers made it impossible to meet emission standards by burning low-sulfur western coal. In order to force middle-western power plants to use high-sulfur coal from their own state, they exempted from control (by scrubbing exhaust) only plants operating on low-sulfur *anthracite* (a specialty coal of low volume found only in the east.) The great gobs of low-sulfur North-Dakota lignite and Montana subbituminous coals were made uncommercial by congressional fiat, along with another lawyer's trick that specified impossibly stringent requirements for new sources of pollution in "non-attainment regions." All of this added up to the nastiest of politics and a strong invitation to backlash.

If they weren't so far apart, North Dakota would probably declare war on Kentucky. As it is, a kind of war is by no means impossible between Pennsylvania and Ohio on the issue of acid rain, which is Ohio's largest single export.* (See chapter 7.)

Dow Chemical's Mystical Doctrines

There is a haunting similarity between the ignorant backlash against environmentalism and the long resistance of people (some sects even now) to the germ theory of infectious disease. Vast complex companies will spend enormous sums to prove the patently absurd.

Dow is the biggest producer of 2, 4, 5-T, the herbicide which gathered ill fame in Vietnam and has been shown to contain as impurity a chemical popularly known as dioxin.

*As tempers become frayed in these nervous inflation years, military exercises between states become conceivable. Not too many years ago the governor of Nebraska threatened a militia action against Iowa because in a typical goof by the Corps of Engineers, a change in the course of the Missouri River had shifted several islands from Nebraska's side of the river to Iowa's.

Dioxin, microgram for microgram, is one of the most toxic substances known. It was responsible for many deaths in Italy and everything we find out about it makes it look meaner. Strange laboratory rituals take place at Midland, Dow's vast city within a city. It seems that for months and years Dow had been trying to prove that dioxin is a by-product of fire—any fire. Dioxin has been with us, according to Dow, as long as men have burned things (now thought to predate the advent of humanoids more modern than *Homo erectus*). The mystic quality of this notion will be appreciated when you realize that dioxin contains chlorine.

The concatenation of chlorine and *all* fire is not even good science fiction. Yet the weird theory was argued at a symposium in all apparent seriousness by a procession of Dow savants.

To top all this, Dow conceived the notion that the federal government was using U-2s, satellites, and just plain reconnaissance airplanes to spy on Dow's Midland reservation. Dow hinted in the darkest terms that the taxpayers were being gouged to allow the United States government to share the company's secrets with its competitors. Such paranoia in large companies is no longer unusual. Dow's physical defense is the same as that of the squid—it lets go with a cloud of ink.

General Motors Proves Diesel Smoke is Wholesome

In another part of Michigan General Motors was engaged in another research project to prove smoke from diesel engines harmless. The money involved in this issue could be astronomical. Although in a later chapter we will delve deeper into the nature of engines and smoke, here is a simplified version of the dilemma:

Under the 1985 deadline, a company's fleet average for fuel consumption must be at least 27.5 miles per gallon. The only sure way to get such a fleet average is to include diesel-engined cars, such as the special Oldsmobile, Mercedes, the Rabbit, and others, which get as high as forty miles per gallon on the road. But the EPA emission standards for 1985 include stiffer carbon monoxide, nitrogen oxide, hydrocarbon, and *smoke* ("particulate matter") limits. *So far nobody has been able to make diesels that meet both the nitrogen oxide and smoke limits.*

The line of reasoning taken by GM is schizophrenic but natural: we can't meet the smoke limit, so smoke must be okay.

The main objection to smoke (and a tremendous one) is its carcinogenicity (cancer-causing capability). Actual carcinogens, such as benzo (a) pyrene, have been extracted from diesel smoke, and the Ames test (a procedure which with amazing accuracy predicts carcinogenicity on the basis of the mutations of standard microorganisms) showed diesel smoke to be ten times more dangerous than gasoline engine smoke. General Motors plodded ahead, using absurdly small doses on laboratory animals and peculiar ways of extracting the smoke particles. When their work was uniformly discredited at a special symposium, they had to resort to an old stall. Decades ago workers in diesel garages in London showed no ill effects. This met only laughter since the London tests had been shelved long ago as hopelessly unscientific.

It turns out that General Motors need not have gone to all that trouble. The steamroller of antienvironmentalism is all warmed up and one can see signs that the atmosphere of the nation's cities will soon be opaque again. The catchword is "You can't take the food from people's mouths to give them a better view of the mountains." This should be paraphrased to "Lung cancer is better than giving up steaks and movies."

There is every expectation that in the campaign to get more coal burned in power plants the "war between the states" will be abolished. In effect, the peace of the dead will descend upon the land because the administration cannot possibly force utilities to put in expensive scrubbing equipment. They will go out of business first (or threaten to go out of business). Of two divergent campaigns—the abolishing of acid rain and the increased use of coal—the latter will come out on top.

The dangerous politics of the antienvironmentalists now identifies antipollution costs as inflationary. This ridiculous notion disappears, as we shall show later, when the reduced cost of medical care is considered in connection with properly policed air.

Choose Your Own Way of Death

Sometimes the backlash has a quality of swinishness reminiscent of the worst excesses of the early industrial revolution. The proprietors of a lead smelter in Idaho took advantage of the extraordinary fact that the EPA did not try to control lead emissions from such smelters until 1978.

Deadwood Gulch, in the town of Smeltersville, Idaho, was once very close to the Bunker Hill smelter. In 1974 there was so much lead poisoning, especially among children, that the company burned down the hundred or so houses of the Gulch and located the workers at a modest distance from the former lead-soaked ground. However, the air and soil are still soaking up lead and the children are still puny. The EPA's attempt to get the state of Idaho to get off its rump was without effect, since the state adopted the company's pigsty theory that it was impossible to distinguish the lead from the smelter from the lead stirred up by cars and trucks using lead-containing gasoline.

One of the many things that lead does is cause irreversible brain damage. On the basis of a brain-damaged child, the

Dennis family of Smeltersville is suing Bunker Hill for $20 million. As is usually the case, money at this level starts bells ringing. The state medical officer, siding with the Bunker Hill company, asserted that unless the people actually *ate* lead, they would remain as healthy as corn-fed heifers.

On the whole the workers disapprove of the Dennis suit. Facing threats to their pocketbooks and the threat to their children's health, they choose to save their pocketbooks. They distrust the "feds" and talk about tying them up in barbed-wire sandwiches and letting them roll out of town.

Bunker Hill threatens to close down if the EPA establishes a blood-level maximum for lead, but the threat is a bit reedy and soprano in view of the skyrocketing price for lead on the commodity market. On the whole the company has a cinch operation. For example, it doesn't worry about fuel prices because it burns by-product sulfur in the smelting operation.

Like dozens of outfits throughout the land, however, it is bristling with eagerness to join any backlash against the trouble-making do-gooders.

Where the Environmentalists Stick Their Necks Out

The me-firsters and the environmentalists are not arranged exactly as Satan's angels were arrayed against those of God on high.

Undoubtedly there has been too much jumping to conclusions concerning all workplace chemicals as sources of all kinds of cancer. As we later proceed through this all-important aspect of the air pollution problem (the basic problem of a "sewer in the sky") we shall try to step very prudently between the known and the merely guessed-at causes of (mainly) lung cancer.

John Higginson, the British authority, founding director of the World Health Organization's International Agency for Research on Cancer, was once something of a firebrand who led many Americans to believe that cancer-causing agents lurk in everything we eat, drink, and breathe. Recently he has denounced that perception as wrong. Or he has changed his mind—or something.

He says, "Now I'm all for cleaning up the air and all for cleaning up trout streams, all for preventing Love Canals, but I don't think we should use the wrong argument for doing so. To make cancer the whipping boy for every environmental evil may prevent effective action when it does matter, as with cigarettes.

"You can't explain when Genoa, a nonindustrial city, has more cancer than Birmingham in the polluted central valley of England. In the United States reports are coming out that there are few differences in cancer patterns between the so-called dirty and clean cities. In fact, the only thing you can say is that air pollution may, and I emphasize MAY, increase cancer in cigarette smokers."

As I shall show later, Higginson seems to be definitely out of date on lung cancer, which has increased in the United States at a far greater rate than expected from cigarette smoking and out of all proportion to other cancers. However, he leaves undiscussed perhaps the most urgent phenomenon with which the last decade has familiarized us—its extraordinarily high incidence of delayed cancer and delayed bronchitis. I myself am suffering from chronic bronchitis caused by cigarette smoking which I gave up fifteen years ago—but too late. As an American antidote for Higginson's premature euphoria, we shall look into a much excoriated book by Samuel Epstein of the University of Illinois School of Public Health, whose *The Politics of Cancer* infuriated the antienvironmentalists. The Occupational Safety and Health Administration (OSHA) in the Department of Labor maintains there is a "massive but silent slaughter" of 100,000 Americans who die each year from exposure to materials in the workplace. (As we know, OSHA people will be the first to be lynched.)

The whole matter of cancer and life-style is a sack of snakes. Why do the Japanese have a lot of stomach cancer but no cancer of the prostate? Why do the Danes have a much higher incidence of colon cancer than the Finns, who in turn have the worst incidence of heart disease on the planet?

These subtleties are negligible in face of the massive fact that the American antienvironmentalists are fixing to set us back a hundred years. They are going to make lung cancer in this country as common as a cold in the head.

2

But the Facts Won't Go Away

If there is one grain of plausibility, it is a
poison.

—Margaret Fuller

The Worst Air Pollution Disaster

I imagine most of us would define the next world catastrophe
in terms of an exchange of nuclear bombs or perhaps of
gigantic mutual squirts of nerve gas. But the worst catastrophe has already happened. It was air pollution on an unimaginable scale. It wiped out all sizable land animals and all sea
animals of any bulk. More important, it came very close to
ending life on earth completely by destroying the photosyn-
thetic plankton responsible for supplying most of the oxygen
upon which all but a few microorganisms (anaerobic) depend
for life itself.

Luckily for us, it happened sixty-five million years ago at
the end of the Cretaceous Period. Not so luckily, as a para-
digm for the future (a future that may be the day after
tomorrow or a billion years from now) it is now almost
certain that the cause of this monstrous contamination was
a collision with an asteroid—an object perhaps six miles in

diameter, which wandered away from the vast horde of its brothers loosely orbiting the sun between Mars and Jupiter.

All kinds of explanations had previously been advanced for the great mass extinction at the end of the Cretaceous, but this one has solid evidence behind it. Luis Alvarez, the Nobel laureate physicist from the Lawrence Berkeley Laboratory, and his son, Walter, a Berkeley geologist, found curiously large enrichments of the element iridium in Denmark, Italy, and New Zealand, all in deposits sixty-five million years old. Now iridium is a bashful element and rather heavy. In the formation of the earth, most of it gravitated inward to the mantle or even to the core. We find little of it in the surface of the moon. But in a body such as an asteroid, where internal gravity is too puny to separate the heavy from the light elements, iridium is found everywhere.

When the asteroid hit the earth, it blew up with such a titanic scattering of small particles of matter (the first smog) that the sun was hidden for many decades. Pieces of iridium-rich dust fell everywhere; probably all of it will never be detected. A little larger collision—a longer period of darkness—might indeed have terminated Earth's story. It was touch and go if any life would survive. Shortly after the extinction, a single-celled plant form known as *Thoracosphaero* became the dominant life form in the world's seas. Its reign was geologically brief, because remnants of more formidable life emerged from the deep seas, where they had taken refuge during the darkness. The seas suddenly were full of sharks and other hungry and interesting things.

The asteroid collision theory explains the frightening swiftness of the mass killing. In the 600-million years of fossil record we can read the record of six major mass obliterations. Were they all caused by clumsy asteroids? Kenneth A. Hsü of the Geological Institute in Zurich thinks that many extinctions, including the Cretaceous, may have been caused by collision, not with asteroids but with comets, most of which fell in the ocean. A comet the size of Haley's (about ten trillion tons) would fit the bill. Such comets are thought to be solid bodies containing large amounts of carbon dioxide, carbon monoxide, and about 10 percent cyanide. A Haley-size comet would contain enough cyanide to give the ocean a concentration of 0.3 parts per million—definitely lethal. By Hsü's model the plants and animals of the Cretaceous period would have been killed in three ways: large land animals by atmospheric heating; marine organisms by cyanide poisoning; and calcareous marine plankton by increased amounts of carbon dioxide distorting the carbonate equilibrium.

Until comets are found to contain iridium this theory has no more validity than science fiction. However, the Alvarez hypothesis also has a few holes. There is too much iridium in Denmark and in the recently discovered deposits in Spain. The concentrations are so discrepantly high, compared with the Italian and New Zealand finds, that only a much bigger asteroid or a terrestrial iridium concentration process of some kind could explain them.

The NASA project to explore Haley's comet by rocket, recently dismissed as expensively vague in objective, would now seem to be concerned with matters of some little importance—such as the future of the earth.

Are We Heating Up or Cooling Down?

The effect of slow but mighty swings in the chemistry of the earth has lately become a popular theme of futurists, because it's so democratic. If the earth becomes another fiery desert, like Venus, only astronauts who flee to Mars or the moon or Io or Titan will escape from being roasted like the fat pigs we are. The so-called greenhouse effect, which consists of an earth whose atmosphere accepts radiation but fails to reflect it, is simulated by a future condition in which carbon dioxide, which does not allow heat radiation to escape, has increased in concentration manyfold.

When you burn coal, you come up with a lot more carbon dioxide than when you burn petroleum, because coal is mostly carbon. When people in the billions are burning anything carbonaceous, the effect on the giant shoulders of the earth is to make them quiver. Since man has had fire, he has become a much worse nuisance to the world than a numberless swarm of soldier ants to a rhinocerous.

The atmospheric concentration of carbon dioxide is now 330 parts per million, about 45 parts per million higher than the estimated preindustrial value. However, there is some mystery about where all the carbon dioxide went that should be in the air, if the calculated amount of burning has taken place.

The cutting and burning of forests, especially in the Amazon valley, is supposed to be a major source of carbon dioxide, but that only makes the budget more cockeyed. Dissolving carbon dioxide in the ocean cannot account for the discrepancy. One acceptable conclusion is that the regrowth of previously cut forests and the enhancement of forest growth precisely because of the increased carbon dioxide in the atmosphere* have roughly balanced the rate of forest destruction during the past few decades.

Some optimists have argued that when you burn high-carbon fuel, like wood or coal, you usually produce a splendid plume of smoke, and that this smoke might have a cooling effect on the atmosphere. This is not necessarily so. It might even have an additional warming effect. If the smoke

---

*Experimentally it has been shown that producing plants in an enhanced carbon dioxide content yields bigger and better crops.

particles are floating over dark things like forests and the particles themselves are light-colored, then they would reflect back solar energy and make us cool. If the particles are drifting over a snowfield, they would make the earth look darker and absorb more energy, thus warming us up. The extraordinary private corporation at Boulder, Colorado, the National Center for Atmospheric Research (NCAR) is working on such global problems. From their data on the size and distribution of smoke particles, NCAR scientists conclude that the overall smoke effect is likely to be warming, thus accelerating rather than slowing down our progress in becoming another hell-like planet such as Venus.

One should avoid the common, mistaken idea that the radical changes men make in the weather are confined to the present, the recent past, or the unhappy future. Carl Sagan and his colleagues have shown how *Homo erectus,* possessing fire, raised so much hell that the change in albedo (surface brightness) of the earth must have been quite evident to observant sentinels from outer space a half million or so years ago.

Some (but not many) of the environmental changes may have been partly due to natural causes. At the end of the last ice age 10,000 years ago, forests may have been changed to grassland almost over night. The Great Plains may once have been an enormous forest, if not an inland sea.

The remains of *Homo erectus* are clearly associated with the residues of fire in sites dated 500,000 years ago. Pre-agricultural people not only caused accidental fires but used fires as a tool to hunt and to wage war.* Indirectly, they caused the formation of deserts. Mostly by means of fire

---

*In 1520 when Magellan passed through the straits that bear his name, he saw so many fires set by primitive natives that he named the region Tierra del Fuego (land of fire).

about 60 percent of central Europe has been converted from forest to farmland during the last one thousand years. The formation of deserts and cleared land, greatly increasing the albedo, more than compensated for carbon dioxide. It made the earth cooler. There is a remote possibility that man will proceed to reclaim rather than form deserts. If so, the albedo increase is only a temporary respite in an inexorable road to oblivion by baking.

If we flatter ourselves that so-called syn-fuels made from coal or shale are going to take the curse off the carbon dioxide problem, we are deluding ourselves. As Roger Revelle and other specialists have shown, the production and consumption of synthetic fuel from coal will release more carbon dioxide than from coal itself.

What will a modest but appreciable increase in carbon dioxide do to us? T.M.L. Wigley and colleagues of the University of East Anglia start out by assuming that all causes of warming broadly cause some change in world climate. Doubling the carbon dioxide content will raise the global mean temperature by about four degrees centigrade. This increase is very uneven, however. The mean temperature increase in the northern hemisphere, for example, will be only 0.6° C. A maximum warming is predicted for high latitudes and continental interiors, including much of North America. Regions such as Japan and much of India may warm less the mean. Unfortunately, rainfall will desert many agriculturally important regions, including our Middle West, Europe, and the USSR, but world-wide the rain will increase 5 percent. We may be buying wheat from India.

With the tremendous shift to coal burning that has been urged on us since the oil crisis, such climate changes could come to pass within the decade of the 1980s. What would follow eventually would be even more noteworthy. In addition to hordes of unhappy farmers, we would have, as the tremendous volume of antarctic ice melted, total drowning out of all coastal cities everywhere on earth. Not only Venice would disappear. New York, for example, would consist of a few isolated peaks of tall buildings with boats scudding between them, probably looking for loot on the upper floors.

The Scandal of Lead

Instructions for separating lead from silver ore can be found in the Old Testament. There is a clear description of lead colic symptoms by the Greek poet-physician, Nicander, in the second century B.C. Pliny learned of the hazards of imbibing lead but, at the same time in his usual slaphappy way, touted the virtues of leaden wine kegs. The Romans mined silver ore for coinage and used the by-product lead for wine vessels and for their plumbing systems. Some historians attribute the curious madness and perversions of the Roman ruling class to lead from wine and water.

Our own popular exhortation "Take the lead out!" unfortunately refers to the heaviness of lead rather than its toxicity.

An utterly preposterous but absolutely true story is represented by the revelations of a gifted chemical scold, Dr. Clair C. Patterson of Caltech. Patterson, helped by platoons of colleagues and assistants, finds that (either due to dirty hands, empty heads, or conspiracy) the concentrations of lead in materials supposedly nearly free of lead have been underreported by literally thousands of analysts—and not by a decimal point but by a thousandfold or more.

The economic and health issues involved are exceedingly important. For one thing they involve the whole canning industry. The mistakes made may have caused the illness and even death of a veritable army of people who are fond of canned tuna.

In this case the mistakes of analysts were in testing the tuna before canning. If the difference before and after canning, with lead solder, is small, the Food and Drug Administration is inclined to shrug its shoulders. Eating canned tuna, the FDA claims, doesn't get much more lead into you than eating cooked tuna fresh from of the sea.

However, as Clair Patterson has proved, the fact is that lead-solder-canned tuna contains at least 4000 times as much lead as the fresh fish. The decline in the quality of analysts is caused, according to the indignant Caltech experts, by what amounts to analyzing with one dirty thumb—a failure to recognize that the choice of meaningful samples is a challenging research problem that can't be dealt with merely by expensive instruments that reduce sample size and increase data output.

A typical case ocurred in 1978 when the Caltech laboratory found that the National Marine Fisheries Service Laboratory in Maryland had made a whopping mistake in analyzing lead in tuna muscle while studying lead in seafood on behalf of the FDA.* It reported an average lead concentration of 0.9 parts per million in fresh tuna muscle and 0.7 parts per million in canned tuna. Caltech's laboratory discovered that the Fisheries Service Laboratory had put the parts per million for fresh tuna too high *by a factor of 1000.* This error reinforced the belief held by FDA that cans soldered with lead elevate the lead levels only minimally.

This was not an isolated incident. The laboratory mentioned is one of hundreds that analyze lead contents incorrectly. I wonder what the canning industry would do if all the analysts were suddenly as meticulous as the Caltech team.

*Patterson and Settle, "Lead in Albacore: Guide to Lead Pollution in Americans," *Science,* March 14, 1980.

Patterson and his co-workers have checked many lead analyses of plant and animal material made by laboratories using the conventional, rapid methods. In virtually every case serious errors were found. Nearly all of the thousands of analyses of lead concentrations in plants, animals, and sediments reported by the Bureau of Land Management are wrong. All of the many analyses of lead in the old stemwood of trees are high by a factor of 1000. Despite over forty years of study and measurements of lead in open ocean waters, all previous analysis of lead in such waters are wrong—most by three orders of magnitude. We are in the grip of a sort of Heisenberg Uncertainty Principle. God fudged.

Comparison of the Caltech estimated values for the concentration of lead in surface sea water of the prehistoric northern Pacific with the present-day value shows that lead contamination, originating mainly from leaded gasoline exhausts, has elevated lead levels by a factor of ten in these waters.

There is a 40,000-fold difference between the lead concentration present in prehistoric albacore muscle and in tuna packed in lead-soldered cans.

What does the canning industry propose to do about this? Go on using lead solder, that's what. The industry doesn't accept the Caltech information.

The response of the Food and Drug Administration to Patterson was more unexpected. One anticipates that canneries will go through the usual pitiful writhings of the crucified capitalist, but a government agency is supposed to maintain some impartiality. However, Ms. Kathryn Mehaffey of the FDA indignantly maintained that banning all lead-soldered canned food would deprive the lower segment of the population of "nutritionally adequate" diets.*

All people in cities and towns in North America today breathe air containing 500 to 10,000 milligrams of lead per

*Chemical and Engineering News, June 23, 1980

cubic meter. The Environmental Protection Agency has recommended a maximum permissible level of 1500. Direct measurements and estimates from mass inventories suggest that the concentration of lead in remote regions is about 10 milligrams per cubic meter. These concentrations are about 100 to 10,000 times higher than the natural concentration of lead in continental air that biochemists believe prevailed in prehistoric times.

A common belief is that the natural concentration of lead in rivers and lakes ranges from one to ten nanograms (billionths of a gram) per gram. This estimate is wrong because most analytical methods for lead in water are too insensitive and the control of contamination during sample collection and analysis has been clownishly inadequate. The amount of lead in the upper ten meters of the Greenland ice cap was about ten tons in prehistoric times. Today the top ten meters contains 4000 tons of industrial lead.

The published estimates of the lead in biomass* are wrong because of erroneous data; thus the extent of industrial pollution of the biosphere is not well understood. Years of accumulation of lead on bark and leaf surfaces has raised the average lead content of trees about tenfold above natural levels in North America.

Patterson's estimate of average amounts of lead in nanograms absorbed in the blood of adult humans is of interest:

Source	Prehistoric	Contemporary urban America
Air	0.2	6,400
Water	less than 2	1,500
Food	less than 210	27,000
Total	less than 210	29,000

---

*Biomass is a term for any piece of material once living.

A lead concentration of 500 nanograms per gram in the American diet is, because of additions from the atmospheric input, equivalent to about 700 nanograms per gram in the diet of people breathing pure air. (In other words, the amount of lead breathed added to that eaten is equivalent to eating 700 nanograms.) A dietary intake of lead at this level will, within four years, double the lead burden of the body. It will raise the blood lead to 650 nanograms per gram and the urinary lead to 900. This borders on the urinary lead-excretion levels of industrial workers who have chemical lead poisoning.

There can be no doubt that the exposure of Americans to industrial lead is several orders of magnitude greater than God designed humans to bear. As the sharp-tongued Clair Patterson again and again emphasizes, nobody recognizes this because nobody knows whether to trust the data. Reagents, nutrients, glassware, controls used in biochemical laboratories are highly contaminated with industrial lead, simply because it is everywhere, and proper precautions are not taken. The professional analysts (always a lower class in the chemical hierarchy) are too lackadaisical to do a good day's job—possibly because of chronic lead poisoning.

Contemporary levels of lead in biochemical systems in cells are so excessive for most Americans that probably numerous perturbations of cellular processes are being caused by excess lead. Since divalent lead masquerades as calcium, biochemical reactions involving calcium are the most likely to be out of order.

Rather than monitor lead exposure by blood lead concentration, in what may be a highly zonked-up biochemical system, the Caltech team suggests it might be better to monitor lead exposures by shift in distribution of lead from the plasma to the red cells.

The Caltech team complains that the 10,000-fold lead pollution factor in tuna packed in lead-soldered cans is largely ignored not only by the FDA, EPA, the National Bureau of Standards but even by Ralph Nader's Public Citizen's Health Research Group. Regulatory agencies must understand that an unrecognized form of lead poisoning may be affecting most Americans and a major part of the world's population.

Lead-soldered cans should be eliminated because they constitute a major source of lead in foods. Half the lead in the American diet originates from lead-soldered cans, since the containers contaminate their contents about tenfold, and canned foods comprise about 30 percent of the American diet.

Another rather mystifying source of lead contamination occurs in the processes of commercial drying and pulverizing. This matter cries for immediate investigation because the American diet contains a significant portion of materials that have gone through a drying and grinding routine.

The experimental task of growing organisms in ultraclean conditions is an obvious research approach, but Patterson et al. doubt that it should be entrusted to investigative persons who cannot even correctly determine the lead content of water.

What does lead do to you, besides making you a poor chemist? Max L. Fogel of the Eastern Pennsylvania Psychiatric Institute has found that ghetto children who eat lead paint off peeling walls first become irritable, show poor muscle coordination, and may graduate to severe brain damage, seizures, and death. Newer studies show that children who have never eaten lead paint but are exposed to constant smaller doses from auto exhaust fumes can absorb enough lead to impair their performance on tests of hand-eye coordination, intelligence, and reasoning.

A multidisciplinary team, composed of Fogel together

with an anthropologist, a biochemist, and a social psychologist, set out to determine the effect of lead on a group of otherwise healthy Philadelphia children. They used a sophisticated technique that takes advantage of the fact that lead from the bloodstream tends to accumulate in the dentine layers of the teeth. When they compared lead levels in the dentine with intelligence scores, they found that children with lowered lead levels had an average IQ of 97, while those with highest lead levels had an average IQ of 80.

God didn't design the brain for protection against lead. Unlike most heavy metals, lead can break through the blood-brain barrier. In the brain the lead may interfere with the synthesis or breakdown of neurotransmitters (chemicals that carry the nerve messages.)

Lead is not the only pollutant that can drive you up the wall. Psychiatrists of the University of Texas Medical School have found that carbon monoxide and nitrogen dioxide may aggravate alcoholism, brain-tissue malfunction, and certain mental illnesses. Near St. Louis over a period of 149 days during the summer and fall, they recorded mean levels of carbon monoxide, nitrogen dioxide, and nitric oxide, then compared the readings with emergency room visits and patient admissions at the Malcolm Bliss Mental Health Center, a city psychiatric hospital. Eventually they monitored over 8000 patients. On days when carbon monoxide increased, so did the daily emergency room visits and hospital admissions. For patients with a broad range of disorders, including alcoholism and brain malfunction, nitrogen dioxide appeared in high concentration.

The surprise was nitric oxide. It seemed actually to exert a protective effect. When concentrations of nitric oxide increased, the number of patient admissions diminished. Nitric oxide can specifically protect individuals from the damaging biological effects of nitrogen dioxide. It is the blessed redeemer. Since the two are almost always present at the same time, straight nitrogen dioxide without the counteracting effect of nitric oxide may be worse than we thought. It may be the real villain in photochemical smog.

Roadway dust is not only a good source of lead but of toxic metals such as chromium, manganese, nickel, and zinc. Urban dusts are worse than rural dusts. It has been established that auto exhaust particles are the main contributors of lead to roadway dusts and that they also do their share in adding lead to dusts collected in the vicinity of buildings having lead-painted trim and situated some distance from a roadway.

How closely are lead and cancer connected? Perhaps because of the immense snow job perpetrated by the Ethyl Corporation and Du Pont, the question has only recently come up. Hans Kang and Peter Infante of OSHA and Joseph Carra of EPA noted that in the case of lead-electrode battery plant workers the number of excess deaths from lung cancer was noteworthy. They also showed that in the test tube lead will favor malignant cell transformation. It has been shown to be carcinogenic to some experimental laboratory animals.

I am worried about something more subtle and far-reaching than cancer. I am worried about lead contamination as a chemical factor in the undesirable lowering of intelligence and of productivity—in general the drop in psychic energy —of the American people as a whole. Professor James L. Sandmeier of UCLA has strongly supported the theory that the fall of Rome was caused by the new-fangled habit of using lead oxide to prevent wine from souring. I see no objection to Professor Sandmeier's thesis. Lead poisoning— chronic plumbism—may be responsible for the decline and fall of the United States of America.

3

Under the Shadow
of the Big C

Cancer is like a dog that whines at your door.
—Proverb

That the public doesn't get the facts on extremely important matters and that certain companies, even states, thrive on products obviously carcinogenic is proved by the fact that people continue to smoke cigarettes. Not even the connection between sexual intercourse and childbearing has been demonstrated more convincingly than the connection between lung cancer and smoking. Since corporate people and their political lackeys continue to keep up the pretense that there is little harm in cigarettes, are we not justified in assuming that they, and people like them, will try to make freely available *anything* noxious and profitable? The answer is obvious. They *are* trying. When you see arguments against the likelihood of cancer in the workplace and cancer in the fumes of commerce, always bear in mind the tobacco billionaires. They are getting away with the greatest con in history. And their methods are models for imitation.

When bland editorials in the rightist press assure you that cancer is on the decline and when sophists such as John Higginson point to Genoa as a seat of cancer and Birmingham as relatively cancer-free, ask what the facts are. What kind of cancer is in Genoa? By using cancer in this broad sense you miss some weird facts.

For example, cancer of the mouth, almost absent in the western world,* is extraordinarily common in southeast Asia. Why is this? Very simple. The Asiatics chew a cocoa-like plant all the working day. They get a mild whizz out of it and are more than willing to take the risk of an agonizing death. When life is really not worth much, one gets consolation from whatever vices one can afford.

Since it scares the liver and lights out of me, I want to take time to document the fact that, contrary to the views only a year ago of Philip Handler, John Higginson, Pollyanna, and the American Cancer Society, the shadow of the Big C in our country is fast deepening, an ominous thundercloud.

The rocket blast that cast a blinding new light on the United States cancer scene was a paper by Earl Pollock and John Horm, statisticians of the National Cancer Institute, published obscurely in the journal of that body during the summer of 1980. In effect, the figures show that the rate of cancer in the United States recently began to rise for the first time in thirty-five years—and to rise with terrifying acceleration. The authors worked with data from the Institute's surveys of cancer incidence from 1969 to 1971 and from 1973 to 1976. Much to the chagrin of the official medical soothsayers, they found a 9 percent increase in all cancers among white males and 14 percent among white females. Previous

---

*Recently a fantastic type of mouth cancer has begun to be prevelant in California, from the act of siphoning gasoline from one tank to another. This is known as the "midnight credit card."

data, collected by the same agency and by the same sampling technique, had shown that up to the 1970s the incidence of cancer was stable or perhaps slightly declining. The new data show that cancer is *very rapidly increasing.*

Is this all due to smoking? Dr. Marvin Schneiderman, an experienced epidemiologist and former director of science policy at the Cancer Institute, showed that less than one-half the increase is due to cigarettes. He was the first to challenge the sainted Higginson and such formidable honchos as Philip Handler, president of the National Academy of Science, who had pooh-poohed the idea that industrial chemicals or emissions were seriously carcinogenic. The cancer rates that have jumped ahead include those of the respiratory tract, bladder, kidneys, liver, and melanoma, lymphoma, and multiple myeloma. Schneiderman subtracted the effect of smoking on lung cancer and of sunlight on skin cancer. Finally, he established that the cancer rate increase for the so-called occupationally related cancers over the seven-year period was 25 percent in both white males and white females—considerably higher than the increase over the same period for all cancers combined.

It should be mentioned that Dr. Handler wrote a gentlemanly letter in effect apologizing for his overoptimism, but the chemical industry has been notably silent, as have defenders of industrial exposure, such as Higginson.

With some degree of pathos, the National Cancer Institute has expressed the hope that these horribly convincing figures will swing the pendulum of public opinion back from its present position of antiregulation toward *more* regulation.

The Incredible Story of Asbestos

Asbestos represents an even clearer-cut example of simple, political evil than does tobacco.

Prior to World War II there were files and files of evidence (all locked up) pointing to the dangers of exposing human lungs to asbestos dust. In fact, Henry Johns, one of the founders of the Johns-Manville Corporation, the biggest supplier in the United States, is said to have died of "asbestosis." This fact is still suppressed. The Germans were sufficiently aware of the hazard of asbestos even before the 1930s to pay compensation claims to workers who had been exposed to the dust and were suffering from one or more of the hideous lung diseases it can cause. World medical literature during the 1930s was full of clinical descriptions of asbestos induced diseases. Yet during and after World War II, we as a nation continued to use the dangerous stuff in shipbuilding and other war industries *with no warnings or controls whatsoever.* A recently released study for the Occupational Safety and Health Administration shows that about two million asbestos-cancer deaths will take place during the next thirty years as a result of exposures that have already occurred. (Asbestos cancer has an unusually prolonged latency period.) That means about 30,000 deaths per year from now until the year 2010—more than the combined death rate from all automobile, airplane, ship, and railroad accidents.

In the proposed "white lung" program the asbestos manufacturers continue to claim that asbestos cancer occurs only when the worker is a cigarette smoker.* Although admittedly the two are worse than one alone, asbestos alone is sufficient, as has been vigorously proved beyond any doubt. The asbestos manufacturers have also tried to get the government involved in paying the gigantic bill for treatment of asbestos inhalance. A federal court in Norfolk has made the

*One of the most ferocious asbestos defenders is John McKinney, president of Johns Manville. He contends in the *Wall Street Journal,* June 30, 1980, that OSHA and other government agencies consist entirely of disgusting clowns, and that goes for the media too. Asbestos never hurt a flea.

rather special ruling that the companies alone must compensate those who contracted the disease in a naval shipyard. If that ruling is broadened and followed by other courts, the asbestos companies will rue that day in the far past when they decided to keep the files locked. As might be expected, the companies have threatened to move their plants to Taiwan or Mexico, where OSHA can't corner them. This, however, would not eliminate the danger to the public, which comes from the product, not alone from the production.

Let me be a little clinical. Asbestosis is a progressive lung fibrosis, easily mistaken for emphysema. Mesothelioma is a cancer of the *lining* of the chest and abdomen and was very common among workers exposed to high levels of asbestos dust during the 1930s and 1940s. It is 100 percent fatal. Then there is lung cancer itself. The choler of John McKinney of Johns-Manville is understandable, since his company, among others, is being sued by victims and their families and the awards are getting bigger.

Quite recently a possible cure for some types of asbestos cancer has been discovered by B. T. Mossman and colleagues of the University of Vermont College of Medicine. This cure employs retinyl methyl ether, a substance very similar in structure to vitamin A.

Dr. Irving J. Selikoff of Mt. Sinai School of Medicine in New York, probably the foremost expert on asbestos diseases in the world, is quite gloomy about the future. Despite years of medical warnings, media scares, school educational programs, and other measures, the accursed material is still in abundant use in the United States and will, according to Dr. Selikoff, account for half a million deaths by the end of the century.

Over 700,000 tons of asbestos per year is still being used in the United States, chiefly in cement pipe, brake linings, paper products, and textiles. The fibers can be found everywhere you look: in schools, homes, office buildings, cars, on the streets, in the air, in gigantic sewer systems, in the waters of Lake Superior. Quite recently its use in some hair blow-dryers touched off a public health scare that had the curious effect of women buying *more* such dryers. They accepted the publicity but were indifferent to the medical scare. The asbestos-filled device was finally pulled off the market.

Dr. Selikoff says he doesn't believe there is any "safe" level of exposure to asbestos. One fiber in one cell is enough to start the dreadful cavalcade of cancer. The only way to eliminate the disease is to eliminate the use of the material.

Cancer from the Sky

It has been known for many decades that the ozone layer in the stratosphere protects us against skin cancer and a number of other insults. It does this by absorbing the powerful ultraviolet rays from the sun. Probably in the early days of the planet the formation of the ozone layer made possible the evolution of complex land creatures, such as human beings, who otherwise would have found it more convenient to lead their lives in the deep sea, protected against the arrows of high-frequency light. (Water in thin layers is no protection, which is why you can get sunburned on a cloudy day.)

The high ozone doesn't have many things to react with except the ultraviolet rays. However, it has recently been realized by two photochemists, F. Sherwood Rowland and Mario Molina, at the University of California at Irvine (not far from that luxury seaside resort, Newport Beach) that certain chemicals which the world produces in high volume can make their way to the ozone layer and start destroying ozone molecules at a fearful rate. The chlorofluorocarbons (Freons), invented by Du Pont and used in enormous quantities as aerosol propellants for hair sprays, deodorants, refrigerants, sponge plastic blowing agents, etc., could not have been more perfectly designed as attackers of our protective fort of ozone. If an alien from that cosmic suburb we now call "outer space" had spent his time in his celestial research laboratory figuring out a subtle way to destroy mankind, he surely would have come up with the chlorofluorocarbons.

In the first place they are remarkably stable in the lower atmosphere. They last at least thirty years, much longer than other potential destroyers of the ozone layer, such as nitrous oxide, which comes off fertilized fields.

Although the Rowland-Molina effect was at first poohpoohed, especially by Du Pont, everything we have found out since adds muscle and fright to the stratosphere battle of the millennium. The National Academy of Science has made several reports which over the past four years have not only increasingly backed the reality of the Rowland-Molina effect, but have induced more drops of cold sweat.

The chemistry involved is an example of free radical chain reactions, which I'm afraid would bore the average reader, but the main scenario is that a single chlorine atom knocked out of the Freon molecule by ultraviolet light can destroy a very large number of ozone molecules. The inability of a large portion of the public to understand the problem is illustrated by the widespread notion that it was the underarm deodorant spray itself that contained the harmful chemical ozone.

This is not going to help much, since the other countries, notably Great Britain, refuse to accept the Rowland-Molina effect (although Sweden is showing signs of agreeing). In the world as a whole Freon propellants are being used increasingly with very little regard for the growing danger of melanoma (a fatal form of skin cancer). The superconservatism of some European scientists may derive from the fact that the theory came out of Irvine, California. If it had emerged from

Cambridge or Sheffield, everybody would be properly terrified.*

There are some unanswered questions about the present rate of ozone destruction, but one main point should be stressed. The calculated chain reactions, being born of light and taking place at great altitude, are incredibly fast. They are not like the muddy reactions which occur at ground level to the accompaniment of human coughs and aerosols of human mucus and coal smoke.

Whatever is going to happen up there is going to happen before the end of the century and the results will be plain. One sure thing is a frightful worldwide increase (perhaps 40 percent) in skin cancer. Certain crops, very sensitive to hard light, such as tomatoes, corn, and sugar beets, may virtually disappear before the century's end. Certain fishes, especially mackerel and anchovies, which are peculiarly affected by hard ultraviolet light in their larval form, may disappear from the seas forever. This is true also of crabs and lobsters. Increased frequency of cataracts among the old people will be accompanied by the mysterious cancer eye syndrome in cattle.

Although scientists, at least American ones, are more or less united on the spray-can theory, there have been excursions here and there. At one time the Concorde Supersonic airplane was believed to produce enough nitrogen oxide in the atmosphere to knock out a lot of ozone. The present consensus is that the supersonic liners produce more ozone than they destroy.

Volcanoes, some of which belch large amounts of hydrochloric acid, have been under suspicion, but the chemistry is

*In spite of the fact that the University of California and Caltech complex alone has more Nobel-laureate-class scientists than any other state or country, it is still fashionable to turn up one's nose at findings that come from California (especially the southern end) and this is true of Ivy League Americans as well as Europeans.

not very compelling. Hydrochloric acid can certainly be blown up to the stratosphere by any strong-lunged volcano, but it is so reactive it might not float long enough to undergo decomposition by ultraviolet rays. There is no certainty about the stratospheric harmlessness of volcanoes, and a more complete analysis of the Mount Saint Helen's eruption may change our attitudes overnight. If hydrochloric acid is an ozone-destroyer, we should be more worried about another source of this chemical in the rocket exhausts from the space shuttle—the astronautic vehicle that NASA has finally launched and recovered after ten years of agonizing and postponing. The projected fifty flights a year would dump some 5500 tons of hydrochloric acid in the stratosphere.

NASA managed to keep this fact below the horizon of the news. Alternate rocket engines that did not emit hydrochloric acid were under somewhat nonchalant scrutiny because at the time the role of chlorine atoms as ozone-destruction chain carriers was known to only a few people who, being chemists, were considered a bit mad by NASA engineers.

Ultimately in July 1977 NASA released a revised draft environmental impact statement for the shuttle. It stated that sixty shuttle launches a year would result in ozone reductions in the Northern Hemisphere of about 0.2 percent. This seemed remarkably pusillanimous; the possible error in the calculation is enormous. I believe NASA has reacted with some degree of dishonesty in the whole matter and has behaved with dissembling secrecy rather than scientific scruple.

Another agent of ozone-layer-destruction comes from outer space. Recent reconsideration of the mysterious Siberian explosion of 1908 focus on the assumption that it was caused by a large meteor which exploded before it hit the earth. The nitrogen oxides, generated when the meteor crashed at thirty miles per second into the stratosphere and giving birth to far-reaching waves of several thousand degrees temperature, are calculated to have reduced the ozone concentration by 45 percent. There is some proof of the connection between the 1908 explosion and ozone depletion. In 1909 the Smithsonian Astrophysical Laboratory was measuring the special distribution of sunlight at Mt. Wilson, California. Their records revealed a distinct ozone depletion continuing through 1911. For years the night skies were brilliant and glowing because of a combination of dust-scattered sunlight and luminescent nitric oxide emissions.

If one big meteor can raise such hell with the stratosphere, what if some gigantic arm started throwing cosmic beanballs at us every week or every day?

In fairness to another ozone scare story which appears to have exerted more fright in the United Kingdom than anywhere else, I mention the notion of J. F. Lovelock in his superscholarly book *Gaia: A New Look at Life on Earth.* Lovelock is thoroughly worried about the proposals for large-scale farming of kelp, which he regards as considerably more malignant than spray cans. In its mysterious and rapid growth processes, kelp produces methyl chloride—a chemical which could ascend straight to the stratosphere and engage in bloody conflict with ozone, after the manner of the chlorofluorocarbons. Don't start a kelp farm, he pleads, for the love of Man!

Ozone as Destroyer

Close to the ground, ozone is no longer our protector.

Most of the rationale of the EPA and state regulations about nitrogen oxides and hydrocarbons is based on the fact that photochemically they combine in complicated ways to produce oxidants of which ozone is by far the most important. We have been stimulating ourselves so long with ozone alerts that people who should know better have assumed in some subconscious fashion that ozone is just a symbol. It doesn't do anything but set off the alert buzzer. After a smoggy day there are no body counts.

Ozone no longer rates even the "Mr. Yech!" logo, a green monster that started in Pittsburgh where to the native child the skull and crossbones means his favorite baseball team, the Pirates, rather than a poison. It took some air travel incidents to show once again that ozone is not just the smell of high voltage electric discharges.

When the price of jet fuel went so high that most airlines teetered on the edge of bankruptcy, the long fliers, such as the B-747 sp's from New York to Tokyo tried to save fuel by flying abnormally high at 50,000 feet or more. During the spring of the same year the pattern of ozone around the Northern Hemisphere changed somewhat, and ozone plumes were known to descend to 40,000 feet.

Suddenly flight attendants began to have all the symptoms of an impending coronary attack. They could hardly breathe and they coughed themselves sick. Eventually it affected the passengers and even the pilots, who for obvious reasons are the last to admit any symptoms remotely suggestive of heart disease. The hostesses were not shy; they never are. And after all there is a lot more breathing involved in lugging food and drink up and down the aisles for hours than sitting in one's seat asleep or drousing through a movie. Thus the hostesses had to breathe a lot more air. After months of imbecilic uncertainty on the part of the airlines, it finally occurred to some bright office boy that what they were breathing was air plus ozone. Analysis showed that in some cases the ozone content of the big cabins was running as much as twice the level stipulated for an alert in Los Angeles or Phoenix.

Even then the airline officials, until faced with lawsuits from sick passengers, thought it would all blow over, and it was many months until charcoal beds or catalytic inlets for the air sucked in from outside were installed on some fleets to decompose the poison. Even now not all the high-flying passenger planes have been protected from ozone poisoning.

These cases of ozone illness at 45,000 feet to and from Tokyo had the wholesome effect of emphasizing to the public that ozone was not just a poetic word for superfresh air but was a toxin among hundreds of other toxins in polluted atmospheres.

Ozone is formed at ground level by a number of processes hitherto unexpected; we shall mention a few. First, what is the possibility that the total ground level ozone is due to invasion from the stratosphere? In other words, is all our blood and sweat to cut down urban pollution a mere expensive diddling while the stuff is falling from above on swooping jet streams?

Jack Fishman of the National Center for Atmospheric Research in Boulder, Colorado, and Wolfgang Seiler of the Max Planck Institute, Mainz, West Germany, have collaborated on studying the world's ozone budget. The theory of ozone being brought down from the stratosphere doesn't account for even a small part of the amount of ozone actually observed worldwide. Furthermore, it doesn't explain why there's a lot more ozone in the Northern than in the Southern Hemisphere. As the result of research flights over remote ocean areas, Fishman and Seiler reached a strange conclusion: most of the excess ozone is being produced by the oxidation of carbon monoxide by the radical OH in the presence of nitric oxide. This reaction had been thought to occur only in polluted areas. On the contrary, it is a lonely oceanic perversion.

Ozone, as might be expected, is associated in a rather grand but mystifying manner with weather. The NASA Nimbus 7 monitoring satellites came up with some extraordi-

53

nary analyses. At higher latitudes there are wave structures of ozone that fit in with the atmospheric circulation. The beginning of northern winds can be predicted from ozone waves. An ozone "minimum" crossing the United States can be seen as a black cloud over the Midwest and this corresponded, in late November, to the onset of winter weather on the East Coast. A few days after the wave the first major snowfall of late 1978 occurred.

Small weather disturbances, which might be missed by ground-based meteorological soundings, can be detected by their effects on the ozone concentration. "Ozonology" in effect may revolutionize weather prediction.

In the study of ozone formation from typically smoggy atmospheres, one recent leader is Professor James Pitts, Jr. of the Statewide Air Pollution Research Center of the University of California at Riverside. His large smog chamber and spectrometric analysis technique are world famous and have been imitated by the Japanese.

One of his discoveries, contrary to EPA theory, was that the formation of ozone by exposing hydrocarbon-nitrogen-oxide atmospheres to sunlight is not limited, as formerly thought, by low temperature. EPA limits of ozone of 0.12 parts per million can be exceeded in a few hours even at subfreezing temperatures.

Pitts also has emphasized the great importance of the free radical OH in reactors leading to ozone formation. This perky radical first runs riot among hydrocarbon emissions, setting up chain reactions which result in nitric oxide being converted to nitrogen dioxide. The latter, a villain on its own, is essential in ozone formation in city atmospheres.

What health hazard tests do we have in addition to the informal ones on the poor flight attendants, most of whom after all were healthy young women? There is growing evidence that ozone, even in very small concentrations, is a sort of all-purpose allergen. It causes asthma and greatly worsens the condition of a chronic asthmatic. It may be enough, indeed, to kill him. Quantitative tests along this line are continuing at the University of California Medical School at San Francisco.

What is poorly understood is the long-time effect of ozone. Does it cause delayed cancer? Pan American Airways settled out of court on suits brought by two stewardesses, one who had developed bronchitis and the other asthma.

But ozone is known to be a mutagen; that is, it can cause profound cellular changes, including changes in the blood and in the germ cells. It is known statistically that airline stewardesses have unusually high rates of miscarriage and their children are often born with defects. They have a long time to nurse their grudges, since the Air Transport Association recently informed the Federal Aviation Administration that the complete conversion to ozone-removal equipment would take six years.

Vinyl Chloride

By 1972 Cesare Meltori of the Bologna Cancer Institute had shown that vinyl chloride, a reactive chemical that polymerizes to form possibly the most popular and versatile plastic of modern times—PVC, or polyvinyl chloride—is carcinogenic. Vinyl chloride as such is a potent air pollutant, causing liver and lung cancer, but residues of it remaining in the solid plastic may also be dangerous. In spite of massive industry lobbying, OSHA stood firm on a maximum one part per million environmental standard, which was passed in 1975.* The vinyl chloride lung cancers were mainly of the type,

*In carcinogens it is now agreed that there is no such thing as a threshold below which nothing happens. Arbitrary limits, such as one part per million, are advanced in order not to put large businesses on the rocks. With all carcinogens for which data are available, the curve of carcinogenicity v. concentration goes through the

adenocarcinoma, not associated with smoking. They were found in a wide range of vinyl chloride/polyvinylchloride operations. Animal tests of the type carried out by Meltori could have been done thirty years ago, but they weren't. "Meat-wrapper's asthma" is well recognized among supermarkets and wholesale meat workplaces, where the employees in packaging cuts of meat use a hot wire to cut and seal the sheet of Saran wrap or the PVC films used for wrapping. Saran wrap, a product of Dow Chemical, is actually a copolymer of vinyl chloride and vinylidene chloride, which has recently been shown to be carcinogenic in rodents, causing angiosarcinoma of the liver.

Using an aerosol propellant hair spray, customers breathed vinyl vapors in the 100 to 400 parts per million range. After much hassling, FDA banned the use of vinyl chloride in all cosmetics, including hair spray (Clairol).

Had vinyl chloride only induced lung cancer and not the peculiar liver cancer, its danger would either have remained unrecognized or its effects would have been ascribed to smoking.

Bis chloro methyl ether (Rohm and Haas) has recently been shown to have much the same carcinogenic effects as vinyl chlorides. It has been discovered, moreover, that this compound can be formed spontaneously in reaction mixtures containing hydrochloric acid and formaldehyde. This places many thousands of workers in danger of exposure to bis chloro methyl ether. For example, many textile workers use formaldehyde in making permanent press fabrics, which are then treated with an acid wash.

---

origin. In other words, there is no threshold. The Delaney Amendment, which simply states that any material which causes harm in any laboratory animal cannot be sold to humans, says nothing about thresholds. In cancer the Delaney doctrine is correct. From that basis the argument concerns only risk versus cost.

Benzene

The National Institute of Occupational Safety and Health (NIOSH) estimates that about two million workers are now exposed to benzene. The shocker is that invincible evidence shows benzene to cause aplastic anemia. This may be cured, but up to twenty years later the victim develops leukemia.

The scare is multiplied by the fact that benzene is often added to gasoline to boost the octane number. About thirty-three million people are thus intermittently exposed to benzene through the use of self-service pumps. Reports from Lund, Sweden, where benzene is more commonly used in motor fuel than in the United States, indicate a high incidence of acute leukemia in gasoline pump attendants. A recent study by Peter Infante of NIOSH involved the investigation of 748 men who had been exposed to benzene from 1940 through 1949 at the Akron and St. Mary's plants of Goodyear, while engaged in the manufacture of pliofilm, a film cast from natural rubber dissolved in benzene. The risk of these workers dying from leukemia was calculated to be about ten times that of the general population.

Benzene is definitely weird in one respect. It seems to have little or no effect on laboratory animals and is negative in the Ames test, which measures mutagenicity. The benzene defenders were put in a peculiarly awkward position. For years most of the industries under the gun had been claiming that toxicity in a laboratory animal did not prove toxicity in a God-fearing human being. Now they were forced to argue that benzene could not hurt human beings, although the epidemiology proved it could, because "human experience had not been validated in animal experiments."

Shell Chemical Company chided EPA for failing to differentiate between a carcinogen and a "leukemogen"—surely an exercise in diaphanous semantics.

OSHA proposed for benzene first a limitation to ten parts per million, then revised this down to one part per million. By this time a new organization, the American Industrial Health Council, was spawned from the Manufacturing Chemists Association, to fight court attempts by OSHA to develop generic standards for carcinogens in the workplace. The first test came in the Fifth Court of Appeals (New Orleans), a body invincibly hostile to environmentalists. The court said "no" to the one part per million proposed on the grounds, not very subtly stated, that it would cost too much. When the issue reached the Supreme Court, its noble hearts could not, of course, be stirred by monetary issues, but it threw the whole matter back into the pre-Delaney-amendment stage. It decided that OSHA had no proof then that ten parts per million was toxic. Why, then, should one part per million be snatched out of thin air? There the matter stands.

Cancer from Small Particles

By far the most worrisome carcinogens are contained in "particulate matter" of smokelike consistency. This hazard has revolutionized the way we look at air pollution. Instead of ozone, nitric oxides, and carbon monoxide, we now recognize that by far the most dangerous urban condition is smoke of a particular kind. Unless the smokes are proved innocent, a smoky city is a place of death.

Part of the agony of this problem is we don't know exactly what we're talking about. For instance, the so-called piggyback theory says that it's not so much the particles themselves—dust, soot, smoke—that do the damage but heavy carcinogenic metals, such as arsenic, zinc, lead, and nickel, that ride into the deepest grottoes of the lung on the surface of the superfine particles.

When scientists get together to discuss whether or not

there is a sort of epidemic of environmental cancer, they start nagging each other. In respect to OSHA's famous statement on the silent slaughter of 100,000 Americans from exposure to workplace carcinogens, Bruce Karsh, Du Pont's medical director, said the 100,000 figure is "an excellent example of highly questionable mathematical adroitness that adds to the striking deterioration in tone and substance of the dialogue over occupational health." (translation: "Your figures are phony and you talk nonsense.")

In the case of auto engines a new measuring instrument has made it possible to measure smoke particle emissions continuously, rather than laboriously filtering them out on a screen. The technique makes use of the photoacoustic effect discovered by Alexander Graham Bell but not of practical use until the development of lasers. If a laser light beam is directed into a cell containing particles, the particles absorb the laser light, heating up in the process. If the beam is rapidly modulated, the particles heat and cool, simultaneously heating and cooling the surrounding air. The resulting increases and decreases of pressure are picked up by a sensitive microphone and its associated electronics.

Ford put this ingenious process to work in demonstrating that Mercedes diesels produce about forty-eight times as much soot as the Ford Cougar Proco.* The Mercedes people were not as impressed with the new technique as some of the bystanders, notably Ford shills.

The problem of particles is one of aerosols—suspensions of finally divided materials of whatever chemistry. Unfortunately, the art of disposing of smokes from industrial stacks and vehicles is very elusive. The Cottrell electrostatic precipitators were at one time thought to be the final answer.

---

*A new stratified charge engine somewhat similar in operation to the Hondas. In a later chapter we shall explain "stratified charge" engines.

Says J. Charles Wilson of the University of Minnesota: "Everybody's precipitating and scrubbing and the baseballs no longer get out."

Still getting out, however, are the particles less than one micron in diameter (a micron is a millionth of a meter). And a curious but discouraging fact is that aerosols of the so-called nuclear mode—generally less than 0.1 micron in diameter—are often generated photochemically, beyond the reach of the bag filters or precipitators. A still smaller aggregation of molecules, called molecular clusters, may play a critical role in the beginning of the nucleation process. But they are less than fifty Angstrom units in size and contain only about a thousand molecules.

While the very small particles reach the pulmonary depths and stay there, the larger particles are collected in the upper respiratory tract, removed by microciliary action, and *swallowed.* They can cause other types of disease, especially if they contain lead. Indeed, it has occurred to me that the extraordinarily high incidence of stomach cancer among the Japanese may have something to do with the absorption and swallowing of an unusual amount of these intermediate particles.

While we talk glibly of particles, we unconsciously assume they are like tiny billiard balls—as in early kinetic theory the physicists assumed that atoms were perfect little polished spheres. Nothing could be further from the hairy truth. Even the smallest particle may have a sort of biological structure like a spider. The vocabulary used by the experts so far does not extend beyond "straight" and "twigged." The time is rapidly approaching when we must be able to say something more interesting, such as "this particle looks like he had a beard and might throw a bomb" or "this particle looks like Marlon Brando."

More important than describing the photogenic qualities of a soot particle is finding out what's in or on it and where it came from. This, suddenly, has become a crucial branch of analytical chemistry. Jaklevic et al. at Lawrence Berkeley have performed automatic X-ray fluorescence analyses for about twenty elements in 34,000 samples of soot or smoke. The elements were selected to identify the particles with the sources: for example, a particle with a lot of arsenic on it is from the combustion of coal. (Such a particle is practically 100 percent certain to be carcinogenic; arsenic in any form has a firmly established reputation for cancer induction.) Vanadium shows the source to be petroleum, calcium comes from limestone, zinc from trashcan refuse, lead from motor vehicles, aluminum and iron from coal and soil, manganese from soil or steel plants. Measurement of the Carbon-14 content can distinguish between fossil carbon and biomass. Such an analysis showed, for instance, that the soot in the atmosphere of Portland, Oregon, is almost entirely from the burning of wood.

Let us return to diesel soot. On the average the mists of carbon particles from diesel exhaust measure less than 0.5 micron in diameter. The EPA estimates that a fleet of uncontrolled diesels equivalent to about 17 percent of the estimated 1990 total auto population would produce some 280,000 tons of particulate matter annually.

Professor William G. Thilly of MIT is one of those who insists with vigor that diesel soot is mutagenic to human cells. He attributes the genetic changes seen in human blood cells to alkyl anthracenes, a member of the clan of polyaromatic ring compounds found originally in coal tar. Early in 1980 General Motors said it had discovered that polyaromatic ring compounds apparently help soot to form in the first place. The company appealed to the refining industry to develop a special diesel fuel containing as few such compounds as possible.

Now this is perfectly conceivable by a simple process involving extraction with liquid sulfur dioxide. With diesel fuel already at a dollar per gallon such a refining step would add enough cost to price diesel fuel considerably above gasoline. And theoretically there is more gasoline available from a barrel of crude oil by simple processing such as catalytic cracking than there is diesel fuel. We would find ourselves in the paradoxical position of paying more per mile with diesel cars than with gasoline cars.

The big problem is that these extremely fine particles tend to float in the air for hours or even days, especially in urban canyons. Over a period of several months, a real swing to diesels of the type now on the market (Oldsmobile, Mercedes, Cadillac Seville, Volkswagen Rabbit, and Peugeot) would drape a deep gray haze over cities like New York.

When the EPA released its proposed regulations for particulate emissions early in 1979, it was evident they were horse trading in the dark. Some autos would have met the standard proposed for the 1981 model year (0.6 grams per mile) with no trouble while others could have done so barely or not at all. But none knew how to meet the standards proposed for 1983 (0.2 grams per mile).

The standards are toughest to meet in the big cars. A 5.7-liter Oldsmobile V-8 diesel puts out over one gram per mile; a 3-liter Mercedes 0.8 grams; a 1.5-liter Volkswagen Rabbit less than 0.25 grams.

The problem of meeting these standards was complicated by justifiable new standards already laid down for nitrogen oxide emissions. By 1981 nitrogen oxides were to fall from two grams per mile to one gram. The only practical way of getting nitrogen oxides down to one gram in a diesel is by recirculating some proportion of exhaust gas back into the engine. *But exhaust gas recirculation sharply increases the production of particulates.* Even Volkswagen admitted it saw no hope of meeting both nitrogen oxide and particulate standards in 1983.

As we have predicted in the first chapter, in spite of the protestations of such men as Hart and Muskie these standards will be steamrollered. The federal government has an immense yen to increase fuel mileage, and dieselization is the only way to get a real quantum jump. Whatever interferes with dieselization, even in California, will be tossed out the window.

The medical situation is not rosy. Recent studies show that the lung cancer mortality rate among nonsmokers has risen significantly since 1935. It is no longer acceptable to subtract any fixed proportion of lung cancer from the total and call it due to smoking. Let us grant that we do not have a lung cancer epidemic, if that is too abrasive a term. But even if we don't, this proves little or nothing, for a very good reason:

The enormous proliferation of chemicals in the air (some of which are certainly carcinogenic) during the last ten years means that the delayed reaction from exposure to these carcinogens will not be scheduled until the 1990s or later. Because we ourselves are not dying of lung cancer caused by a gigantic smear of chemicals (there are some 23,000 chemical compounds in diesel exhaust alone) has no relevance to the health of our children or grandchildren, or even to our own health twenty years from now.

The chemical industry has grown exponentially since the late 1930s and early 1940s. The production levels of synthetic organic chemicals have doubled every seven years and the total production is now over 175 billion pounds per year. The EPA lists 44,000 chemicals in common use. It has been reported at one time or another that 1500 of the approximately 7000 chemicals tested are carcinogenic.

It is interesting to trace the production histories of benzene, perchlorethylene, vinyl chloride, acrylonitrile, chloroform, carbon tetrachloride and trichlorethylene. These are known to be carcinogenic. *But widespread and high-level human exposure to these substances has taken place only since the 1960s.* Even if these chemicals have had only a small effect on the current overall cancer rate, they may still have a very large effect on the future cancer rate.

This is where John Higginson fails to qualify as a perspicacious observer. He forgot the asbestos story. In considering environmental cancer we are watching only a peak of the great iceberg unless we continually bear in mind that *environmental cancer is slow but sure.* Don't ever overlook the question of latency, even in yourself. The wild oats you once sowed may be a thirty-year-old crop.

In the Panzerkrieg process that one can see ahead (for example in the virtual omission of nitrogen oxide standards in diesel exhausts) one cannot fail to discern the very ominous effect of momentum. Even if the particulate emission standards are nominally reduced, waiving the nitrogen oxide requirement will allow a deeper penetration of the market by diesels because of lower production costs. The result will be a veritable flood of diesels. The total amount of diesel soot is then bound to increase exponentially. We will be drowned in gray dust after a few years. In twenty years there will not be enough hospitals to accommodate the wretches whose lungs have been chewed out by soot carcinogens.

Tobacco

We don't intend to report the whole classic horror story of cigarettes. However, there are certain aspects of smoking that have been attacked so far only in dentists' and doctors' offices, carrying signs saying, "Thank you for not smoking." This means sitting next to a guy who says "Mind if I smoke?" In one sense the passive smoker gets the worst of it. He gets the unfiltered smoke.

A study of the University of California at San Francisco followed a report in 1979 from Beth Israel Hospital in New

York and Harvard in Boston that found poorer lung function in the children of parents who smoke. When exposed to the fumes from somebody else's Marlboro or Salem the tubes and sacs that make up the small airways become scarred. In the passive smokers in the study at least 10 percent of their tubes and sacs were injured. Many of the patients looked like refugees from a bad apartment house fire.

The conclusion was that nonsmokers who work in the same office with smokers receive the same bombardment of the small airways as if they themselves had smoked about eleven cigarettes a day, often more than the smoking companion had consumed.

I am not so annoyed as I once was at the little old lady who gets up in the restaurant and waves her umbrella ferociously at tables where smoke is billowing.

A new chill of fear surrounds cigarette smoke and possibly explains most of its cancer-forming properties. This is the relatively high concentration of chemicals known as nitrosamines, which is now the most fashionable way to die of cancer, and will be discussed below.

There are some peculiar anomalies about smoking. A high degree of correlation is shown between the present shockingly high lung cancer mortality rate in nineteen different countries and their per capita cigarette consumption *thirty years ago.* Three countries fail to fit the curve: France, Japan, and Ireland.

The lung cancer rate in France is the lowest of the western world, yet cigarette consumption is among the highest. The answer is probably that French smokers inhale less than, say, Americans. But why? The reason is that the French prefer Gauloises, made with a black variety of tobacco rather than the blond Burley blends of American cigarettes. Black tobacco smoke is highly alkaline while blond smoke is acid. The nicotine from alkaline smoke is much more rapidly absorbed through the mouth and tongue, allowing the smoker of French cigarettes to satisfy the craving for nicotine without inhaling. The Japanese get by with the same habit. The custom of *Kazami* involves puffing without inhaling. The case of Ireland is unexplained, but whoever expected the Irish to conform to anyone's curve?

It is pretty well established that there has been a decline in cancer rates in Great Britain since the Clean Air Program was started in the mid-1950s. From 1947 to 1970 in the United States increases in lung cancer rates of 10 to 20 percent have occurred which can't be accounted for by smoking. This seems to mean that causes of lung cancer exist in the United States which are absent from Great Britain.

On the other hand, tobacco smoking does not affect merely the lungs. In addition to the well-recognized effect on coronary conditions, it causes cancer of the lip, tongue, mouth, larynx, pharynx, esophagus, bladder, pancreas, and probably the kidneys and liver. The well-known medical statistician, Dr. Joseph Berkson of the Mayo Clinic protested: "I find it quite incredible that smoking should cause all of these diseases."

The tobacco makers, on the other hand, don't admit that tobacco smoking causes *any* disease. If tobacco were prohibited, the states of North Carolina and Kentucky would promptly secede from the Union. Tobacco would compete with marijuana for leadership in the drug traffic.

Jimmy Carter remained aloof while his Health, Education, and Welfare Secretary Califano, who called cigarette smoking "slow motion suicide," was stuffed down the tube under orders from the tobacco lobbyists. It is not clear how Carter was able to inhale enough political expediency and, at the same time, keep his conscience viable, while promising to lend federal support to tobacco growers on this theory that such assistance and the health dangers of tobacco are "separate issues." This is like giving an alcoholic a case of Vodka on the excuse that Christmas is coming. *Conservatively estimated, 300,000 American deaths per year are attributable to tobacco.* If these had been casualties of a war, an immense public outcry would have brought the troops home.

As things stand there has never been a successful court case against a tobacco company for causing the death of a heavy smoker. Cigarette ads have been taken off TV, but along with them have disappeared the strong antismoking commercials. Furthermore, since cigarette advertising has shifted to the newspapers and magazines, there has been a strange editorial silence in print, with the exception of propaganda emanating from the tobacco people. Their Madison Avenue slaves are always thinking up new theories and putting them in the mouths of unknown (and possibly nonexistent) professors. The latest whizbang is the genetic caper. This claims that some people, predestined by their genes to get cancer, are also by nature predisposed to smoke. In other words, *cancer causes smoking.*

As a footnote, it should be noted that filtered, low-tar cigarettes may well have increased the danger of lung cancer. This is because in order to get the same nicotine rush the smoker puffs faster, inhales more deeply, and gets through a larger quantity of tobacco per day.

Nitrosamines

In its slow and often staggering run the Environmental Protection Agency has succeeded in officially designating as hazardous (causing cancer) only seven pollutants: arsenic, asbestos, beryllium, mercury, vinyl chloride, benzene, and radioactive substances. There are thousands more that deserve the label, and among the most important are the nitrosamines.

Nitrosamines, proved to be powerful carcinogens by experimental animal tests, are formed whenever an amine, which may be a fragment of a protein molecule, reacts with a nitrogen oxide, nitrous acid, or molecules containing the nitrite group.

As is so often the case, the nitrosamine story began to develop quickly, once a reliable analytical tool was devised. The Thermal Energy Analyzer, invented by the Thermo Electron Cancer Research Center at Waltham, Massachusetts, is capable of analyzing for nitrosamines below the parts-per-billion level.

Of about 130 nitrosamines so far tested, 80 percent are carcinogenic in more than 20 different animal species and no species has been found to be resistant. The lowest level of dimethyl-nitrosamine so far tested in rodents and found to be carcinogenic was 50 micrograms per kilogram (or about 5 parts per billion), which is equivalent to an entire lifetime dose of less than 30 milligrams.

Aside from one source, so unexpected that we shall mention it last, tobacco smoke contains the most deadly nitrosamines. Nicotine itself is an amine and can react with the nitrogen oxides present in the smoke. The "side-smoke" that the passive smoker unwillingly inhales contains more nitrosamines than that inhaled by the active smoker. It is quite possible that nitrosamines are primarily responsible for the lung cancer caused by smoking.

Since time immemorial, nitrate has been used to preserve and cure meat. Early European cave paintings show the use of saltpeter for this purpose by Cro-Magnon man. The typical pink-red color of cured meat is due to the reaction of nitrite (reduced from the nitrate) with myoglobulin, a muscle protein related to hemoglobin, to form reddish derivatives. Here we have a double, maybe a triple dilemma. Is the risk of long-delayed cancer from the meat treatment more than the risk of botulism? Furthermore, are the nitrites or nitrates themselves carcinogenic? There is some lingering doubt about this, but most people would take the carcinogenic gamble rather than the botulism.

Nitrosamines have been deliberately used in many cutting oils and in the processing of rubber. The smell of the inside of a new car is the smell of dimethylnitrosamine from rubber coating applications. It is a deceptively pleasing odor but will doubtless be replaced by "Charlie."

During one short period beer and even Scotch whiskey were believed to be contaminated with nitrosamines because amine-containing malt was exposed to smoke which included nitrogen oxides. In this country only one popular beer, Coors, used an indirect method for heating the malt and could therefore brag it was the only brew in the bars that wouldn't cause cancer. With commendable agility all domestic and foreign brewers either promptly changed their malt cooking process or treated the beer with sulfur dioxide, a process known as "sulfuring." Although Scotch whiskey is still under a whiff of suspicion, the "peat smoke" taste of Scotch would be eliminated if the malt were heated indirectly, and one can hardly imagine such a lordly beverage being submitted to sulfuring.

Many common, over-the-counter and prescription drugs contain amine groups which can be nitrosated in the stomach to produce high levels of nitrosamines. Some examples: chlorpromazone, methadone, disulfiram (ant abuse), aminopyrine, and phenmetrazin.

Much worse is the cosmetic situation. It may be that beauticians, as suggested by recent studies, have more cancer, particularly in the lung and bladder, than coal miners. Nitrosamine levels up to 48 parts per million have been identified in commercially available cosmetics, including baby lotions. Max Factor's Ultralucent whipped creme makeup has a nitrosamine content of 48 parts per million.

Next comes Revlon Moon Dip at 3.7 parts per million.

Nitrosamines have been detected at low concentrations over certain manufacturing plants—for example, a plant in Baltimore that makes a rocket propellant known as unsymmetrical dimethyl hydrazine.

A richer source of nitrosamines is automobile exhaust, which may be the most potent source of lung cancer on the freeways. Of approximately seventy registered soot or fuel additives used for carburetor detergents, more than one half are amines. They are readily nitrosated in the exhaust to form nitrosamines. To my knowledge no one except General Motors has given this extraordinarily important chemical smog problem any serious study.

Peter Mapes of Temple University, who with John Barnes was the first to show that dimethyl nitrosamine was carcinogenic to rats, also had shown that this nitrosamine is metabolized in a similar manner by humans.

This particular compound has been twice used as a murder weapon and perhaps more uneventfully in dozens of cases that didn't come to police attention. It is technically the recipe for a perfect homicide. After ingestion it is metabolized within a few hours; by twenty-four hours not a trace can be detected in body tissue. The first murderer was a chemistry teacher in West Germany who was sentenced to life for killing his wife. The German was a little stupid. He brought his hospitalized wife the nitrosamine-poisoned food. She became suspicious and had the food analyzed. The nitrosamine showed up. Her death nevertheless occurred as the result of severe liver dysfunction with signs of cancerous lesions identical to those seen in experimental animals treated with dimethylnitrosamine.

The second murder took place in Omaha, was even more stupidly carried out, and certainly more cruel. A biologist working at the Epple Cancer Research Institute was sentenced to death for killing the husband and infant nephew of his ex-girlfriend. The murderer put the dimethylnitrosamine in lemonade and milk. He used excessively large doses and the drinks proved lethal too quickly to avoid suspicion. A twenty-eight-year-old man died immediately from brain hemorrhage and an eleven-month-old boy from liver damage; three other people partook of the drinks and have been warned that they may contract cancer. The object of the murderer's affections, the ex-girlfriend, drank neither of the poisoned refreshments and is still fit as a fiddle.

Now for the bombshell. All other sources of nitrosamines pale compared to the hitherto unadvertised prevalance of amyl and isobutyl nitrites, now sniffed as sexual amplifying drugs in positively enormous quantities. Amyl nitrite is usually known by the street name of "popper" or "snapper" because it is legally distributed as an antiangina heart drug in 0.3 ml crushable glass ampules wrapped in a gauze jacket. You pop it before inhaling. Isobutyl nitrite is usually distributed as a 12 ml bottle with a screw cap.

In effect these nitrites have become the poor man's cocaine. Their use, starting about 1930, has climbed faster than the national debt. The volatile nitrites can be inhaled either during foreplay (producing floating sensations, increased skin sensitivity, and loss of inhibition) or just before orgasm. Users report the climax to be intensified and prolonged.

The vastness of the business may be gauged by the number of brands of isobutyl nitrite: Locker Room, Rush, Bullet, Aroma of Men, Dr. Bonanas, Cat's Meow, Satanic Scent, Hi Ballo, Black Jack, and Krypt Tonight are only a few.

Sensory inhibition of erection has been noted by 5 percent of male users. Some men find that amyl nitrite helps prevent premature ejaculation.

Thirty years ago amyl nitrite was widely used in New York City artistic and theatrical circles of both heterosexual and homosexual persuasions, most of whom could not afford cocaine and wanted a stronger rush than they could get from marijuana. Today the nitrites, especially isobutyl, are more especially identified with homosexuals. The San Francisco market is said to be larger than the Los Angeles or New York markets. It is estimated that 230 million doses of these nitrites are produced each year. One has a label that states: "Warning: excessive inhalations may lead to euphoria." Since the nitrites readily find amine groups to react with within the body to form nitrosamines, the warning label should change "euphoria" to "death from lung cancer."

4

The City of the Lost Angels

So may the city that I love be great
Til every stone shall be articulate.

—W. D. Foulke

If I give a whole chapter to my home city, *El Pueblo de Nuestra Senora La Reina de Los Angeles de Porciuncula,* it is not because it is the worst smogged city in the world (that is probably Ankara) or even the Western Hemisphere (that is probably Sao Paulo) or even in the United States (that is probably New York), but because more intensive study has been devoted to it—and because I love it. I was very much affected by an essay by Richard Reeves in *The New Yorker,* painting in almost Hogarthian grotesquerie the troubles that beset a family living in the Mulholland Drive hills: brush fires in summer, mud slides in winter, smog the year round, the constant dread of earthquakes.

The lady of the house told Mr. Reeves: "It takes a certain kind of person to live here. We came back. We all came back. We're damn fools, but the trees come back, and so do we. It's a constant battle. Nature keeps trying to take over here. But it's beautiful, and it's where we want to be."

It *is* beautiful. On the rare clear days (perhaps a day after a rain) the San Gabriel mountains sparkle voluptuously. One's past comes hauntingly back—the past of a canyon ringed with giant eucalyptus trees, smelling in the morning of sage, manzanita, pepper trees, and Ragged Robin roses. Picnics took place where Chavez Ravine, the Rose Bowl, and Eagle Rock now stand and in our backyard on Mount Washington Drive, which to me will always seem a pathway of delight, though it is probably now a ghetto. (Ghettos have a way of springing up like colonies of poison oak in the lovely parts of El Pueblo.) I am told that Mount Washington itself, once served by a long incline or cable car, is now a collection of junky old houses. The view is unmatchable anywhere else in the world. One sees down the endless sweet stretch of the San Fernando Valley to the north; the San Gabriels to the east; and to the west Santa Catalina Island looming like Bali H'ai in the long gleaming ribbon of the Pacific Ocean. Mount Washington should be better than the Santa Monica mountains behind Bel-Air and Beverly Hills, but so foolish are the sociological urges of rich sheiks and the barons of our enormous untaxed subterranean cash flow that property in the latter region is valued roughly at a hundred times the value of Mount Washington real estate.

From my boyhood in a smogless canyon I can recall certain things that now appear to be of scientific interest. For example, I never saw lightning nor heard thunder until the family moved temporarily east. I can never forget the utter terror of crossing Narragansett Bay in a ferry with lightning bolts assaulting us as thickly as shells exploding at the battle of Verdun. My sister recalls the same peculiar absence of thunderstorms in the Los Angeles of our youth. Did the smog bring the lightning? Or was the peculiar meteorological syndrome that gave birth to the inversion (the hot air layer that on smoggy days holds whiskey-colored pollutants such as nitrogen tetroxide close to the ground) implicated in the appearance of thunderstorms? It was as if Nature, in her absent-minded complacence in having created a beautiful little city, suddenly remembered: "Oh, Migod, I forgot to give you thunder and lightning. Well, I'll order it. Coming right up." And so on certain days the Los Angeles of today is as noisy with thunder as St. Louis or Wichita.

I have mentioned that New York has the worst air of any North American city. The peculiar reason for this is not the fault of New York's citizens but of the uncontrolled burning of coal in the Ohio Valley. This interstate, even international, traffic in polluted air is perhaps the most tangled political and legal problem we have, but in New York the combined effect of automobile pollution and wind from the west fortify each other. The winds have added sulfur oxides to the more usual mess primarily identified with auto emissions alone.

The problem in Los Angeles involves practically no sulfur compounds. It is the classic auto exhaust syndrome realized so many years ago by that genial Dutchman at Caltech, Professor Haagen-Smit. Nitrogen oxides, free radicals, and hydrocarbons undergo a complex series of photochemical reactions that produce oxidants during the day, such as ozone and peralkylnitrate (PAN). These customarily disappear during the night. During a very hot, windless day, with the inversion layer as low as 300 feet, the city is ringing constantly with ozone alerts.

It would be the height of optimistic folly to say that photochemical smog is getting better in Los Angeles or even that it is not getting worse. During the second week of September 1979, Los Angeles had the most "smog episodes" or "Stage 2" alerts (defined as a time when the ozone averages over 0.30 parts per million over a one hour period) since 1954. There were eight consecutive days of practically uninterrupted alerts. October 1980 was even worse. The Los Angeles school system and adjoining districts canceled all high school football games. At the Los Angeles Coliseum, where UCLA went ahead with its Saturday night game with Purdue, the Boilermaker fullback, an asthmatic, went into breathing convulsions and had to be carried off the field. (Remember, this was nighttime, when the oxidants were supposed to be going to sleep).

Conditions were admittedly terrible all around. The temperature was as high as 108°F., and there was an unusually tight, low inversion layer. The circumstances were not improved by a large number of brush fires and a bus strike that resulted in heavier than usual auto traffic. During these second stage episodes, industries of all sorts, including dry-cleaning establishments and beer-bottling plants, are supposed to chink up all the vents; residents are advised to curtail driving, stay indoors, and avoid playing tennis or even swimming. (As we shall see later, the advice to get indoors may be fatally obsolete).

What might happen if similar conditions prevail during the 1984 Olympics in Los Angeles (assuming that this international ritual continues after 1980)? The possibilities are gruesome enough to suggest that the Olympics be moved to some relatively smog-free place—say Fairbanks, Alaska. Although dates have not been set, likeliest ones would be late July and early August, when hot weather is probable. Dr. Stonar Horvath, physiologist at the University of California, Santa Barbara, has concluded that at ozone readings of 0.5 parts per million (which were reached in 1979) athletic performances would decrease by 10 percent. "At least there would be a marked decrease in performance in distance events. But certain combinations of heat and smog would create a disaster, and I'm talking about athletes keeling over. Symptoms would include aorta chest pains."

Horvath suggests that the 1984 games be held in the spring or at least that distance events be scheduled at night. That idea was echoed by Dr. Stanley Rokar, an Los Angeles pulmonary specialist, who said, "I would be fearful of having marathon runners compete in smog like this."

Remember the first marathon winner, Pheidippides, who brought the glad news of Cyrus's defeat to Athens? He collapsed and died. At Los Angeles in 1984 we might have to institute mass burial for a platoon of Pheidippideses whose only message was the ambulances are coming, the ambulances are coming!

The setback in the Cahuenga (or Los Angeles) Basin smog situation during the past few years has not only caused various governmental tempers to flare but worried cities not yet beset by such sickening inversions, including Tulsa and Wichita. Under the 1977 Federal Clean Air Act Amendments, regions that don't make "reasonable progress" toward meeting a stringent set of emission standards by 1982 face Washington-imposed restrictions on growth. With the present temper of Congress and the administration, such restrictions would cause an outbreak approaching the status of civil war. And the resulting pollution would, I am afraid, be no less than disastrous. In the impending bloody victory of the antienvironmentalists, I would be ready to join a shoot-out against them, but I'm too old and cowardly.

Of course, the federal government is supposed to have indirect ways of stunting a city's growth, through the lamentable reliance of cities upon central government grants. Under the Federal Clean Air Act areas that aren't likely to meet national air quality standards by the end of 1982 must have vehicle inspection programs to make sure that the catalytic exhaust converter equipment is working. According to the EPA, six regions of California, including Los Angeles, San Francisco, and San Diego, aren't likely to meet the 1982 standards.

Under the law the state was to have authorized a car inspection program by July 1979. Actual inspection wouldn't have to begin until 1981 or later. In a letter to the governor,

EPA said it would begin action to stop the money for sewage treatment plants and highways unless the state legislature established an inspection program within thirty days.

The legislature continued mulish. A coalition of Republicans and rightist Democrats is promoting the controversy as a state's rights issue and may succeed in indefinitely blocking passage of a test plan, despite the EPA threat of sanctions.

The fiery maestro of this state's rights faction is William Campbell, Republican minority leader of the state Senate. He contends that EPA is exceeding its authority by threatening sanctions and by allegedly demanding that the inspection program be carried out by federally centralized inspection centers rather than by ordinary service stations. (Campbell has the idiotic notion that these difficult analytical procedures can be carried out by the average, teen-aged, pimple-faced attendant.) "Congress didn't give the EPA the power to call for an annual inspection or a centralized one," he roars. "This is an example of Congress losing control of the monster called the EPA, and the monster is running amuck."

Although the California legislature has turned up its nose at EPA-mandated inspections of antipollution devices, it should be noted that this intransigence does not apply to all of the state. Los Angeles and Ventura counties, for example, play along with EPA. (This is another signal of the long discussed possibility that the state will break in two. Contrary to the belief of Easterners who know less of California history and geography than they know about Finland, this would not simply divide the state into a land of delightful intellectuals (north) and grubby moral majority freaks (south). The most important effect is that it would leave the north with most of the fresh water. Some kind of treaty would have to be negotiated—in addition to arrangements already in effect—to assure Los Angeles and San Diego of enough water from the wild northern rivers to supply a future metropolitan area of about twenty million souls.)

Let us see in a calmer spirit how the failures of smog control, especially in the Los Angeles Basin, have come about.

Despite a billion-dollar effort there has been no progress over the past several years. In the last two years air pollution has worsened frightfully. These facts were officially conceded in a letter to President Carter from the South Coast Air Quality Management District (the air pollution control agency of the 6000 square miles of the Los Angeles Air Basin).

The reasons for the sad picture are, primarily, that the highly touted catalytic control devices for auto exhaust haven't performed up to expectations. The catalytic devices deteriorate sooner than expected because of tampering, illegal use of leaded gasoline, and poor maintenance or adjustment. You put what amounts to a catalytic refinery on a shuddering muffler and the only thing the customer notes is that if he backs off the highway, he can easily start a brush fire. This is exhilarating to teen-age drivers. The average auto mechanic won't even touch the converter, unless he is paid to take it off. In states which mandate annual check-ups, the catalytic converter commonly doesn't get a look, let alone a test. I have yet to see an auto mechanic's examination or manual that even refers to the chemistry of the pollution removal process. This is not surprising since the average auto mechanic is not encouraged to learn anything fundamental about the very process of combustion itself.

The advent of the exhaust catalytic converter has had some as yet not fully analyzed effects on the composition of L. A. smog. Any sulfur in the gasoline is oxidized quantitatively to sulfur dioxide, which is not generally the case without a catalyst. This does not present a sulfur dioxide problem of the same scale as the burning of high-sulfur coal. It means, however, that in the more advanced areas of smogology in L. A. a new factor has been added. As has been emphasized, we are now more interested in fine soot particles and their chemical baggage than in any other kind of pollutant. Dry nitrogen dioxide does not react with soot particles separately, but it does react in the presence of sulfur dioxide. It is creepy little facts like this that turn out to ruin a hundred thousand lungs.

Aside from the unworkable gimmicks, everybody admits the summer weather recently has been lousy. Also decisions by federal and state energy regulators have forced some utilities in the Los Angeles Basin to use fuel oil instead of natural gas* or nuclear power.

Interagency cat-and-dog fights distort the picture. The Air

---

*Unexpectedly, natural gas has again become one of the country's largest sources of energy. This is because of recent discoveries in Anadarko Basin, the Tuscaloosa trend, and the Overthrust area in the Rockies. It is deep gas and therefore expensive (about $4.00 per thousand cubic feet) but there is enough of it to carry us well into the twenty-first century.

There is a dramatic but so far almost totally theoretical extrapolation of the recent discoveries of deep natural gas zones. (Incidentally, one reason for their popularity is that gas produced from 15,000 feet or deeper escapes price regulation.) Thomas Gold of Cornell, the well-known co-author with Fred Hoyle of the steady-state theory of the universe, believes that methane (natural gas) may exist in extremely deep levels of the crust or the mantle as carbon leftovers from the evolution of the planet. This theory says, in essence, that most methane trapped in the earth's crust got there not by conversion of biological carbon but by outgassing primordial carbon that has been trapped in the center of the earth since the planet was formed. Gold is certain that by very deep drilling we shall find everywhere in the world enough gas to meet the energy demands of the planet's population for thousands of years. Even if this beautiful fantasy turns out to be fact, we are still dealing with an unrenewable source. But it would surely give us breathing room in more than one sense. Besides being the most innocuous of all the hydrocarbon fuels (in California, methane in the exhaust does not count as a hydrocarbon pollutant), the geographic impartiality of the Gold theory would make noisome cartels like OPEC impractical, since anybody with enough money and know-how to drill deep enough would hit the jackpot anywhere he chose—in the Antarctic, the middle of the Atlantic, or the South Bronx.

Quality Management District, which bosses industrial pollution, puts most of the blame on unexpectedly high auto emissions. The State Air Resources Board, which polices vehicle emissions, blames industrial pollution and the goddamn weather. (Everybody but the Chamber of Commerce goddamns the weather.)

Everyone, absolutely everyone, agrees that the smog is getting worse (although a couple of clear years in succession could change the falsely monolithic nature of this opinion. Average people only seem to remember the last three—possibly four—years of smog).

However, one indicator that can't be laughed off is the number of days when the air in the Basin is rated "very unhealthful" by the EPA. (Air is rated "very unhealthful" when it contains at least 0.20 parts per million of ozone.) In 1978 there were 76 such days in Los Angeles County, compared with an average of 62 days in 1972–77. In the eastern half of the basin the number of such days in 1979 totaled 72, compared with an average of 47 days in 1972–77.

The number of "hazardous" days—a semantic term supposed to make the cold chills run up and down your spine, but which simply denotes ozone peaks of over 0.35 parts per million—has actually declined since the 1950s. There were 11 such days in Los Angeles County in 1979 compared to 33 in 1969. No other locality in the world, except possibly Ankara or Athens, gets this high.

The Los Angeles Basin, particularly in the summer, is probably the most poorly ventilated site in the world for a major city, again with the possible exception of Ankara. Inversion layers normally occur 200 days of the year. In 1978 inversion layers were lower and lasted longer than normal; sunny days were more frequent, and the wind speeds lower.

Although the weather is always being insulted, both federal and local meteorologists believe they have proved that weather conditions cannot account for the bulk of the recent smoggy bloom. The Air Quality Management District takes each day's highest ozone reading in the Basin, adds all the high readings for the June–September smog season, and averages them. In 1979 the maximum readings averaged 14 percent higher than those for the previous six years. Adjusting for the weather, the increase becomes 8.7 percent. Conclusion: the weather can't take all the blame.

The resident scientific expert, who ascended to the throne once occupied by Haagen-Smit, is James N. Pitts, Jr. of the University of California at Riverside. Somewhat cagily he manages to blame everything in the last few years, except mudslides and homosexuality, on auto emissions. State tests began about three years ago on late model cars. The results were laughable—if one can laugh when asthmatics are choking for breath. Over 50 percent of the autos failed to meet the California emission standards. The Air Quality Management District claims the catalytic devices on half the cars that flunk have been tampered with, meaning actually disconnected, presumably in a mistaken attempt to improve power. Nationwide EPA studies show about 10 percent of the catalytic converters have been deliberately short-circuited. (If you can't do this yourself, you can get an unscrupulous mechanic to do it for a separate, unreceipted ten bucks. This is part of the subterranean cash flow.)

Federal pollution laws require that unleaded fuel be used in 1975 model and later cars, since this was the year the catalytic mufflers came in, and the catalysts are rapidly poisoned by lead. But EPA finds that a large percentage are using leaded gas. The 1975 and later models have specially narrowed gas tank openings, requiring the use of the slender nozzle reserved for unleaded fuel or gasohol. The leaded-fuel perverts either use special funnels or enlarge the size of their tank inlets with crowbars.

The Value of Catalytic Mufflers

Since the maintenance and integrity of a catalytic muffler seems to be the crucial question, at least in Los Angeles, as to whether or not smog conquers all, a few explanations are in order.

The converters are either monolithic (alumina made porous by a carborundum process and painted internally with small amounts of platinum, palladium, and/or rhodium) or bed-type collections of catalyst pellets (General Motors). Not only are these very expensive catalysts, which serve to oxidize the carbon monoxide to carbon dioxide and unburned hydrocarbons to carbon dioxide and water, very susceptible to lead additives in the gasoline; they are also poisoned by small amounts of phosphorous compounds coming from the crankcase oil. (For some years all premium motor oils contained zinc dithiophosphate as an inhibitor of bearing corrosion.)

Recently, since nitrogen oxides have been increasingly identified as prime conspirators in automotive smog, a so-called three-way catalyst system has been devised in which the key component is rhodium. This is intended to reduce the nitrogen oxides catalytically to nitrogen (not all the way to ammonia, which would be a fearful odor nuisance on Rodeo Drive, Beverly Hills). Until now the standard way to get the nitrogen oxide content of the emissions down to bearable amounts has been to recycle part of the exhaust gas into the engine, thereby cooling the maximum combustion temperature and diluting the oxygen. It must be emphasized that the nitrogen oxides are not formed from anything in the fuel but by reaction of the nitrogen of the air with the oxygen of the air under high-temperature conditions. When this was first accomplished industrially, it was called the Haber process and enabled Germany to fight World War I without importing nitrate from Chile.

The catalytic converters have certain disadvantages. Aside from susceptibility to toxins, they will oxidize even the minute amounts of sulfur in gasoline to sulfuric acid in the exhaust. Under certain peculiar conditions they produce cyanogen or hydrocyanic acid, both of which are good for excoriating mammals but not for improving the healthfulness of city air.

The sulfur problem is the most serious. If the sulfur in Los Angeles gasoline increased even slightly (due possibly to greater use of Alaskan crude in refining), Los Angeles would suddenly share the sulfur-oxide problem that bedevils the Northeast.

What Are the Real Health Hazards in Los Angeles?

I think I have made it plain in the third chapter that I regard delayed lung cancer from toxic smokes and soot and from nitrosamines as the cause of future excess deaths in any smogged-up city.

The cancer problem from polyaromatic hydrocarbon emissions from ordinary gasoline-powered cars, although not as spectacularly threatening as diesel vehicles, easily may be the worst danger Los Angeles faces. This is because there are so many jalopies still lurching around the city. As shown in a brilliant analysis by Japanese auto scientists, the average emission rate of polyaromatic hydrocarbons (mostly of the carcinogenic sort) depends on the age of the car (in mileage) and the age of the crankcase oil (also in mileage). In cities like Los Angeles where every fifteen-year-old has something to drive and can buy a jalopy for practically the price of the scrap steel left in it, this adds up to a lot of automotive soot. I am not convinced that the nitrosamine problem is not even worse, but it is a problem too new to speculate about any further.

Ozone, as we have seen, is a kind of all-purpose mischief maker: if you have a tendency to allergies, it will sharpen this tendency. If you are a semiasthmatic, ozone will give you a diploma into full asthmahood. It is glad to help you on your way to full-fledged emphysema or heart disease.

The occurrence of lead dust in compounds containing chlorine, bromine, and oxygen has been shown in Los Angeles to depend on the average speed of the traffic. An observed large increase in lead in 1977 at one particular site is easily explained by the opening of an additional northbound traffic lane, which resulted in higher traffic speed.

Because of its dryness, Los Angeles has something possibly more serious than the acid rain, which is the subject of chapter 7: acid dust. Caltech scientists collected the dust by coating flat plates with glue and exposing them over a period of several months. They found that about twenty times more acidity had reached the floor of the Los Angeles Basin in the form of solid particles and gases than as rain. The acid (mostly nitric) was sufficiently corrosive to burn holes in a leaf surface. Unlike rain, acidified fine particles can penetrate buildings and other areas not reached by rainfall. There is something spooky about this. You take refuge in your house and slam your air-tight door. But the fine dust follows you in, like a ghost. The ghost is again from the automobile.

Of the standard members of the Los Angeles photochemical smog community—carbon monoxide, nitrogen oxides, and hydrocarbons—the latter two are reported as especially dangerous because of their tendency photochemically to form ozone, PAN, and other oxidants. If you had your pick and could remove either hydrocarbons or nitrogen oxides, which would you aim at? Hydrocarbons are most threatening in the United States, while the Japanese are more afraid of nitrogen oxides.

Nitrogen dioxide by itself is a bad thing to have around.

In very large amounts (150 parts per million) nitrogen dioxide is lethal. In 1929 nitrogen dioxide and its dimer nitrogen tetroxide (the compound that gives smog its dusky wine color) killed nearly all the patients in a Cleveland hospital. In this case the nitrogen oxides were released from the accidental burning of a storeroom full of old-style cellulose nitrate X-ray files.

As noted previously, nitric oxide may be not only harmless; it may soften the effects of nitrogen dioxide. Levels of nitrogen dioxide, however, as high as fifty parts per million will cause chronic, usually fatal lung disease, such as *bronchiolitis obliterans*. Ehrlich and others have shown that preexposure to nitrogen dioxide at levels above one part per million increases the mortality of animals later exposed to bacteria. In other words, nitrogen dioxide wipes out the immune system, mainly by interference with the microphage activity. Increased morbidity from bronchitis has been observed among elementary school children exposed to nitrogen dioxide for two years and in infants exposed for three years.

In a series of experiments with his big photochemical cell, Pitts and his colleagues detected and "fingerprinted" (developed time-concentration profiles) of nitric acid, formaldehyde, ammonia, ozone, all the nitrogen oxides, peroxy acetyl nitrate, (PAN) and scores of other chemical personalities in samples of smog from the Los Angeles Basin.

From his studies of real and simulated atmospheres, Pitts warns that Los Angeles smog is not a show with a few stars; it is a circus with almost numberless and perhaps still unknown actors. The health impact of ambient photochemical smog results not just from nitrogen dioxide and ozone but from a spectrum of "trace" gaseous and particulate pollutants which coexist with the major critical species. For instance, while the presence of PAN and nitric acid has been established, their interaction with nitrogen dioxide and ozone and the resultant effect on health has not yet been clarified.

Nitric oxide itself seems to be beneficial, according to Pitts.

As a chemical species nitrogen dioxide may interact directly with respiratory tissues. It may be further oxidized to nitric acid aerosols which have sometimes directly fatal effects.

In a lengthy review of experimental human studies, Carl Shy and Gary Love of the University of North Carolina, noted nitrogen dioxide's ability to alter lung functions. Long exposures make people "feel funny." It lowers the lung's ventilating capability, increases its sensitivity to allergens that constrict the bronchials, and in general weakens the lung's defenses against infections. Even at low limits it increases, like ozone, the susceptibility of a patient to asthmatic attacks.

According to the painstaking twenty-year-long studies of M. Evans and O. Freeman of SRI International the amount of tissue damaged by nitrogen dioxide depends on the concentration of this chemical, the age of the animal, *and the presence of vitamin E and selenium in the system.* (Vitamin E has for several years been known as a good thing to have in your blood when venturing out in smoggy weather.) German studies show that animals surviving large but sublethal doses of nitrogen dioxide and continuing to live for a long time in its presence develop a fatal emphysemalike disease. The Japanese are beginning to show the disastrous combined effects of nitrogen dioxide and ozone.

Lately, more medical attention has been paid to the non-respiratory functions of the lung; for example, its ability to regulate local and systemic blood pressure and flow, its vascular permeability, and the formation of platelets necessary for the process of bloodclotting. The lung has a say in these activities through its control over circulating levels of the vasoactive hormones, such as the prostaglandins, angiotensin, and serotonin. The effect of nitrogen dioxide in prostaglandins is extremely important, if only because prostaglandins (which may be regarded as almost ubiquitous minihormones, with a message for nearly every cell) have become recognized as extremely prominent actors in the great drama of the body.

Dr. O. Menzel of Duke University's Medical School showed that nitrogen dioxide causes the formation of arachidonic acid, precursor to the prostaglandins, and at a later step in the life of the organism both nitrogen dioxide and ozone inhibit the conversion of arachidonic acid to prostaglandins. This latter inhibition rips up the synthetic pathway to metabolites, such as thromboxane and TXA, which increase blood pressure and aggregate platelets, processes which can lead to blood clots and narrowing of the arteries.

As in so many cases here we have a medical dilemma. A known toxin has a way of doing some good. This is like the old remedy for syphilis. Mercury has a specific kill effect on the syphilitic spirochete, but it also has a thousand ways to do you harm.

Prostaglandins are very busy little things. They regulate local blood pressure, flow, and permeability of capillaries in the lungs. The prostaglandins may fine-control the delicate balance between perfusion and ventilation in this low-pressure, high-flow system. It is like being in the control room of a gigantic turbine plant through which all the water of Niagara Falls converges. This is easily toppled. An early measurable symptom of emphysema first signals an imbalance in the relationships: perfusion is increased; ventilation is cut down.

Emphysema is a progressive disease that begins with edema (fluid on the lungs). Nitrogen dioxide can induce edema in rodents—a syndrome that, however, can be prevented by feeding the rodent victim massive doses of vitamin E.

As far as it has been examined, the parallel with man is perfect. Prostaglandin metabolism never returns to normal in a man who is exposed cyclically and repeatedly to nitrogen dioxide. If nitrogen dioxide produces edema in man in the same manner as it does in rodents, vitamin E may prove a specific pill of choice, especially to urban dwellers and cigarette smokers (or even marijuana smokers). I assure you it is better for you than cocaine.

They Called the Wind Maria

The surprising mobility of smog was first discovered in southern California. It was noticed that under the influence of the prevailing westerly breeze, the witch's brew, starting in downtown Los Angeles, ended up in the small cities of the Inland Empire—Riverside, San Bernardino, and Fontana. It is often possible, if slightly horrifying, to stand at a point near Riverside (perhaps the hills above the old Glen Ivy Hot Springs) and watch the smog creep up from Los Angeles. In 1979 the trajectory was right over Highway 10.

In the past this wind was redolent of oranges, with a taste of sea salt. Today in its remorseless advance across Orange County and into San Bernardino and Riverside Counties, it brings smog. The orange trees have long ago been exchanged for toxin-spewing cars, and Orange County has everything that Los Angeles County has, except age. (The population of the great areas that compose the Cahuenga plain increased by another half million in the 1980 census.)

In the late 1960s, almost as suddenly as an earthquake, smog instead of orange pollen came to the little cities of the Inland Empire. Orange County had become just a part of the

Los Angeles spread. The Santa Ana Canyon became for western Riverside County a source of smog as bad as Los Angeles—in fact, worse. As Senator Gary Hart said, "What goes up, usually comes down worse." Certainly this was true of the once delightful little city of Riverside. The sewage in the air, as it started in downtown Los Angeles, took occasion during its daytime trip to Riverside County to undergo further malign photochemical reactions. More ozone was formed than disappeared. So incensed were the proud people of Riverside that in the early 1970s Mayor Ben Lewis threatened to sue Los Angeles County and Orange County, as years before the quiet foothill city of Pasadena and the village of San Gabriel at the foot of Mt. Wilson only ten miles from Los Angeles had vainly called for the waves of smog to recede. But their anger, and that of the mayor of Riverside, proved to be as powerless as King Canute's animadversions against the saucy sea. Riverside now bears such names as Smog Capital of the West and Smog City.

At least its citizens exert a level of activism long dimmed in the smog-weary western areas. Riverside County calls a "first stage smog alert" when the ozone reaches 0.027 parts per million, while Los Angeles County and San Bernardino wait until the level is 0.12 parts per million and then the "event" is termed "second stage."

As Professor Pitts remarked of his hometown, if Riverside managed a drastic reduction in its own auto emissions, the improvement would be mainly noted in Palm Springs, forty miles to the east. Thus again we perceive the effects of the Maria-like winds.

A remarkable and on the whole dismal discovery came from the gloom of pollution damage in the Inland Empire. High towns in the San Bernardino Mountains, such as Big Bear and Lake Arrowhead (scene of Raymond Chandler's *Lady in the Lake*), believed quite safely above the inversion level, were found to have some of the highest smog readings in the state. You cannot escape the smog, it seems, by mere upward physical movement. This may prove a serious disappointment to the new owners of four-million-dollar homes in the Santa Monica Mountains, whose sole hope in escaping hell was certainly a physical rather than a spiritual ascent.

Walter Westman of UCLA has confirmed the unreliability of the inversion layer by examining the damage done to California coastal sage scrub. He finds that regional oxidant levels, even at considerable altitudes, are causing deterioration in the sage scrub communities. The effect is that of an enormous cataclysm on a human community. The rich and poor alike die. Only a few tolerant species survive, and these tend to be monotonously alike.

The UCLA scientist does not argue that this danger is occurring *above* the inversion levels. Rather, he notes that damage to shrubbery is worse, *just below* the inversion ceiling.

This narrow band of air may possess very peculiar qualities. In the case of migrating insects, for example, most of them (locusts, midges, even mosquitoes) swarm just at the interface of the inversion. This is a happy hunting ground for martins and other swallows who make a living by gulping insects on the wing.

The smog of Los Angeles may be historical in at least two respects: (1) because of the overall cultural and scientific intensity of the people in the area, smog—if it is ever to be defeated—will be defeated here; (2) as the second-largest metropolitan area in the country, Los Angeles has too much money power to give up without a fierce expenditure of sheer business energy.

I remember from my school days a football song: "You can't beat L.A. High." I must in my heart continue to believe you can't beat El Pueblo.

5

Other Capitals of Lung Disease

An air that kills from yon far country blows.
—A. E. Housman

In the horse-and-buggy days such places as Phoenix and Denver were regarded as gentle sanctuaries in which to recover from tuberculosis or other pulmonary disorders. Now physicians in these cities often warn asthmatic people to get out of town. Denver is a mess because of the "Los Angeles disease" of atmospheric inversion and excessive auto traffic. Denver has big shoulders, looks down (literally) at every one, and has preserved its air of independence. It always does the wrong thing. (The Brown Palace Hotel is perhaps the only luxury hostelry in the world where men are not allowed to have a drink with women to whom they have not been formally introduced.)

A typical Denver mistake was its recent decision to buy diesel buses instead of electrical ones. For this error it was promptly scolded by the Environmental Protection Agency, but scoldings by this agency are what Denver can most easily shrug off. Colorado is one of the delinquent states, and because it has failed (at the time of writing) to come up with an auto pollution control program, the EPA will cut off about $300 million for water and sewerage projects. If this goes through, Colorado will be the first state to be spanked so publicly and noisily. Governor Lamm blames it on his legislature.

Although not much publicity is given it, the city of Denver faces by far the most dreadful pollution possibility in the world, with the exception perhaps of some Siberian cities which the CIA may be able to identify, but which otherwise are tagged "Top Secret." Denver has an unbelievable amount of nerve gas stored, of all places, at the airport. This agent is of a type with which I am familiar, since years ago I visited TVA country as a consultant to try to iron out some technical troubles they were having with chemical engineering. It is G-B, a waterlike fluid containing both phosphorous and fluorine. I recall the examination of the pupils of my eyes, before and after, and being furnished with a kit, including a vial of atropine, the only known antidote. Pigeons were flying all over the place, inside and out, since they act as sensitive living probes, much in the manner of white mice in a deep coal mine.

This kind of nerve gas acts by skin contact or breathing. Both ways it kills almost instantly by destroying the enzymes which neutralize the acetylcholine, the transmitting substance that serves the autonomic nerve system. All kinds of unpleasant things happen to you in a few seconds after a drop has touched your flesh but the end result is strangulation as the nerves which control breathing go out of whack.

The reason the nerve gas is stored in Denver is that it was used experimentally on the high plains, where it killed innumerable sheep. Encased in 888 steel barrels, "protected" by cement, it stays in Denver because the Army is afraid to move it. Suppose one of the barrels sprang a leak; everybody in the airport would be killed.

In its present flimsy location, the danger of an accident in which some or all of the barrels were involved in an airplane crash, is too much for the Denver honchos to think about. They pretend the stuff isn't there. An explosion that resulted in the wide dispersion of a few million droplets of G-B could not only wipe out the population of Denver but that of all eastern Colorado, along with parts of Nebraska, Kansas, and Wyoming.

The Booby Prizes

If one were to rate the big cities of this country by air pollution, New York and Los Angeles are easily the worst (two-thirds of the days of the year are "unhealthful"). Cities with over two hundred unhealthful days are Denver, Cleveland, Louisville, Riverside, Anaheim, Chicago, Philadelphia, St. Louis, Washington, and Jacksonville, Florida. (Jacksonville is a real stinker for its size. The Great Stocking Riot of 1949 happened there, when women's hosiery rotted on their legs.) Coming up to high smoggishness fast is Tennessee, mainly because of coal burning by the TVA, but the smog also has a photochemical origin. Ambient quality standards for ozone, carbon monoxide, and smoke have been exceeded over the past three years in Knoxville, Memphis, and Nashville.

From a global standpoint the decennial Review of the Organization for Economic Cooperation and Development (OECD) of the United Nations is worth attention. Worldwide there had been an upward trend in sulfur dioxide pollution during the 1960s which decreased during the 1970s in some countries, notably Japan. The Japanese succeeded in reducing sulfur dioxide emissions by over 50 percent between 1970 and 1975. Emissions of sulfur dioxide per unit of energy consumed were also reduced in Canada (which, however, still has the worst sulfur record of all industrial nations), in the United States, Finland, Germany, Sweden, and the United Kingdom (which still is almost as high as Canada). In France the emission of uncontrolled sulfur dioxide has greatly increased.

Efforts to control particulate matter emissions have been more successful in a number of OECD countries than attempts to control sulfur dioxide. Between 1970 and 1975 smoke was reduced 50 percent in Germany, France, and the United Kingdom but only 30 percent in the United States.

The biggest groan of bad news concerns nitrogen oxide emissions. They are increasing, and increasing fast all over. The most important increments were in Canada, Finland, France, Germany, Japan, the Netherlands, Sweden, and the United States. In Japan a brief *decrease* in nitrogen oxide emissions took place after 1974, but this is still Japan's worst air problem.

The Japanese Formula

All things considered, how does Japan do so well? A study of the economics of pollution control in Japan by Thomas K. Corsh of the EDCO Environmental, Inc. of Cincinnati and other accounts by Japanese–American friends give some hints.

Japan is a crowded, homogeneous country. When they get an idea in their heads, it goes around like sheet lightning, and all citizens march front and center. They are extremely health conscious. In response to increasing public pressure the Japanese government in the late 1960s set up a complex system of ambient and emission standards based not on available technology *but on health effects.* The Japanese philosophy was the exact opposite of that expressed by Inco about capping its Sudbury nickel smelter. If the emissions threaten health (say the Japanese), to hell with the business feasibility. They will find a way to stop the emissions and worry about the bill later. The dazzling success of this notion has never been quite explained to American technologists, let alone American businessmen. Japan's only failure remains the control of nitrogen oxides.

One reason for Japanese austerity in the control of pollution is the series of horrible poisonings that took place in the 1960s. Most of the residents of Minamata and Niigata were paralyzed or killed by mercury poisoning from contaminated fish. The splintering of bone tissue and excrutiating pain of Hai-Hai ("ouch-ouch") disease in Toyama was attributed to cadmium poisoning. Many deaths from acute asthma, bronchitis, and emphysema in Yokkaido were blamed on the mammoth petrochemical complex located there. In a typical Japanese scenario in one of the Minamata cases the president of the Japan Chisso Company had to bow down in silent supplication before the victims to express his penitence.

The Japanese make it easy. At first, companies could depreciate at 60 percent on their environmental investments. The government banks loan at minuscule interest on environmental projects. But enforcement is brutal. It is left up to the prefectures (corresponding to our states) and, contrary to United States experience, the prefectures wield a faster, heavier club. Hai! Hai! is heard on all sides, but it is only through such crackdowns and slappings around that the atmosphere of Tokyo has been changed from unbearable to merely toxic. On some days one can even see Mount Fuji.

I think part of Japan's general answer lies in opening the books. I have been deeply impressed by the number of frank, revealing, very advanced studies on various aspects of combustion and automobile air pollution that appear in the Japanese essays put out by the Society of Automotive Engineers. Do you want to know how, exactly, the Mazda rotary engine works, and how it can be improved? Do you know the design that makes the Honda stratified charge principle work and yield such extraordinary fuel economy? It's all there in the SAE papers, mostly abstracted in the magazine *Automotive Engineering.* The audacity with which this private information is made public denotes either foolishness or complete confidence. I think it is the latter, because the quality of the research is the highest I have ever seen since the days of David Ricardo, the British automotive genius. The Japanese are ahead of us in all aspects of automotive engineering. They are also ahead of the Germans.

Spending for air pollution abatement by Japanese industry increased rapidly after 1965 and reached a peak of nearly 18 percent of total expenditures in 1975. (Our boys holler like stuck pigs if it is suggested that the percentage approach 5.) By October 1975 over one thousand flue gas desulfurization units had been installed. Operating expenses for pollution control remained high. At many copper smelters it represents 30 percent of production costs.

The total investment for pollution control by industry between 1965 and 1975 was 5.3 trillion yen (about $15 billion). In comparison with other industrialized countries, this is very high, as shown in the following table:

PRIVATE SECTOR INVESTMENT IN POLLUTION CONTROL

	Percent of total Private investment	*Percent of Gross National Product*
Japan	4.0	1.0
United States	3.4	0.4
Netherlands	2.7	0.3
Germany	2.3	0.3
Sweden	1.2	0.1
Norway	0.5	0.1

The Japanese are firmly of the opinion that the polluter must pay. This approach is designated the Pollution Pay

Principle (PPP). In a very clever way the Japanese arrange things so that the cheater gets cheated. For example, the inlet water to a plant on a river is downstream of the outlet water. If the riverside plant pollutes the stream, the pollution thus makes an immediate visit back to the plant.

In the PPP system costs are borne by the polluter rather than the government. The costs are then passed on in increased prices, so the consumer, not the taxpayer, bears the burden of pollution controls. Japan has extended the original PPP to include the restoration of polluted environments, the administration of monitoring and surveillance programs, and compensation for victims of pollution—even those who must travel some distance to swim because waters at nearby beaches are polluted.

Of great interest is the way PPP applies to sulfur dioxide emissions, since these are a planetary problem. In Japan all major sulfur dioxide emitters must pay a penalty for each cubic meter of sulfur dioxide released, even if the plant is in compliance with the appropriate emission standard. The tax rate is based on the nature of individual development and pollution in the area. Rates in some specially designated regions are as much as seven times those in less developed areas. The penalty in a designated area could amount to as much as 17 percent of the cost of a fuel containing 3 percent sulfur. The total proceeds from the sulfur dioxide penalty in 1976 was $110 million, the proceeds being used to reimburse certified victims of respiratory ailments and to pay for research on these diseases.

Taxes, which economists call "selective differentiative," have always been a key element in the Japanese economy— a principle not unlike the "supply side" tax doctrines of Reagan's advisers. The initial depreciation allowances for pollution control equipment was first boosted vigorously in 1967 in Japan. A first-year depreciation write-off of 50 percent was permitted through 1976 on new pollution control equipment. Depreciation at this level amounts to a zero interest loan, and the equipment glides in almost as if Santa Claus had delivered it.

Business firms in Japan are assessed a tax on fixed assets. A 50 percent reduction in this type of pollution-free production is permitted in the year following installation. Tariff revenues from imports of high-sulfur fuel oil have been assigned to refineries to offset the costs of subsequent desulfurization. But some of the costs have been charged directly to the electric power industry, whose flue gas desulfurization costs are lowered by burning the cleaner oil.

A lot of this seems freakish to us. We had better get to know it well, because it is beating our pants off. The ability of Japanese firms to absorb high pollution-control expenditure, compete with us in prices and quality, and at the same time raise hell on the Ginza every night is partly due to the historical business structure of the country. Prior to World War II the economy was directed by giant financial conglomorates called *Zaibutsu,* often controlled by single families whose reach extended to all aspects of modern business. Immediately following the war strong antimonopoly and anti-restraint-of-trade laws, imposed by General MacArthur, broke up the Zaibutsu. Enforcement of these laws relaxed in the early 1960s and the largest groups returned, much to the strange and sadistic delight of the people. They preferred their weird economic hierarchy to an American form of economic democracy, which was as incompatible with their temperament as the game of American football. These modern associations, *keiretsus,* have flourished in the last twenty years.

The three largest *keiretsus*—Mitsubishi, Mitsai, and Sumitoma—together account for about 40 percent of the capital of all the firms listed in the first section of the Tokyo Stock Exchange.

At the top of the most modern *keiretsu* are certain banks, which may exercise working control, through indirect corporate financing, over twenty or thirty major companies within the group. Each controlled company in turn may have minority interests in a hundred or more baby-sister companies, so the total number of firms associated with a single *keiretsu* may run into thousands.

The Japanese business style itself also has an effect on pollution control expenditure. It must be remembered that the rate of capital ownership is less than one half that of the United States. In 1968 only 22 percent of total Japanese corporate assets were provided by capitalization. Rapid economic growth has prevented many firms from accumulating capital from internal sources. The tax laws also favor debt financing by allowing interest to be deducted from income, as in the U.S.

The importance of debt in Japanese business provides some freedom from stockholder sniping. Investments can be made more easily without regard for immediate profitability. This is why apparently nonproductive investments that don't promise a rapid return on capital, such as pollution control equipment, are more feasible than in the United States.

The most heartening aspect of the Japanese pollution control system over the past decade is that the control efforts have paid off. More income came in as a result of these efforts than went out in the form of higher prices.

But Japan is in trouble with nitrogen oxide from a huge proliferation of automobiles, not all of which wind up in California. Tokyo is one of the most dangerously polluted supercities in the world. There is a discouraging trend away from the magnificent rapid mass transit system, epitomized by the famous "bullet trains" from Tokyo to Osaka, to mass purchase of automobiles. The people are getting rich enough to resent being pushed and squeezed into commuter trains. The Japanese have natural sense but they also have dignity.

Some Good Ones—Some Bad Ones

In scooting around this pretty blue globe one can hit a lot of sour spots, then suddenly a sweet one or two.

Moscow, a kind of twin to Chicago, has still more smog, mostly due to trucks and cars and an overly social inversion layer. One asks a sophisticated Muscovite why Moscow, with the best public transit system in the world, is building so many private cars, especially big ones. "Why not?" he asks, puzzled.

"Well, you don't need them and they're starting to stink up the city."

"People want the cars."

But to the technical visitor, Russian questions are all about air pollution. Do catalytic converters really work? How else can you regulate emissions?

There is a cable car which runs from the outskirts of Alma-Ata in Central Asia to the heights of its nearby mountain. As you go higher and higher, the city lies flat and obscured with that unmistakable color of nitrogen tetroxide. The smog is already worse than Denver, and one realizes that in a country like Russia, where trucks and cars are still scarce, there is a lot of emphysema and lung cancer ahead.

In Russian textile mills both noise and particulate pollution are extremely high. The decibel level is an incredible 98, and the air glints with fine dust. Rub your finger along a wall and you come up with a wad of fine lint. The big, healthy, and noisy women who work in these mills will cough and die with the old, familiar brown lung.

Jumping from one hellhole to another, one pauses in Mexico City, then at Sao Paulo. Population predictions by most demographers agree that in the early twenty-first century, Tokyo-Yokohama will be the world's largest city, with Mexico City second, and Sao Paulo a close third. Of the three hopelessly smogged metropolises, Sao Paulo seems the worst. Rio de Janeiro calls Sao Paulo *chato,* which means a crab louse, but also has the connotation of dull and humdrum. You have to have the patience of a *chato* to endure the air. This gigantic city is so smothered in smog that even an Angeleno's eyes will sting and his lungs and stomach simultaneously want to turn upside down. The city is shrouded perpetually in a photochemical haze so thick that the World Health Organization found that strange pulmonary adaptations had occurred in the children—adaptations that allowed most of them to live. On most days Sao Paulo smells like a garage on fire. It is little wonder, as we shall see later, that Sao Paulo has made the most vigorous strides of any world community in switching to alcohol fuel.

We must not overlook Venezuela, which has always rivaled Brazil in everything but size. However, as a charter member of OPEC this country is in the enviable position of being able to pollute itself sick with its own oil fumes. In Caracas premium gasoline sèlls at 35 cents a gallon and the Caraquenos buy 500,000 gallons a day. The location of the city is unfortunate. Four million people are jammed into a beautiful but narrow valley. They are all choking to death. From time to time it has even been suggested seriously that the great capital be moved out of its geographic trap. Some relief is hoped for from a subway system scheduled for completion in 1983.

Now let us jet to Athens. Unless we are in remarkable shape, even a few days stay in this glory of Greece may make us too ill to do anything but crawl into a plane and return to fragrant Los Angeles.

Athens is incredible. Hemmed in by mountains and thus

afflicted with a Denver-type smog, its modest acreage is crammed with nearly four million people. Over 100,000 people from outlying provinces move to Athens every year, with the result that 40 percent of Greece's population are squeezed into the capital. Athens not only has automotive photochemical smog; it is well supplied with sulfur dioxide from burning high-sulfur coal, and the sulfur dioxide converted into sulfuric acid aerosols eats away at the marble of the Parthenon, the Erechtheum, and other treasures on the Acropolis. They will be gone long before the end of the decade. With few parks, trees, or oxygen-producing plants, the city is strangling to death—but to the accompaniment of the greatest street noises of any city in the world.

If you have the urge to see Ankara, forget it! This is the worst of all. Cramped in a small round valley like the caldera of an extinct volcano, the city runs on a high-sulfur lignite fuel. And the population has the highest known rate of cigarette smoking in the world. When Kemal decreed that Ankara become the new capital, his advisers warned him the locale could hold only about 50,000 well-behaved people. The population is far over three million and growing with that insensate animality that seems to inflict all extremely unattractive spots in the universe.

Let's return to the states by way of Australia. In this continent at last we have found a smog-free, paradisical metropolis—Melbourne. Compare this delicious place with its big brother, Sydney, a typical stinker, and return straightway to Melbourne. The Lord blessed it a peculiarly propitious geography, providing a natural air-conditioning system. Nothing ever happens in Melbourne, but who cares? For the smog-weary and the happening-weary, Melbourne is the capital of the universe.

We return to the states, landing at San Francisco. This bonny city has a serious smog problem but generally nobody notices it. Some weird theories have been advanced. It is suggested, for example, that biomass emissions (that is, from plants) are responsible for the high ozone levels observed in the San Francisco air basin.

It is probably impossible, for reasons of protocol, to find out why President Reagan believes nitrogen oxide smog is caused by trees. During the October 1980 near-panic, Reagan landed in the false dark of the Los Angeles afternoon, murmuring "tragic!" Did he mean that it was too bad all the eucalyptus and palm trees in the city would have to be cut down?

As a matter of fact, natural emissions from trees, low as they are, are overestimated, because the plastic bag method normally used for measurement is unreliable. Terpene emission rates at ground level are not representative of emissions near the canopy top where ventilation is high. It is true that terpenes are more reactive than the hydrocarbons in man-made pollution. But rural atmospheres, which may be loaded with terpenes, are, contrary to Reagan's chemical theories, low in nitrogen oxides. Under these conditions hydrocarbons tend to act as scavengers rather than photochemical ozone generators. So where terpenes make their greatest showing, they have the least effect.

Blaming pollution on live plants requires a sort of science-fiction state of mind. Nationwide the greatest concentration of natural hydrocarbons (necessary to start the ozone-producing reactions) are the terpenes over the forests of North Carolina. The total hydrocarbons produced by plants compared to those wastefully emitted by autos is absolutely negligible.

Nevertheless, people of the Bay Area Air Quality Management District keep on insisting that their ozone trouble is from some mysterious vegetable monster and not from their automobiles. Sometimes I think . . . but I will not allow myself to be accused of the old prejudice said to persist between Los Angeles and San Francisco. After all, I went to school right across the bay at the University of California. There is certainly room in the state for three such essentially great and lovely cities as Los Angeles, San Francisco, and San Diego.

6

Air Pollution Moves Indoors

THIS OLE HOUSE is gettin' shaky, THIS OLE HOUSE is gettin' old, THIS OLE HOUSE lets in the rain, THIS OLE HOUSE lets in the cold*. . .

—Stuart Hamblen

I have mentioned the case of finely divided acid dust that follows a man into his Beverly Hills home and is impossible to get out again without resort to exorcism. Actually the problem nationwide, and especially in the Northeast and Middle West, is not one of outdoor pollutants invading one's house but of pollution *produced* indoors. The dilemma has confronted us quite suddenly, mainly because of two changes in American life-style: (1) the meticulous double-glazing and crack-caulking, the improved siding, thorough wall and ceiling insulation, and such measures taken in the laudable interest of saving energy, and (2) the massive switch to wood stoves and wood fireplaces.

This may help us in our energy conservation but we may

*Copyright 1954 by Hamblen Music Co., Inc.

find outselves in the ironic position of conserving ourselves to death. Most of us, working men and women and children included, spend about 92 percent of our twenty-four-hour day in a house or a building. Toxins inside the four walls are therefore about eleven times as significant as air pollution outside. These domestic toxins were not so important in old-fashioned homes that leaked air in and out and were correspondingly expensive to heat or to cool. As an almost savagely passionate conservationist, it breaks my heart to say it, but growing evidence points to the wisdom of a return to the porous house, with the wind whistling through the cracks.

What is this indoor air pollution? No moralist need tell you that the chief enemy is cigarette smoke. (Since the sudden rush to burning wood this may be dubious, but we shall tackle this ticklish question a little later.)

John D. Spengler of the Harvard School of Public Health says that indoor sulfur oxide runs about 20 to 70 percent of outdoor levels. Indoor nitrogen dioxide values can *exceed* outdoor levels by a factor of two, depending on the type of cooking. Spengler studied homes in six communities: Kingston, Tennessee; Portage, Wisconsin; Steubenville, Ohio; St. Louis, Missouri; Topeka, Kansas; and Watertown, Massachusetts. He monitored sulfur dioxide, nitrogen oxides, ozone, respirable particulate matter, total suspended particles, and the sulfate and nitrate fractions of the particulates. Continued measurements in kitchens with gas burners showed levels of nitrogen dioxide up to one part per million. Gas hot-water heaters are a rich source of this dangerous chemical.

Increased breathing troubles are noted in bronchitis patients in hazy houses. Many specialists, such as Dr. Spengler, have concluded that past data on the effect of air pollution may be absolutely meaningless. True responses outdoors may have been biased by the neglected influence of indoor exposure. This should, after all, have been obvious. If a person spends ten hours sleeping and watching TV at home, then works another eight hours in an office full of smokers, the brief outdoor exposure in getting to and from work can almost be factored out of the equation.

In every community examined by Spengler the indoor effect of nitrogen dioxide was remarkable. The overall ratio of the presence of nitrogen dioxide indoors and outdoors is less than one for homes with electric stoves and higher than one for homes with gas stoves. Clearly there are people walking in the relatively clean outdoor air of Topeka that have the same or higher indoor exposure to nitrogen dioxide as people living in the polluted air of Watertown, Steubenville, or St. Louis. The indoors difference between homes using gas and electricity is greater than the difference between homes with the same fuel and, except for Steubenville, ranges from three to seven times greater in pollution for gas.

The British pulmonary expert R. J. Melia has reported that children in homes with gas cooking had more instances of lung disease than children in homes with electric cooking. Girls showed a higher incidence than boys, which Melia suggested may reflect more time spent in the kitchen.

The continuous measurements of nitrogen dioxide from gas stoves add up to a sharp signal of distress. These high levels can last for minutes or hours.

Carbon monoxide is nearly as worrisome a pollutant as nitrogen dioxide.* The Canadian couple, T. D. and E. Sterling, have studied the amount of carbon monoxide emitted by gas stoves in various kitchens. The houses involved were occupied by nonreckless people, namely the faculty, staff and students of Simon Fraser University of British Columbia.

---

*Ozone doesn't enter the picture because of the absence of direct sunlight.

A gas stove will always produce a little carbon monoxide even if the gas-air mixture is well adjusted. However, the Sterlings found that using more than one burner reduces the immediate air supply. Also air may be partly cut off by pots placed over the flames in a cooking configuration. Tests showed rapid build-up of carbon monoxide from the stove. The increases varied directly with the number of burners lit and the number of lit burners with pots on top. The amount of carbon monoxide in all the house space varies inversely with the volume of the house, because carbon monoxide diffuses very rapidly into whatever space is available. This is significant because it means that the lungs of a baby asleep upstairs know what is going on in the kitchen immediately.

In one set of measurements the initial levels of carbon monoxide in the houses varied from 3 parts per million to 8 parts per million. In each kitchen four burners were lit and covered with pans. After twenty minutes the carbon monoxide in the kitchen ranged from 20 parts per million to 120 parts per million. Only four values were below 50 parts per million, the eight-hour threshold limit for industrial exposure adopted by the American Congress of Governmental Industrial Hygienists.

The houses examined by the Sterlings were standard old-fashioned ones. They cite more alarming reports of actual carbon monoxide poisoning in highly insulated houses.

Houses Built for Cancer

The indoor pollution we have mentioned so far is, in effect, the same as that produced by automobiles. The fact that it is made by smokers and gas stoves fails to tag it with the mark of the beast. But the new insulation craze, for which the government grants tax relief, has brought the fear of cancer. We can skip over the nitrosamines from your bacon and assume you are not a closet sniffer of amyl nitrite, but we cannot overlook two serious carcinogens, radon and formaldehyde.

The formaldehyde comes from the slow decomposition of formaldehydeurea foamed resins now sold in enormous amounts as stuffing for insulating modern houses. In this case the resin is pumped in liquid form into the walls of homes. When the foam insulation solidifies, any formaldehyde that is not used up evaporates and escapes into the house.

Experiments with small animals show that formaldehyde is definitely carcinogenic.

Radon gas is a natural end-product of uranium decay. Uranium is not found only in specialized products, such as mine tailings; it occurs naturally in nearly all soil, concrete, and brick. It is just there. Usually the basement air of a modern home, blocked off from the rest of the house, is a collector of radon gas from the bricks, cement, and soil and is a good place for a slow and painful execution. EPA's specialist David P. Rosenbaum is convinced that 10 percent of all lung cancer is now caused by indoor radon. He believes if all Americans were to reduce the ventilation of their homes by one-half, the increase in indoor radon would eventually result in 10,000 to 20,000 additional lung-cancer cases every year.

The EPA is in an odd predicament because indoor pollution is by no means clearly within its jurisdiction. Massachusetts has banned the use of formaldehyde-urea resin foam insulation and Connecticut has strict requirements. The Department of Energy, fearing the collapse of its heat conservation program, will set a standard limiting the amount of unreacted formaldehyde in liquid resin.

Even if the EPA decides it has jurisdiction over home

pollution,* it will have trouble putting together a program that makes sense.

Better ventilation? Various devices have proved insufficient. The health benefits of humidifiers are negligible. Available evidence suggests that although humidified air may enhance perception of comfort, for ordinary healthy people (*are* there any ordinary healthy people?) humidifiers have sometimes been the cause of confusing respiratory symptoms and irreversible lung damage.

Dr. Donald Proctor of Johns Hopkins Medical Center has concluded that the lung is a highly efficient air-conditioning system that warms incoming air to body temperature and saturates it with water vapor before it reaches the bronchial passages. Even when the air is very dry, the nose is an effective humidifier. Proctor's studies suggest that reports of upper respiratory irritation commonly attributed to dryness of the air are more likely due to the high levels of pollution that can build up in indoor air where homes are tightly sealed to keep down heat loss.

It is only fair to concede that the Association of Home Appliance Manufacturers make no medical claims for humidifiers, they do maintain that humidifiers help plants and furniture. (Your sofa really appreciates this tender loving care, and reciprocates by concealing all your spare change and your car keys.)

Numerous cases of an allergic lung disease called *hypersensitivity pneumonitis* are linked to organisms that thrive in humidifiers, particularly the centralized units through which warm air passes. Sometimes outbreaks of humidifier fever (often confused with Legionnaire's disease) may occur among groups of workers in a centrally humidified office.

---

*The Clean Air Act Amendments of 1977 don't merely play down the importance of indoor pollution. They ignore it entirely.

Symptoms of humidifier fever may include shortness of breath, coughing, fever, and general malaise. If not detected early, permanent damage can occur as lung tissue is gradually and irreversibly destroyed. Yet the symptoms are very easily confused with those of other disorders and may continue for years before they are linked to the heat-loving bacteria and fungi that thrive in humidifiers. If you are an asthmatic feeling most the time like the bottom man on the bottom team of the league, I suggest you disconnect your humidifier.

The health effects of indoor pollutants are very serious. Let me give you a good reason why they are possibly the most serious of any we have so far considered in this book.

At Portland, Oregon, Peter Breysee, professor of environmental health at the University of Washington, pointed out that mobile homes now contain more formaldehyde-urea particle-board and insulation and on the average have less ventilation than ordinary homes. Mobile homes are an increasingly popular form of housing. Dr. Breysee and many alert doctors across the country have theorized: *indoor pollution may be responsible for great increase in the sudden infant death syndrome ("crib death").*

For many years this phenomenon, in which a healthy baby dies suddenly and unexpectedly, has been as mystifying to physicians as it is horrifying to parents. New evidence from a number of quarters now points to abnormalities in respiratory control. Autopsies show that a very high percentage of the victims have an abnormal increase of muscle in the small pulmonary arteries. This increase was believed to be caused by chronic underventilation of the lung. The baby had not been breathing enough. Could this be because the air the baby is forced to breathe is full of garbage?

This essential clue may explain why crib deaths occur as often or oftener in lovely modern homes as in tenements. I have a hunch that this may prove yet another tragic instance of our lack of knowledge and of perceptivity in the whole field of air pollution.

The Fresh Air Fiends Were Right

Take the ideal demonstration house at Mt. Airy, Maryland. Here in the crisp, clean air sits one of the nation's most energy-efficient houses. The double-insulated, triple-glazed windows, and polyethylene caulking have cut energy use one-third to one-half below a conventional house of the same size. But this pride of the National Association of Home Builders is rotten with humidity, odors, and pollutants. The accumulation of radon gas inside the model basement is one hundred times higher than in a typical homestead most of us were brought up in.

John Stolwijk, epidemiologist and member of a World Health Organization Committee looking into such problems, says "There's more damage done to human health by indoor pollution than outdoor pollution."

Recent advances in engineering and building materials have helped reduce air infiltration rates in modern houses and buildings. The rates have ebbed as low as one air exchange every ten hours, compared with an air exchange every two hours in a typical American home. Sweden, Denmark, and West Germany recently issued indoor standards for certain pollutants and installed special ventilation systems, but except for some state and local building codes setting minimum ventilation standards to control odors in public buildings, regulations don't exist in the United States.

Consider the radon problem. In a certain part of Texas researchers measuring radon emissions from wellwater found that in one home the levels of radon gas in the bathroom far exceeded the working level considered safe for uranium miners.

Charles Hess, an outspoken physicist at the University of Maine, says, "Natural radiation (radon) is more dangerous than the man-made stuff released from the crippled Three Mile Island Reactor, because people are exposed to it for a lifetime, not just a few days."

Radon-222, which is the immediate decay product of radium-226, is the heaviest member of the noble-gas family and the only member of the uranium decay series which is a gas at ordinary temperatures. Its very existence is somehow insulting to commonsense. Radon readily diffuses through rock and soil and is present in underground mining caves.* Radon has a half-life of 382 days and decays to the isotopes of polonium, lead, and bismuth. These so-called radon daughters are born as single atoms that attach themselves readily to aerosol particles and so gain access to the lung. In an atmosphere of radon gas the main radiation dose comes from the inhalation of the radon daughters.

Furniture, carpets, drapes, tablecloths, pillows, and such furnishings pose their individual problems—not because they are malevolent but because we are near them so much of our lives. Most of the stuff in a livingroom contains formaldehyde, asbestos, ticks, or fungi from potted plants.

Self-cleaning ovens are a dreadful air-pollution peril. Government research facilities in Berkeley found that in less than an hour a single over heating to self-cleaning temperatures can yield enough carbon monoxide and nitrogen dioxide in a tightly sealed kitchen to exceed the existing United States ambient air quality standards for these pollutants.

---

*One can think of radon as possibly the most beneficient way to cause mutations. Can we credit the sudden emergence of that brilliant prodigy, Cro-Magnon man, to the fact that he spent a lot of time in caves?

Hygiene products, aerosol sprays, cleaning agents, air-fresheners, solvents, adhesives, and other household products, according to Dr. George Barch of Tulane University Medical School, "subject the human body to a constant, unrelenting chemical trauma. By tightening up the American home and filling it with patented junk, we may be transforming it into a virtual gas chamber."

Sulfur oxides or nitrogen oxides in combination with high moisture level inside houses can cause the phenomenon known as acid rain, which can stain the furnishings, damage the lungs, and make the dog old before his time.

Some people have suggested installing air-purification systems in home similar to those in submarines, but the Home Builders Association says that would boost the cost of a building by $55,000.

Bernard Saltzoar of the University of Cincinnati has suggested cheap monitors to see whether your house is poisoning you. What is needed, he says, is a simple low-cost personal monitor-dosimeter that can be worn like a badge. Certainly this is a switch. Ten years ago such monitors were being worn in Denver to see whether it was safe to go outside. We have made progress. We are going to be outdoors folks, after all—just to escape the dangers of staying at home. But what will the TV industry have to say?

Burning Wood

New England is witnessing the rebirth of the use of New England forests, a trend growing so fast that it outruns the government statisticians. To many old people it is simply a return to normalcy—abnormalcy and, in fact, devilishness being long represented by oil heating. Now wood fuel is in such demand that whispers can be heard in the still woods that windfall profit taxes on the wood dealers should not be regarded as outlandish.

As always happens when the price of an accessible commodity shoots up, there are thieves. Timber rustlers, especially in the Northwest, are stripping America's natural forests, either for construction timber or firewood. The pirates range from suburban residents, who ignore restrictions and load station wagons with fresh-cut timber, to professional crooks who load five-ton flatbeds in the middle of the night. Most daytime thefts are given an odor of sanctity by aid of a Federal Use Permit, issued by the Forest Service. This allows a citizen to take up to ten cords of firewood from a national forest each year at no charge. However, the wood must be "dead and down," and of no commercial value.

Says one Portland, Oregon, forester: "A guy has just paid $500 for a wood stove and another $500 for a chain saw, has rented a trailer and driven sixty miles. He finds no dead and down trees, so he takes anything he finds, fallen or standing. You're limited to ten cords a year. But at $100 a cord for firewood, the commercial timber rustler will take the ten cords one day, then come back the next day for ten more, or cut at night. At $850 a day profit, they'll cut standing trees."

Wood played the early hero in the New England drama of energy and continued to be the primary fuel for New Englanders until the latter part of the nineteenth century. By 1850 there were thirty-six steam-powered sawmills fired by wood in Maine alone. Coal became standard fuel in the United States later than in Europe, primarily because of the shockingly high rate of deforestaation in the industrial countries abroad. The classic case of ancient Lebanon has always been held up by Congregational preachers in Vermont as an example of what happens if you chop faster than you grow —and at the present rate of chopping Vermont could well become another Lebanon.

In the United States as a whole it was not until the 1970s that energy from coal surpassed indirect solar energy, in the form of wood, water, and wind as the primary industrial fuel. Petroleum before OPEC had, of course, taken the lead by about twenty furlongs. By the time of the Arab oil embargo of 1973, the use of wood for house heating had declined so markedly that even in woody Vermont, fewer than 1 percent of the households used wood as a heat source.

The shift back to wood occurred partly from snobbism and partly from freezing to death. In 1980 we found 20 percent of homes heated primarily by wood and more than 50 percent partly so heated. Home owners found that the price differential between wood and oil was suddenly so large that even with the $500 spent on a stove, they could save hundreds of dollars the first heating season. Perhaps one half of all wood now burned in New England houses is cut by the home owner. Wood cutting and wood splitting parties are becoming popular. About two million wood stoves will be sold in the winter of 1981; only 150,000 were sold in the energy fateful year of 1973.

Whether the average home owner embarking on a wood-burning campaign really saves any money is questioned by the following somewhat satirical accounting that appeared in the Salina County, Illinois, *Bureaucrat:*

Stove and installation	$ 458.00
Chain saw	149.95
Gas and maintenance for chain saw	44.60
Pickup truck, stripped	8,379.04
Truck maintenance	438.00
Replace rear window of truck (twice)	300.00

Fine for cutting unmarked tree in state forest	500.00
14 cases of Michelob	126.00
Littering fine	50.00
Tow charge from creek	50.00
Doctor's charge for removing splinter from eye	45.00
Safety glasses	49.50
New living room carpet	800.00
Paint wall and ceilings	110.10
Chimney brush and rods	45.00
Fifteen-acre woodlot	9,000.00
Replace coffee table chopped and burnt while drunk	75.00
Divorce settlement	33,679.22
Total first-year cost	54,132.81
First-year savings in conventional fuel	62.37
New cost of first-year wood burning	54,070.44

Not everybody has such a bad year as this Michelob drinker, but for the generation that now owns most of the New England real estate, advice from their elders is recommended. Not surprisingly, there has been a spate of fires caused by ignorance, poor equipment, or sloppy installation.

A fast-burning, light softwood, such as pine, makes a good kindling, but to hold a stable fire you need oak, maple, or hickory. In California eucalyptus is splendid, but not pepper. Apple holds a fire well at night and has a pleasant aroma.

White birch looks beautiful in the grate, but the serious stove connoisseur is not impressed by its heat value and tends to regard it as a city dweller's wood. The experienced wood-burner will use nothing but hardwood, except for kindling. It has a much higher heating value per cord and does not give as much creosote or as many sparks as pine, spruce, or fir.

Some more free advice, mostly from Professor Colin High of Dartmouth College: Never cut wood shorter than you need for your stove. Cut your wood in the fall when the sap is thinned. Split it in the winter, since frozen wood falls apart easier. *Cut at least a year before you burn.* There is a tremendous difference in the burnability of dry and green wood. Find wood which splits easily (ash and birch) and doesn't need a lot of diddling around with hammer and wedge (elm and locust).

For people who buy their wood cut, split, and delivered, prices range up to $200 per cord, and this makes wood more expensive per BTU than oil, even if the wood is dry. When wood is burned green, its moisture content is about 50 percent and its heating value is 4200 BTU per pound, compared to an average 8500 BTU per pound for bone-dry wood.

There is an old Vermont saying that wood warms you twice: once when you cut it and once when you burn it. Maybe knowing you're not dependent on OPEC would send a third wave of warmth down your skinny old spine.

Professor High points to several benefits that the growth of a large wood energy market could have in the New England forests. There would be a chance to market the large quantities of rough or rotten trees that abound in these woods as a result of a long history of selective cutting of the high-quality trees, combined with a lack of forest management to augment high productivity stands. My impression of New England foresters is that they don't take their jobs as seriously as the boys out in the Northwest or in the Southeast. I think they spend most of their time writing poetry.

Sweden plans to grow fast-rotation trees that can be harvested every three years; they are experimenting with willow and birch. The trees are mowed down and the wood collected in the winter. Next spring new shoots rise from the stumps and are nurtured, since as future trees they don't have to use energy in establishing a new root system. The United States has developed machines that reduce a sizable tree, branches and all, to chips, each about the size of a dollar, in thirty minutes.

Loggers who can afford whole-tree harvesting machines are going to see a bonanza. Such equipment increases productivity enormously and reduces the job hazards associated with traditional logging. Whole-tree chipping reduces the slash after logging which many landowners and picnickers find so repulsive. A slash is an ideal habitat for many snakes, including—as I know to my own distress—copperheads and water moccasins.

To keep costs down loggers will have to invest a lot of money in feller bunchers, skidders, and chippers to deliver firewood at a competitive price. Large machines do this best in clear cuts (operations where whole slices of forest are cut down) and there is no doubt that clear cutting is bound to be as popular in Vermont as in the Amazon. It has a somewhat brutal and generalizing effect on the forests. Although in the most important respects whole-tree harvesting produces the same overall effects as traditional logging, it does remove from forests a higher proportion of the biomass (the total living organism we call a tree). Whole-tree harvesting reduces the amount of wood and leafage left to decay on the forest floor, thus in effect taking natural fertilizer from the soil.

Professor High believes that "energy plantations" of fast-growing trees, harvested on short rotation with whole-tree harvesting methods would be the key to produce wood quickly and cheaply. This would be more like agriculture than forestry and might cause erosion and water-quality problems. But there seems little doubt that whole-tree harvesting is here to stay, even if chemical fertilizer has to be put into the equation.

The Bad News About Wood Burning

Wood burning, although a good source of radiant heat, produces a wide range of emission products. Although wood has very little sulfur, it has everything else and more. The amount of carcinogens in most wood smoke exceeds that in coal or diesel soots. It also likes to burn to give off our dear friends, nitrogen oxides, hydrocarbons, and carbon monoxide. If I had a baby, I would sooner leave it outside on a snowbank than in a well-insulated house heated by wood stoves and fireplaces.

The highly suspicious smoke particles from wood are controllable after a fashion in industrial boilers. Particulate emissions from home fireplaces, stoves, and furnaces are not controlled. Many small towns in valleys where temperature inversions occur on cold winter nights are already going through the agony of truly dangerous pollution events. When wood stoves are run closed for long periods of time, the pollution problem—like the creosote problem—increases and the amount of toxic organic matter released can be much higher.

The particle pollution from wood burning has been a concern in Portland, Oregon. Using a radiocarbon technique that identifies smoke from wood specifically, John Cooper of Oregon Graduate Center found that the combustion of wood accounted for over one-third of the *respirable* particulates on a cold winter day in a Portland residential area. It is ominous that the smoke from burning wood contains such a large percentage of superfine particles that can explore deep in the lungs.

Even old-fashioned New England farm women admit that burning wood has its disadvantages. A Vermont lady says, "Every time you open a goddamn wood stove, something comes out. It forms a film on my walls. The curtains and furniture get as dirty as the hinges of Hell."

Residential wood stoves, unlike commercial and industrial boilers, are not subject to state and federal pollution controls. In Missoula, Montana, the city-county health department requests that residents stop burning wood on days when air pollution reaches a certain level. If you know Montanans and know how cold it gets in Missoula, you will not be surprised to learn that these formal requests are not highly honored. Vail, Colorado, a very fancy place, forbids more than one wood or coal furnace in new houses—but wood stoves are exempted.

Although in Vermont wood is a sort of declaration of independence, the state officials point out that the type of wood-burning industrial boiler that heats the state hospital in Waterbury emits four times as many smoke particles as an oil boiler despite mechanical controls that filter out most of the golf-ball-sized crud.

Aside from the carcinogens and the other indoor pollutants, the most singular and important discovery about the combustion products of wood is the high percentage of nitrous oxide. This very weird chemical, called laughing gas, was hitherto thought only to occur as a by-product of nitrate fertilizers, and then only in amounts too modest to scare even the scardey-cats like me. The National Center for Atmosphere Research (NCAR) at Boulder has found that nitrous oxide is released in large quantities when *wood is burned.* Why this has not been observed before is one of those analytical-chemical mysteries like the monstrous, self-perpetuating error in lead analysis uncovered by chemists at Caltech. Unlike most other combustion products, nitrous oxide has no place to go. As ecologists say, it has no sink in the troposphere. It can only wander upward, trying to fly over the land of Oz. But up there it finds a sink and destruction. Transformed to nitric oxide and nitrogen dioxide, it joins happily in catalytic chain reactions that leads to the decomposition of ozone.

The implication of the NCAR scientists is plain: burning a lot of wood is equivalent to releasing a lot of freon aerosols. We are back to melanoma cancer, the obliteration of crabs, shrimps, and mackerel, and all the rest.

7

Acid Rain and Willful Winds

It isn't raining rain, you know, it's raining
violets.*

—B. G. Sylva

The high mobility of smog is a relatively modern realization and therefore not very well covered by the Clean Air Act (1970) and its amendments (1977). That is also why we now have both interstate and international legal ruckuses. Let me give an outrageous example of the portability of smog.

The North Pole in springtime is the smoggiest place in the world. Flying over the Arctic thousands of miles from the muddy skies of New York, London, or Hamburg, pilots often spend hours in a haze so thick that looking straight down is the only way to see anything. This piece of atmospheric drama was first encountered by reconnaissance planes in 1959, plotting the now popular great circle flights between Europe and California. Some pilots believe the Arctic is more

*From "April Showers," copyright by Warner Bros., Inc. (New York), lyric by B. G. Sylva, 1927.

124

dangerous than the incredible traffic at Chicago's O'Hare Airport, since the visibility aloft is frequently reduced to less than five miles.

All the chemical evidence shows that the arctic haze has its origin about 8000 miles away in the same polluted air that produces acid rain in the United States and Europe. According to Kenneth Rahn, an acid-rain specialist from the University of Rhode Island, the most likely source of this pollution is Europe. Rahn believes the spring hazes are relatively uncontaminated but during the winter the arctic haze consists largely of droplets containing sulfate and organic matter with smidgeons of heavy metals, such as vanadium and manganese. Over the winter 1976–77 excess sulfate (above that contributed by natural sea salt) increased twentyfold to about two micrograms per cubic meter at Barrow, Alaska.

If the sulfate and vanadium in the winter smog at Barrow started out as part of a typical parcel of urban air, a much larger proportion of the vanadium than of the sulfate was lost en route. Although sulfate particles drop out continuously, their concentration would tend to be maintained by the conversion of sulfur dioxide to sulfate. Rahn is suggesting that peculiar weather conditions in the arctic winter allow the polluted aerosols to stay in the air longer than expected and to produce the rather nasty pollutant concentrations observed.

We are familiar with the great voyages of fine particles from active volcanoes*, but Joseph Prospero and others at

*The largest eruption of which scientists have evidence occurred 75,000 years ago in Tobe on Sumatra. It left a caldera now filled by Lake Tobe, 100 kilometers long and 30 kilometers wide. It produced an ash deposit big enough to have covered an area as wide as the United States. Dust from the Tambora eruption in 1815 in Indonesia affected the world climate drastically. New Englanders called 1816 the "year without a summer." Snow fell in August. In England during two years after

the University of Miami have shown that desert dust travels farther than we had imagined. Some of the fine dust—lifted as high as 6000 meters by storms over the Algerian desert—doesn't come down until over the Barbados, 7000 kilometers away. At times Algerian dust may even reach Florida or Mexico.

Left to themselves these dust particles (up to twenty microns in diameter) would fall short, but several processes intervene and prolong the voyage. One is the input of lifting energy from the turbulence between the dust layer and the northeast trade winds that cut under it. Removal by rainfall is minimized by the rain-suppressing effect of the warm dust layer itself, which is enhanced by the dust's absorption of heat from the sun.

Another example of long-distance particle travel is the jaunt that dust from the Gobi Desert of Mongolia makes out into the Pacific. In 1971 a Japanese research group headed by Kenji Isono, reported that they had observed dust pass over Japan from Asia and days later collect in Hawaii and Alaska. They concluded that a single surge of dust from the Gobi had drifted across the Pacific for well over 10,000 kilometers.

The Arctic has its own ways of maintaining its aerosol population. One is the short, direct path that air masses follow from pollution sources in the middle latitudes into the low-lying Arctic. In contrast, the sources for pollution of the Antarctic, one of the cleanest places on earth, are farther away and the winds between them and the 3000-meter-high interior follow long, rising spirals. The Arctic, like the Antarctic, is more or less of a desert. Barrow, Alaska, receives only ten centimeters of precipitation a year and most of that

---

Tambora blew up, the temperature averaged 5° F. below normal, and the price of a sack of flour in London doubled.

in the summer. Thus pollutants that would be ordinarily removed by rain or snow are commonly found in the air, especially in the winter, which is the time when greater amounts of sulfate and gray organic matter show up on aerosol sampling filters at Barrow.

One reason Rahn and others are reasonably confident of the theory of European origin of Artic pollution is that they have found excess vanadium all around the Arctic, but they can't find a likely source for it other than the major industrial centers of the middle latitude. For reasons that entirely elude us, vanadium is a natural component of crude petroleum and is concentrated in heavy industrial fuel oils. Atmospheric chemists have found that when excess vanadium is detected in the air, it invariably is a pollutant from the burning of residual fuel oils. The vanadium in the air at Barrow doesn't have a local origin because vanadium-laden heavy fuels are too thick to be used in the Arctic.

Several chemical clues point to Europe as a likely source for the fantastic factor of arctic pollution. Samples collected in Greenland, which straddles likely routes from the United States, contained several times less sulfate and vanadium than those collected at Spitzbergen, which is due north of Scandinavia. The ratio of sulfate to vanadium progressively increases from western Europe through northern Norway to Spitzbergen. The relative proportion of manganese from heavy industry and vanadium appear the same in Europe, Spitzbergen, and Barrow, but differ from those in New England or New Jersey.

The best path between the European source and the Arctic appears to be northeastward into the European USSR, northward into the Arctic, and thence on to Barrow. Travel time: twenty days.

United States pollution, therefore, can be judged guiltless of the pall around the North Pole.

The Vicious Rains

The innocence of the United States, however, ends right there. Acid rain propelled on the summer winds is a problem that recently has raised more hell than the issue of busing black and white school children.

Some winds have always been devils, especially those that sweep down the mountains, such as the *Foehn* in southern Europe, the chinook in the Rockies, and the Santa Ana in Los Angeles. They are accompanied by outbreaks of violence and suicide. Such winds are supposed to have a high ratio of positive to negative ions.*

Because of wind, a good case can be made for Hartford, Connecticut having the foulest air in the country. I hasten to add that this is not Hartford's fault. The Environmental Protection Agency cannot find any source for bad air in Hartford. The aerial garbage blows in from New York, New Jersey, and even Baltimore. There's nothing that the EPA can do but try to suppress the pollution in the New York area. That in turn would mean stopping the sulfur oxides from being generated in Ohio and riding the evil west winds into the northeastern states.

Perhaps the most sensible overall study of photochemical air pollution in the northeastern United States was made by William Cleveland and T. E. Graedel of Bell Laboratories.

Although it might be thought that since nitric oxide and hydrocarbons are the main building blocks of ozone synthesis, areas with large emissions of nitrogen oxides and hydrocarbons would have the highest ozone concentrations. That is not the case, as we already discovered in southern California. Areas which are as far as forty-five to sixty

---

*The ion theory has a hint of scientific validity but has become somewhat of a sham. Generators of negative ions (the supposedly soothing ones) are sold at huge prices but are actually dangerous since most models produce ozone.

miles downwind of major sources of primary emissions, and which themselves have fewer emissions, can have the highest ozone concentrations. (The similarity between Los Angeles–Riverside and New York–Hartford is remarkable in regard to ozone, although it differs massively in that sulfur emissions are important only in the northeastern mess.)

Some of the Bell Laboratory conclusions:

1. Reduction of primary emissions of hydrocarbons and nitrogen oxides in the New York area would reduce the concentrations of many trace contaminants but is not likely to have real effect on concentrations of ozone within the region itself, since the latter is determined by the ozone already in air transported into the region from Ohio.

2. The ozone peaks in concentration are increased by approximately 20 percent as a consequence of primary emissions in New York City and material transport. As a result Connecticut has the highest ozone level in the Northeast and perhaps in the country.

3. Both within and downwind of the New York City region, four of the five undesirable secondary products (sulfate, peroxy acetyl nitrate, nitric acid, and acrolein) would decrease substantially if the amount of nitric oxide is reduced but would respond only slightly to reduction in hydrocarbon concentrations.

But what is acid rain? In parts of the eastern United States and western Europe precipitation has changed from a neutral pollution two hundred years ago to a dilute solution of sulfuric acid and nitric acid today. In the most extreme example recorded, in a storm in Scotland in 1974, the rain had the acidic equivalent of vinegar (pH 2.4). The pH scale is logarithmic. The lower the value, the more acidic. Complete neutrality corresponds to a pH of 6.0. At normal concentrations and pressures of carbon dioxide (a weak acid), the pH of rain and snow would be 5.6. Soil particles are usually slightly alkaline. The ammonium ion in rain and snow tends to increase the pH.

Maps of mean pH of rain show a central region of high acidity that had spread from Belgium–Holland in the late 1950s to most of Germany, France, the British Isles, and southern Scandinavia by the late 1960s. At the time of the pH of 2.4 in Scotland, values of 2.7 and 3.5 were recorded on the western coast of Norway and in Iceland.

Tall stacks turn local problems into regional problems. In 1955 only two stacks in the United States were over 180 meters tall. Now essentially all stacks being built are over 180 meters. By 1975 at least fifteen stacks taller than 300 meters had been built in the world. The nickel smelter in Sudbury, Ontario, has a superstack over 400 meters tall. Some 1 percent of the total sulfurous emissions in the world comes from this one smelter. During the last decade the annual emissions of sulfur dioxide from Sudbury, Canada, have equaled the amount emitted by all the volcanoes of the world. The deposition of sulfates has been noticeable on the Greenland ice caps.

Dry deposition of sulphur dioxide or its oxidation products has been the chief way to poison people *near the emission source,* while wet deposition dominates in remote areas of northern Europe and in the eastern United States.

Certain geologic structures are peculiarly sensitive, such as areas with siliceous bedrock (granite, quartzite, and quartz sandstone). These rock types won't dissolve and won't buffer acids. Typical structures are the Pre-Cambrian Shield of Scandinavia, the Canadian Shield, the Rockies, New England, the Adirondacks, and the Appalachians. In lakes and streams exposed to acid rain in these regions, the fish population has been totally destroyed. We will discuss this loss later on.

Other subtler effects may turn out to be more perilous. The rate of decomposition of organic matter is slowed, presumably because vigor of bacteria and fungi is reduced. Bacteria generally do worse as scavengers in an acid environment. Indeed changes occur at all levels of the food web: phytoplankton, zooplankton, and fish, all of which, if they survive at all, decrease in number of species.

The Environmental Protection Agency has ruled that from 70 to 90 percent of sulfur dioxide must be removed from the emissions of all *new* coal-based power plants. The old plants, which remain largely uncontrolled, are doing the damage.

We must emphasize that many environmental costs are hidden, particularly the ones associated with synergistic effects of the stress that acid puts on organisms: for example, decreasing their resistance to pathogens and predators.

Looking at data from August 1977 researchers at New York University Medical Center noticed some curious things. They found that the air over New Jersey, which two days before had been stagnating over the Ohio River, had a much higher sulfate level than the air just a few miles away over New York and Long Island. In the summer air can stagnate over an area, undergoing a sort of chemical masturbation process, for two, three, or even more days at a time. This is just what is needed for the conversion and toxifying of pollutants. The air masses then can carry the smog across half a continent.

Winds in the Northeast tend to be windier than elsewhere, affording less stagnation time. Thus distant sources tend to dominate urban sulfate levels in summer, whereas local sources are now more important in winter when winds are less active. The Northeast is at the wrong end of a countrywide sewer in the sky.

Acid deposition is a better term, although it will never be used as commonly as acid rain. Only about half the acid in the atmosphere comes down as rain or snow. The other half comes down in dry deposition, by impact, by adsorption on surfaces, and by dissolving directly in lakes and oceans. The ground, however, gets the same amount of acidity either way.

It takes about one day on the average for coal-plant sulfur dioxide to convert to sulfate. Actually the process for this absolutely crucial oxidation is complicated and obscure but probably involves reactions with ozone, peroxides, OH radical, and ammonium sulfate. Sulfuric acid is the immediate product, but sulfate salts are commonly formed. Both ammonium sulfate and ammonium bisulfate, which appear to be the major forms by which sulfuric acid disguises itself, are strongly hydrophilic (they love water). Thus they form droplets, readily contributing to the familiar haziness of summer, and rain out quickly.* The average residence time for sulfate aerosols is about a week. In winter it's closer to five days; in summer, ten days. Under certain conditions, sulfur and nitrogen compounds generated in the United States can reach Europe.

The path followed by nitrogen oxides is still uncertain but seems to be similar to that of sulfur dioxide. Nitric acid is formed in about a day, and the acid aerosol is deposited in about a week. Nitric acid, in fact, forms about one-third of the acid rain in the East. And in the long run nitrogen oxides may prove to be a much more worrisome problem than sulfur dioxide. Technologies exist to keep sulfur emissions under control. But nitrogen forms too many oxides. There is really no adequate technique for nitrogen oxide control. If there had been, the automotive industry would have put it

*It is discouraging to realize that the magic morning haze in the pecan grove is simply a by-product of sulfur smog.

to work twenty years ago.

Although the acid rain problem is mostly of eastern concern, it has been found recently that in the southern and western parts of the United States, pH values between 3.0 and 4.0 are common during storms. However, acid rain in the far-western United States, near Los Angeles, San Francisco, and Seattle, is produced primarily by nitric acid, pointing the finger at autos rather than power plants.

The acidity of precipitates in some parts of Scandinavia has increased by two-hundredfold during the past two decades. Acids from the sky, however, are hardly a new terror. In England in the early part of this century, acidity in the vicinity of Leeds, a heavy coal-burning city, was 75 percent attributable to sulfur compounds, while the pH in rain and fog dropped below 3.0 on occasion.

The behavior of acid clouds is unpredictable. At night and in the early morning, ground-based inversions can isolate the pollution plume aloft, so that it stays up there until conditions allow it to perch, like a flock of crows, at ground level.

Lake Sensitivity

Each lake has a threshold of acidification beyond which everything important dies, even mosquitoes. The threshold value of Scottish lakes is at a pH of about 4.6. In Sweden increased acid loadings have resulted in over 15,000 fishless lakes.

In the United States low thresholds exist in the lakes of the Adirondack State Park of New York and the Boundary Waters Corner Area–Voyageurs in Minnesota. In the Adirondacks the threshold has been exceeded for several years. Fish have stopped reproducing, and over one hundred lakes are fishless. Parks of eastern Canada, thanks mainly to the International Nickel Company, are barren of fish.

Like the Adirondack Park area, the Minnesota lake region rests on acidic bedrock and thus provides the recipe for the acid sensitivity of the midwestern states. Upper Michigan, northern Wisconsin, and northern Minnesota have this unfortunate type of bedrock.

The absence of dramatic pollution, other than fish killing, is deceptive. Pollution over a long range of time and distance usually doesn't exceed conventional air quality standards. But like delayed cancer in the human predicament, there are signs of permanent reduction in tree growth in the acid rain areas. Plant pathologists predict a decimating effect on crops such as lettuce, spinach, or chard, of which the foliage is the edible portion. Even at a pH of less than 3.0, acres of crop leaf surfaces become spotted or necrotic. An extensive screening program to look at the effects of sulfuric acid rain on virtually every crop of the United States was finished by the EPA in the summer of 1980. It would take another book to list these results, but it can be said that indeed virtually every crop is affected.

There is no doubt that Ohio has the highest sulfur dioxide emission rate of any state, nearly twice the total rate of 4,700 tons a day in the six New England states, New York, and New Jersey combined.

Pennsylvania, a proud dominion, rich in forest, field, deer, and streams, is being soaked by the most acidic rain anywhere in the country, possibly in the world. On September 19, 1978, a notable shower fell on Kane, located one hundred miles from the state's western border. According to the Pennsylvania Forestry Associates, it had a pH reading of 2.32. That beats the Scottish record. In most of Pennsylvania's lakes the trout, bass, and pickerel are gone. Frogs no longer call their girl friends—they're dead too.

Acid rain ruins the paint jobs on about one million houses a year. In the rural area of Clarion County, Pennsylvania, the rain is so acid it's eating away the plumbing in homes with rooftop cisterns. Roughly 15 percent of the homes had lead levels which exceeded standards set by the Safe Drinking Water Act of 1974. Even the dew is acid enough to shrivel a dandelion.

In Pennsylvania's lakes and streams the added acid causes a shock from which hatching fish cannot recover. Increased acid affects a food chain, replacing normal plants that live on lake and stream bottoms with mosses and fungi. This is a sort of return to the early eons of the planet, before fish evolved. The fish die because there's nothing left they can eat.

In some desperation men have dumped tons of limestone into acidified lakes and are even toying with breeding an acid-resistant fish. But as a zoologist remarked, "Breeding an acid-resistant fish is like breeding a gas-resistant canary for miners." The intimation is stark: "Today the fish; tomorrow, the fisherman."

If the fish aren't killed, they are most likely rendered poisonous by an extraordinary mechanism. In normal rivers the highly poisonous mercury wastes fall to the bottom and are avoided by prudent fish. In acid waters, however, the mercury is readily transformed to the compound methyl mercury, which is easily absorbed and even relished by fish. It doesn't poison them, but it does poison human beings who eat them.

Pennsylvania is suing the EPA to enforce sulfur dioxide standards in Ohio. Two coal-fired plants near Cleveland currently are emitting sulfur dioxide at four to five times the allowed rate. They are old plants and therefore relatively untouchable by EPA. The state of Ohio is not about to oblige Pennsylvania, New York, New Jersey, or any other state. The "oil backout" legislation, representing Carter's attempt to get utility plants to burn coal, would cause approximately a 20 percent increase in acid rain in the Northeast.

Strange Quirks of Wind and Weather

We are beginning to realize that the world is not only connected by enigmatic climatic and weather relationships, but the behavior of the troposphere vis-a-vis the stratosphere is full of mysterious rituals which seem to make no sense.

Let us return to the problem of ozone, since so much is known about its association with air pollution in general. In recent years Chester Spies of the Battelle Memorial Institute has observed high ozone concentrations in many rural areas that were previously thought to be immune to the effects of photochemical smog. His studies suggest that the concentrations of ozone at any given location is the result of (1) ozone from the stratosphere, (2) ozone generated by autos, (3) ozone formed by precursory chemicals accumulated in high pressure weather cells and transported many hundreds of miles over several days (regional ozone), and (4) ozone formed in urban plumes downwind of cities. Ozone associated with high pressure systems tends to blanket large regions of the country and, when superimposed on background and locally generated ozone, can result in concentrations exceeding all standards. Ozone formed in urban plumes is combined with ozone from these other sources, and forms hot spots in the regional ozone blanket.

To determine the maximum distance ozone can be transported within an urban plume, such plumes were investigated under conditions where the plume extended out over the ocean. This is ideal, owing to smooth terrain and lack of scavenging emissions.

As the research aircraft moved from one point to another, the ozone concentration increased dramatically. The maximum ozone along the path was found directly downwind of the urban center. Concentration levels proved that the urban plumes of ozone extend for at least 150 miles. A subsequent study of a Boston plume showed a maximum reaching distance of 250 miles. Even at such distances the ozone concentrations approached twice the federal standards. An air mass can move rapidly enough to traverse 200 miles between New York and Boston during the course of a single day.

On such a typical day the ozone patterns at 9:00 A.M. show the effect of the previous evening's high ozone in the northeast part of the region. Since the overnight concentration of ozone within stable layers aloft was probably even higher than the surface concentration, it seems plausible that much of the morning ozone is actually left over from the previous evening. This concept of a sort of Sky of Oz region, above the inversion layer, where chemical snakes are kept away, for a time at least, from destructive encounters, is an important new contribution to the damnable complications of pollution theory. By noon there is a definite intrusion of ozone-rich air into Connecticut from the southwest. The fact that wind speeds averaged over thirty miles per hour throughout the day is entirely consistent with the theory that this band of ozone represents the smeared-out urban plumes from the complexes in New Jersey, New York, and southwest Connecticut. Air from Philadelphia enters Connecticut after passing through the New York metropolitan area.

The mass trajectories indicate that the air arriving at Simsbury, Connecticut, during most of the day had passed over New York and Philadelphia, and to some extent even Washington and Baltimore. The air arriving in Groton during daytime and evening hours had passed near Baltimore—up the Atlantic coast of New Jersey and across eastern Long Island. In this particular pattern Groton received very little input from New York and Philadelphia.

Measurements of Freon-11 were made to provide a means of distinguishing between urban and rural air. The sources of F-11 emissions are cities, so that air passing over urban areas has higher amounts of F-11 than rural air. Since F-11 is essentially inert in the lower atmosphere, it can be used to trace the movement of urban air and its ozone. The following table summarizes the data:

Source of Ozone	Contribution to Total Ozone Burden
Background and rural emissions	20 parts per billion, daily average
Regional ozone, associated with High pressure	70–150 parts per billion, hourly average
Ozone generated within urban plumes	150–250 parts per billion, hourly average

These numbers are surprising and in a sense, discouraging. They indicate a shifting and whirling scene, impossible to understand.

Atmospheric mixing experiments now confirm a process which rapidly mixes air between the troposphere and the stratosphere and may force a reevaluation of air quality standards for ozone as affected by man's diddling in the chemical balance of the stratosphere.

The driving force behind this rapid mixing is what air pilots dread—clear air turbulence. This treacherous condition is created when the high-speed jet stream lines up with a cold front. This occurs most often in the midlatitudes during the spring. The boundary between troposphere and stratosphere, known at the tropopause, actually folds under these conditions, resulting in totally unpredictable situations, including insertions of stratosphere air downward and troposphere air upward. A small airplane may suddenly stall or go into a wild loop.

A Colorado mystery that has irritated atmospheric detectives for years can only be explained on the basis of the crazy new aerodynamics. Data for a rural area at an elevation of 2900 meters near the Continental Divide show remarkably low pH values for the rains. A sharp downward trend in pH over the past three years is associated with increasing amounts of nitric acid. In other words, this domestic Shangri-La is afflicted with severe acid rain. But where in the world is it coming from?

The site is located in the Como Creek Watershed, Boulder County—six kilometers east of the Continental Divide. The area in a 400-kilometer radius around the watershed has an extremely low population density, except for a strip along the Rocky Mountain front range (Fort Collins, Boulder, Denver), 20 to 50 kilometers east and 1300 meters lower in elevation. But the wind never flows from Denver toward Como Creek. The next closest urban area is Salt Lake City, 600 kilometers west, and Phoenix, 400 kilometers southeast. Considerable weather-pattern data show that air movement is from the northwest over a region of very low population density.

The tests started in June 1975 and were reported for three years. The downward trend in pH and upward trend in nitrate cut across seasons and across years with very different weather patterns. Nitric acid, primarily an auto emission, is the component responsible for the observed *increase* in precipitation acidity.

Only two possibilities appear reasonable: (1) complex and unsuspected mechanisms are moving the pollutants substantial distances (westward and upward) from the Denver urban corridor, contrary to the prevailing pattern of air mass movement, or (2) very profound changes in rain chemistry are occurring in the western United States because of big increases in the release of nitrogen oxides from multiple sources through the west. The former possibility seems to fit in better with the "crazy aerodynamics" phenomenon, of which clear air turbulence is one frightening embodiment.

Is it any wonder that people still talk about the weather? The weather is more mysterious than Mata Hari, and it seems likely that if we are to control air pollution, we must also gain some degree of dominance over, or at least obtain much more information about, the weather.

Acids from Volcanoes

The recent eruptions of Mount Saint Helens have focused attention on volcanoes as competitors of sour coal burning power plants in vinegarizing the downwind pastures, lakes, and automobile paint jobs. Although we have concluded that some volcanoes may be a source of serious trouble to the ozone layer by tossing great storms of hydrochloric acid into the stratosphere, what about the effects on the lower air?

So far Mount Saint Helens has been curiously well behaved as far as ejection of sulfur dioxide is concerned. During the steam phase of the eruption, it put out only about thirty tons per day, compared to hundreds of thousands of tons from other active volcanoes in the Pacific area. However, do not look down your nose at Mount Saint Helens. The eruption was twice as powerful as Vesuvius. Luckily there was no Pompeii nearby.

The ash, although not of the dangerous quartz type that causes silicosis, is acidic enough to ruin the turbine blades of jet engines. At the time of writing, no other unusual effects had been noted that threaten the salmon or the bears. The eruption on May 18 was catastrophic only because it steam-rollered people and animals with the sheer bulk of ash or mud, not because it poisoned them. However, the story is not over. Doubtless someone will come up with a Mount Saint Helens syndrome.

One interesting aspect of the eruption could stand more investigation. Radioactively speaking, which was more dangerous, Three Mile Island or Mount Saint Helens? The volcano blew out about three million curies of radon gas. Three Mile Island released ultimately about 2.5 million curies of radioactive xenon gas. But conservatively speaking, a curie of radon, because of its superactive daughters, is regarded as at least a thousand times more dangerous than xenon. Thus the volcano was and remains the more fearsome source of radioactivity.

Mount Baker, the northernmost volcano in the American Cascades, came close to erupting six years ago. Vapor clouds rose from the main vent, Sherman Crater, a few hundred feet below the 10,778-foot summit. Fumeroles in the crater suddenly discharged steam and hydrogen sulfide, a foul and dangerous poison. Its acids killed the fish in its own mountainside streams and some of its snow-packed slopes were stained yellow. Baker did not erupt at that time but if it had, doubtless it would have been meaner than Mount Saint Helens.

8

Nuclear Energy versus Coal

Coal is a portable climate.

   —Emerson

We are going to need both nuclear energy and coal in very large amounts before the end of the century. After petroleum, they are really the only big games left in town. Which is the most dangerous, which is the most expensive, which is the best all-around bet? Viewing the problem globally, one can say that the intensive development of industrial nuclear energy should reduce the possibility of its *military* use. Wars occur when the have-nots mobilize against the haves. Nuclear energy is safer for the world because it is cheaper and easier to give the world nuclear energy than energy in any other readily available form.

From the previous chapter, we have learned that the burning of high-sulfur coal in power plants is an ingenious way to produce dilute sulfuric acid, kill lake fish, and retard the vegetation for hundreds, even thousands, of miles from the smokestack. But, of course, that is not the whole story.

My experience with nuclear power goes back not only to the early days of "excursion" research* at the Idaho Falls Laboratory (where the goal was to see how far you could get off the beam without burning somebody up), but I was indirectly connected with the Manhattan Project before the explosions at Hiroshima and Nagasaki.

Of the two means of producing energy (burning coal and splitting atoms) I much prefer to split the atom. Operating a nuclear reactor can be a very routine business. Nuclear reactor operators are not all dumb, but many exist in a state of glassy-eyed boredom. Greater computerization and less of an aggregation of buzzers and lights would improve the efficiency of the job. Dr. Edward Teller has made the noteworthy suggestion that very smart talking computers be installed in every control room. With the high IQ robot, the operators could carry on a question-and-answer conversation. The computer would further educate them, as it dispelled the boredom.

The curious fact has been overlooked entirely or looked at cross-eyed, that more damage has been caused by *radioactivity from exposure to coal dust and coal ash than by exposure to uranium or plutonium isotopes in nuclear power plants.* The mining, handling, and burning of coal are intrinsically about a thousand times more dangerous than the transformation of fissionable materials into electric energy.

To counter this observation, the antinukes, if they are momentarily confused, always start talking about solar energy. That is a good thing to talk about, if we define our terms. In the long look, of course, coal and other fossil fuels are solar energy. Gasohol is solar energy. So are windmills and the thermal currents of the ocean. But generally the

---

*An excursion in a nuclear device is usually a deliberate operation outside those limits prescribed as standard.

antinukes seem to have in mind *direct* solar energy. "I can set a piece of paper on fire with a magnifying glass," they seem to say. "Why can't you run an industrial plant the same way?"

Specifically they are talking mainly about photovoltaic cells—devices for converting sunlight directly into electricity. There is a grandiose dream for setting up thousands of miles of photovoltaic cell networks above the stratosphere, converting the rich outer sunlight into microwaves, and beaming them down to earth receptors which will transform them into conventional electric power. This is a good dream —for the twenty-third century. By that time it may be competing with a still more dreamy dream: nuclear energy from fusion rather than fission.

The trouble with direct solar energy is its extraordinary expense. The hardware bandits had it priced out of human reach even before the first authoritative books on it were published. The most recent estimate of direct solar energy cost has been made by the Department of Energy's Solar Energy Research Institute at Golden, Colorado. They figure that direct solar energy for industrial use will be competitive when petroleum reaches $436.00 per barrel (more than ten times the present price.)

The Crooks Who Nearly Killed Nuclear Energy

Unfortunately, a nearly deliberate and successful attempt has been made to multiply the expense of nuclear energy to an infinite horizon at which everybody but the customer gets rich. It is not hazard, nor is it over-theatricalized episodes such as Three Mile Island that have caused the decline and fall of nuclear energy in this country; it is the unconscionable brigands who made it two hundred times more expensive to buy nuclear plant hardware than five years ago.

As for safety, it is unwise to sneer too indifferently at the modest dangers that do lurk in the sequence of operations of nuclear energy. But since Three Mile Island the ignorant press has made matters very sticky. One example is a story that was headlined in every newspaper in the United States: "Cracks Found in Reactors!" Actually, the cracks were not in the reactors but in the turbines that convert steam to electricity. The cracks had nothing whatever to do with nuclear reactions; cracks are found every day in one or more of the innumerable steam turbines used in coal, gas burning, or hydroelectric utility plants all over the world.

According to Dixy Lee Ray, former governor of Washington and ex-chairman of the Atomic Energy Commission, being killed in a nuclear accident is as likely as being bitten by a poisonous snake while crossing the street in Washington, D.C. Hazel Henderson, perhaps the most intelligent woman in the country, points out that if this were so, the insurance rates would be reasonable. But they are not. "The cause," she states, "is not prudence based on rational analysis of the hazards but because, in real life, we are now dealing with a disequilibrium economy that piles risks on risks. We don't know how to *model* probability under these conditions. The underlying logic of insurance breaks down."

Nevertheless, all nuclear plants *are* insured. This happens in different ways. One method of insurance is single private insurance for liability—Something like $140 million per plant. There is also mutual insurance. Under this system each company which operates a reactor is supposed to contribute about $5 million to a pool. The total liability adds up to about $500 million per plant. Congress has provided a makeshift policy of $500 million per nuclear accident—a figure that the Supreme Court has noted is a good "starting point" for calculation.

The worst accidents have already happened. The Public

Health Service estimates that from 1946 to 1960, one thousand uranium miners were needlessly and recklessly exposed to radioactive gases present in the air of mining tunnels. The Service estimates that as many as 1,200 deaths from lung cancer could result. Yet it appears that the future lung cancer incidence from coal radioactivity is going to far exceed the uranium mining and shipping fatalities. One reason is that such coal plants are often located in large cities and thus expose the surrounding population to more radioactivity than do normally operating nuclear reactors of equivalent power.

I am personally sold not only on the "Model-T-type" light-water reactors that Westinghouse and General Electric have produced, but on the great economies that have been laid out in perspective for us in the form of *breeders.* *

Theoretically the breeder concept results in more available energy delivered to the fission process than taken out of the process in the form of heat. No laws of conservation are broken, but in the breeding system energy that would otherwise stagnate for eternity is made accessible for immediate use. In the classical breeder the load is 80 percent uranium-238 and 20 percent plutonium. In the breeding process neutrons from the splitting of plutonium-239 convert uranium-238 (or thorium) to additional plutonium-239. You get more fissionable plutonium atoms formed than you split. How can you lose?

According to Jimmy Carter and other timorous spirits, you lose your soul and the world. Terrorists and gangster nations, confronted with all this plutonium-239, will grab off

---

*Although this is a good word, I must admit to being repelled by most of the language of the nuclear bureaucrats. In nuke-speech, for example, an explosion is an "energetic disassembly." A fire is a "rapid oxidation." Rather than speak forthrightly of plutonium contamination in the reactor vessel, a spokesman delicately acknowledged that plutonium had "taken up residence" there.

enough to make fission bombs with which they can threaten the world of good Christians and start wars popping off all over. The earth will then be destroyed by ten-thousand fire crackers. I cannot buy this science-fiction conspiracy. For one thing, artificial plutonium-239 is so contaminated with plutonium-240, it would destroy more terrorists by premature detonation than the target of terrorism. From personal experience I know how hard it is to make an atomic bomb that really works, even if you have a blue print. For the same amount of effort the terrorists can get more explosion from dynamite. (If I want to spend Fitzgerald's dark night of the soul worrying, three o'clock finds me having nightmares, not about nuclear bombs but about nerve gas.)

Because of Carter's timidity and the wild greed of manufacturers and mine owners, we find ourselves left about half a decade behind the advanced nations, such as Russia, France, and even Germany, Japan and the United Kingdom. France with its Super-Phoenix has the most sophisticated breeder now in operation, but several Russian units are about on a par.

The American people as a whole have always voted for and will (I believe) continue to vote for nuclear energy. What they are voting for, however, is a good clean house, run by competent people, who seem to be in good supply in the Chicago area (perhaps the most successful center of nuclear energy on earth) but rather thin in some places.

It is obvious that the most important part of the United States public that needs reeducation on nuclear energy is women. In June 1980 a Pro-Nuke was set up to make personal contacts, not with the Clamshell Alliance, not the Sierra Club, but with women, all kinds of women. The bright idea evolved of using women as traveling spokespersons *for* the nuclear industry. Nuclear Energy Women (NEW), a Washington-based group of female nuclear engineers, manufacturers, and utility-company representatives is the rallying group for the potential army. I think the women on the listening end will be reasonable, especially as they don't have to face up to formidable young men with beards and extraneous sex appeal.

Among the "unscheduled outage" problems (another euphenism) are valves that are not only as expensive as if they were cast of gold, but that simply won't work. It doesn't seem to matter which of the major valve manufacturers in the United States the valves come from. The problem has ominously accentuated. During the late 1960s the Atomic Energy Commission (AEC) would find two defective valves per plant per year. In 1972 the average had climbed to over 8 percent, and today the figures are classified, which certainly does not mean a decrease.

Milton Shaw used to point out the fact that the Navy has the power to impose standards on manufacturers who make parts. Until the AEC (or its 1975 version, the Nuclear Regulatory Commission) gets such a power, Shaw suggests that policing the industry with routine inspection is "like pushing a brick around with a wet noodle."

The trouble at Three Mile Island was primarily defective valves and incompetent operators. Some of the troubles there and elsewhere could only be created by men who are dead-tired, drunk, drugged, or so absent-minded that they don't belong to the world of the late twentieth century.

The Swedish vote to continue with nuclear energy is very encouraging, since there are more antinuke college students in that country per capita than perhaps anywhere else in the world (except Cambridge, Massachusetts, of course). The Swedish ballot was not merely a "yes" or "no" affair, like the one in Austria, which resulted in total and immediate abandonment of the country's first nuclear power station. The Swedes gave voters three choices. The two "yes" options on the ballots, which proposed to halt the development of nuclear energy over several years after first increasing the number of reactors, received 58.1 percent of the vote. A proposal to dismantle the country's operating reactors over a period of years received 38 percent.

The vote seemed to show that nuclear programs could still win substantial support a year after the Three Mile Island incident. In West Germany, where fourteen nuclear reactors are in operation but further development of nuclear energy has been practically halted by court action and lack of political decisiveness, the Swedish vote seemed to have a bracing effect.

The Waste Disposal Problem

There are well-known methods of disposing of the radiation wastes, and it has become now a political and economic rather than a technical problem.

The classical solution of burying the wastes in salt domes is still feasible, except that states with salt domes suddenly claim they have other things to do with them: they are going to dig them out and start underground Disneylands; they are going to use them for low-cost housing; they are going to have underground football stadiums; etc., etc.

The costly, but technically feasible, process of forming capsules of strong glass, ceramic material, or titanate around the patches of radioactive waste, then burying the masses in granite underground formations, will probably end up as the best choice. It is not astronomic in cost as might be imagined, because the amount of wastes from even very large nuclear plants is almost ludicrously small. They are still smaller, of course, from breeder reactors.

Objections to such a straightforward process of disposal consist of cries that over 250,000 years the artificial deposits won't stay put. The earth moves too much to be sure a waste disposal mass will stay in the same place. Alvin Weinberg, a sort of revered sultan of nuclear energy and formerly head of the Oak Ridge National Laboratory, neatly disposes of this silliness. He points out that in Gabon, Africa there is a uranium mine in which natural reactors operated two billion years ago. Several tons of plutonium and billions of curies of radioactivity were found. Yet the plutonium and the reactivity remained immobilized. If the earth can retain radioactivity so well by chance, he asks, cannot modern technology do better?

If for unaccountable reasons burial in the earth is politically improper, the nuclear wastes can always be wrapped in rockets and shot into the sun, where they would find a warm welcome. A less expensive way of garbage disposal is to shoot the wastes into an orbit midway between Earth and Venus, about 14 million miles from Earth.

Coal Must Also Go Ahead

Since I wrote last on coal*, two crucial developments have come ahead fast. The first and most important is a means of burning coal so that it doesn't emit sulfur dioxide and cause the tragedies of acid rain depicted in chapter 8. The second is the perfection of the system, mainly pioneered in Russia, of producing useful gas from coal by partially burning it underground.

The gasification or liquefaction of coal in surface facilities is a somewhat sick goose. There is still a lot of big talk and big money running around, but somehow one feels a lack of drive and enthusiasm. One understandable reason for this is the environmental penalty. The conversion of power plants

*Energy and the Earth Machine New York: Norton, 1976.

from gas or oil to coal is proceeding at a slow crawl.

Coal combustion, according to the Fuels Sciences Laboratory, occurs in two stages. During the first stage the fresh coal particle decomposes, converting itself to gases and char, with the gases burning in a little flame surrounding the char particle. When the production of gases stops, the flame attaches itself to the char particle and the second stage of combustion is the burning of the stubborn and nasty little piece of carbon. The formation of nitric oxide occurs during both stages, but this is not the Haber process nitric oxide we are all too familiar with from the automobile. It is nitric oxide resulting from the burning of organic nitrogen compounds in the coal itself In shale oil there are huge amounts of such organically bound nitrogen.

The behavior of mineral matter during combustion when you burn coal may determine whether or not you have a practical process. Most of the coal mineral matter is converted to glass. The importance of the glassmaking reactions are: 1. The slagging and fouling characteristics of the product determines a big part of the cost of combustion. How do you separate the ash at the end of the line? Does it in fact hopelessly *foul up* the line? 2. The glass forming process forms extremely small particles. Electrostatic precipitators are not effective but human beings are quite efficient in collecting them and cuddling them, just as Cleopatra cuddled the asp. 3. Many of the toxic elements present in original coal tend to be present in high concentration in the submicroscopic particles. On this surface its toxic elements are present not as inert glasses but in such a form that they are readily absorbed into the body fluids.

Another problem—and one with an element of, we might say, almost chemical mystification—is the emission of unburned hydrocarbons, almost all carcinogenic polynuclear aromatics. Such emissions represent a failure of the combustion process to go to completion. In classical combustion-engineering lore, it was believed that all such failures were due to imperfect mixing and could be eliminated by some gadget or process like a glorified Cuisinart. More recently researchers have become aware that these are real chemical limitations on the combustion process. The embarrassing question comes up as to whether one can really burn polynuclear aromatics. Combustion is a so-called free radical process which cannot be started up unless the reactants are present in certain minimum concentrations, the flammability limits. It is conceivable that there are other minimum concentrations at which a combustion process decides it must stop.

The factors that control the length of time necessary to burn a coal particle are only partly defined. With oil in dwindling supply it would be highly desirable to follow governmental wishes and burn coal in previously oil-fired boilers. But the boilers generally lack ash-handling facilities. This problem may be avoided if one uses ash-free coal. There is a greater difficulty, however, in that these standard boilers lack the firebox volume needed for the larger coal flame, a problem directly related to the length of time needed to burn coal particles.

S. C. Morris and others at the Brookhaven National Laboratory have studied some of the problems of conversion of coal to gas and oil, as mandated in the Power Plant and Industrial Fuel Act of 1978.

When coal is converted to gas or oil by hydrogenation,* the emission of the hydrogenation plants will not add to the

---

*In this case the hydrogenation of coal refers to the high-pressure catalytic reaction of hydrogen gas with coal. It is generally regarded as much more expensive than the Fischer–Tropsch process, in which the coal is first converted to mixtures of carbon monoxide and hydrogen gases, which are combined catalytically to yield liquid hydrocarbons, but also, if desired, alcohol.

pollution, even in a densely populated area. The automatic sulfur removal during hydrogenation may be an elegant alternative to the chemical washing of flue gas to remove sulfur dioxide in the burning of ordinary coal.

Probably the first coal liquefaction plant to be built under the Synthetic Fuels Corporation program will be the so-called SRC-11 (solvent refined coal) complex,* Gulf Oil's very expensive show at Morgantown, West Virginia. In addition to the United States Department of Energy, this is supported by money from West Germany and Japan. But there is a ding-dong fight brewing which, even before the pumps begin to grind, will make the placid town of Morgantown feel like the eye of a hurricane.

As of late 1980, EPA had turned all its guns on the energy department's tentative draft of an environmental impact statement. The National Resources Defense Council and the National Wildlife Federation were also pouring stink bombs into the redoubt. The biggest complaint is the poisonous nature of the process streams, wastes, and end-products: benzene, aniline, indole, quinoline, phenol, and cresols.

EPA is being difficult, perhaps because its authority in the whole "synfuels" program is shaky. It refuses to issue a guidance document and threatens that formal regulations cannot be drawn up for another two years. Ultimately one hundred permits will be required for each new synfuel facility.

All is not jam and bourbon during hydrogenation, however. The liquid fuels produced by direct liquefaction contain carcinogenic polycyclic organics, as do the tarry and oily effluents of many liquefaction or gasification processes. A large pilot liquefaction plant at Institute, West Virginia, op-

---

*Solvent refined coal is not what it sounds like. The phrase indirectly conveys the fact that during hydrogenation (the pivotal step) a special liquid fraction of the coal is used to disperse the rest.

erating between 1952 and 1956 caused a lot of skin cancer and pretumorous growths in the plant workers.

What Gulf and the Department of Energy fear most is an outright legal challenge by the National Resources Defense Council and the National Wildlife Federation. As John Stenger of the Department of Energy said, "Anybody with a fifteen-cent stamp can bring us to court and stop the whole project."

It was to avoid such vulnerabilities, of course, that then-President Carter originally proposed the overriding energy board designed to go around kicking everybody in the teeth who seemed to have that fifteen-cent stamp.

The Brookhaven team compared health effects from (1) coal combustion with flue gas desulfurization, (2) combustion of solvent-refined (hydrogenerated) coal, (3) low Btu gas produced from coal, and (4) coal combustion in a fluidized bed.*

The technologies were assembled into various supply-to-end-use trajectories by means of the Brookhaven Energy System Network Simulator. Although this is an increasingly popular way to solve complicated problems, my personal experience with it, as with nearly all elaborate computer systems, is that the answers you get are often either absolutely unintelligible or absolutely absurd. It is possible that we are putting too great a strain on computers. In the case of a supercomputer which was asked a highly sensitive, extraordinarily complex military question with several connected answers to yield and five-star generals hanging on its every word, the computer finally answered simply "Yes." Dumbfounded, one five-star general demanded, "Yes, *what?*" The computer replied, "Yes, *sir!*"

One of the things the analysis shows is that emissions of

---

*We shall have a good deal more to say about this particular process later.

air pollution from direct combustion are less than those of central-station electrical generation because of the large differences in the trajectory efficiency. To translate: if you burn coal in a furnace at home, you do not put out as many total emissions as the electric plant does in burning coal to generate the same amount of electricity you would need if you threw away your home furnace. The reason is the well-known excessive loss of power in electrical transmission.

Burning coal with a flue gas scrubber, burning solvent-refined coal, and fluidized bed combustion give greater emissions than the use of low Btu gas from coal.

Electrical transmission lines have the largest land requirements of all combinations considered.

The compressors used to pump gas through pipe lines produce most of the nitrogen oxide in that particular trajectory.

The projected health effects from mining are, of course, much worse underground. Per unit of fired energy achieved, coal mining kills nearly three thousand times more people than uranium mining. For this reason, if for no other, the use of surface-mined coal, a much safer commodity, is expected to increase at a far greater rate than deep-mined, in spite of all the bizarre legal impediments that the states with deep, high sulfur coal deposits can dream up. The Brookhaven projection also assumes that electrical power plants operating on the basis of coal combined with flue gas desulfurization and fluidized bed combustion bring the coal to the power plant via five hundred-mile rail hauls.

One can make some good guesses at local health damage from a typical eastern, uncontrolled, coal-fired power plant. The peak is 120 premature deaths per year of operation. This plant emits 150,000 tons of sulfur dioxide annually, resulting in about one premature death per thousand tons of sulfur dioxide.

In its recent reincarnation as a flower-child, General Motors has made available to power plants its invention of a "side stream separator" which is 50 percent more efficient in knocking out particles from combustion exhaust than the "bag house" or other particle collectors for coal-fired plants. It boosts from 66 percent to 90 percent the efficiency with which fine dust particles (under ten microns) are removed from the stack gases. The three-part system consists of a fabric bag-filter, a centrifugal fan, and interconnecting ducts through which boiler exhaust passes while being cleansed of particles.

Under the labyrinthine restraints imposed by the 1977 Clean Air Act Amendments, coal hydrogenation technologists can shift the source of pollution from electrical generation and end-use to the conversion sites. And under the bubble concept, now accepted by EPA, it is the total pollution emerging from an imaginary bubble enclosing a plant or complex of plants (that may be as big as a town) that counts. Single units under the bubble may, for instance, squirt nerve gas all over the place, as long as the nerve gas emerging from the bubble is within tolerable limits.*

Under the 1977 amendments it may be easier for the new power plants and services to be built in what are described by the 1977 laws as *nonattainment areas.* In this way clean fuels can be manufactured from coal in remote locations.

The 1970 law provides full credit in new source performance standards for pollution removal during coal conversion. Significantly the amendments do not require that pollution generated in the course of hydrogenation be considered at all.

---

*The bubble concept is essentially immoral. It assumes that you can kill your own people with pollution, as long as you don't pollute anybody outside your property. It is designed to the perfect satisfaction of such stink holes as textile mills, where people die with brown lung after a few years of exposure to lint that never leaves the bubble.

Coal hydrogenation plants are likely to be located at the mine mouth or at least remote from the major population centers where the energy will be ultimately used. From the health standpoint this will reduce the death rate, at least of many innocent bystanders.

The introduction of coal hydrogenation will affect acid rain production. Shifting the location of sulfur dioxide emissions to the dry western states should result in less acid rain in the Northeast. Total sulfur dioxide emissions are likely to change because of the low sulfur content of the western coal.

The causes for cancer of the lung, skin, and scrotum in the coke oven and gas works have invariably been polycyclic aromatics. Cancer risks increase with increasing process temperature; beta-naphthylamine, a bladder or pancreas carcinogen, has been found in gas works and coke ovens. Cancer of the kidney is seven times as likely for coke-oven men as for steelworkers.

British men with over five years experience on top of gas ovens had 69 percent excess lung cancer and 126 percent excess mortality from bronchitis, compared to those in the gas works. These men are exposed to greater concentrations, in particles, of 3, 4-benzpyrene, three micrograms per cubic meter of which is six hundred times the normal London concentration. North American coke-oven workers are also peculiarly vulnerable if they work *on top* of the ovens. Still, when you talk with them, the answer frequently is, "What the hell business is it of yours?" Some of the worst backlashers in the United States are among those who are the front-line victims of the war between pollution and the human race. With the converse attitude the Japanese have far lower cancer rates among coal-gas workers.

Cancer of the scrotum, the first lesion to be linked with an occupation, in this case chimney sweeping, has been generally reported in workers exposed to coal oils, tars, and soots.

157

First reported two hundred years ago, it has not yet disappeared, although now it is rare. It can be eliminated completely with adequate industrial hygiene.

During coal hydrogenation, hydrogen sulfide, carbonyl sulfide, and carbon disulfide are formed. The latter two are removed from synthetic gas and concentrated in a sulfur-recovery unit. Hydrogen sulfide is so blatantly dangerous* that it should not be used at all in high school chemistry courses.

How to Solve the Sulfur Dioxide Problem

Sulfur dioxide, as an invariable pollutant of the flue gases of power plants burning high-sulfur coal, can be easily removed by a single process.** When the gas is passed through water containing lime or some other alkaline substance, the sulfur dioxide is oxidized to sulfur trioxide. This reacts with the lime to form calcium sulfate, which is removed by bag filters, by electrical precipitation, or by other means. This process, called *scrubbing,* is very expensive and results in a colossal waste-disposal system for the by-product calcium sulfate.

To my knowledge, there is not any commercial power plant in the country actually doing this scrubbing.

Fluidized Bed Combustion

Instead of scrubbing, you can remove the sulfur as a dry product by using a so-called fluidized bed combustion process. The idea for this probably came from the petroleum industry's wide use of suspended fluid bed catalysts. Pioneer-

---

*It is not uncommon for "tank gaugers" who measure the volume of oil on hand in sour-oil tanks to die and fall off the roof of the tanks leaking hydrogen sulfide.

**It is well to bear in mind that 85 percent of our unmined coal contains so much sulfur it cannot be burned in conventional boilers without breaking the air pollution laws.

ing work on fluidized bed combustion was carried out in Great Britain. In the special furnace finely divided coal was burned in a granular, moving bed of limestone or dolomite plus residual ash from previously burned coal. Limestone and dolomite react with sulfur dioxide to give calcium plus magnesium sulfate.

Fluid bed combustion takes place at about 950° C., which is lower than the 1650° C. used in conventional coal-fired boilers. At the lower temperature, slag is not formed and the volatility of alkali salts is reduced. Because of lower temperature, the formation of nitrogen oxides is greatly reduced, and most of the sulfur dioxide reacts to form the sulfates mentioned, which are withdrawn from the system along with the ash.

For a pressurized fluid bed combustor which burns coal containing 4 percent sulfur, the results from a single run are as follows in parts per million:

	Fluid Bed Product Range	Average	Presently Allowed by EPA
Sulfur dioxide	40–100	70	650
Sulfur trioxide	5–6	5	no standard
Nitrogen oxide	40–100	70	500 as NO_3

Heat is continuously extracted from the fluid reactor bed. This is accomplished either with immersion cooling tubes or by supplying excess combustion air to carry away the heat. Heat transfer between the bed and the cooling tubes is very efficient, since it is both by radiation and by convention. The coefficients of transfer can be up to ten times larger than in conventional gas-to-surface heat-exchange systems. The lower temperature also reduces corrosion and fouling of the heat-exchange tubes. However, tube erosion is still a problem.

In atmospheric-pressure fluid bed systems, which currently are attracting such interest, combustion heat is transferred to water circulating in the immersed tubes and converted to steam for a turbine. In a pressurized system, coal can be burned at pressures up to as many as ten atmospheres (140 pounds per square inch). The hot gases leaving the bed not only make steam but are also expanded through a gas turbine for additional power generation. For both systems, the reduced boiler size results in an important reduction in capital and maintenance.

Fluid combusion has the potential for much superior burning efficiency, which can be as high as 45 percent for a pressurized plant, compared to about 34 percent for conventional units with add-on emission controls (scrubbers).

While sulfur dioxide and nitrogen oxide emissions are largely wiped out by fluidized-bed combustion, we don't know what other hazardous pollutants may be emitted in the process. We are in the dark, but somebody's law or other will doubtless provide us with a viperish new toxin.

The available compilation of substances, *The Universe of Potential Pollutants,* includes those known to be present in coal, those known to be emitted from combustion processes, and those known to be toxic. The list contains 803 substances —612 organic and 191 inorganic. The list is being revised, updated, and modified as new knowledge is obtained.

The so-called Threshold Limit Value is the average concentration of toxic gas to which the normal person can be exposed without injury for eight hours per day, five days per week, for an unlimited period. Since sulfur dioxide and nitrogen oxides from fluid-bed combustion operations are already well below permissible concentrations, the interest shifts primarily to the control of particulate matter.

The current technical control devices are scrubbers, cyclones, bag-house filters, and electrostatic precipitators. Scrubbers remove both sulfur dioxide and particulates (the particle dust is washed out) hence a nonchemical scrubber, perhaps just water, might suffice for a fluid-bed combustion unit.

New control techniques are being developed, such as pre-treatment methods to increase sorptive capacity of limestone and dolomite. Precalcination of the limestone for pressured fluid-bed combustion units make it as effective as the more expensive dolomite. Sulfur dioxide capture by dolomite is unaffected by flame temperature. However, sulfur dioxide removal by limestone is greatly enhanced by higher operating temperature, which improves the calcination of the calcium carbonate. Past studies have shown that nitrogen oxide emissions are generally lower for fluid-bed combustion than from conventional boilers. An increase in operating pressure may reduce nitrogen oxide emissions even further.

By 1985 environmentally safe fluidized bed combustors are expected on the United States market. This is the first time that the development of a major new technology has proceeded hand in hand with an in-depth assessment of its environmental effects and a concurrent development of required pollution control techniques.

There is still a disposal problem. The Department of Energy has ten projects going to develop uses for the spent bed materials in agriculture and in soil stabilization for construction sites.

From 1970 to 1973 much of the research and development for this spectacular process in the United Kingdom was financed by United States agencies. In 1974, however, the situation changed. The British government authorized the National Coal Board to implement a Plan for Coal that would increase the annual output to 150 million tons. President Carter's parallel ambition was to pick our annual production up to at least a billion tons, but we never got close.

The fluidized systems at first appeared inappropriate for ordinary industrial boilers (laundries, apartment houses,

Buckingham Palace) because it requires crushing and drying the coal before firing and the use of a tall combustion chamber. The deep, churning bed would have to have a high-power air fan.

But was it necessary to crush the coal first? How about just washing it?

It must be remembered that the fluidized bed at any given moment contains very little coal (less than 5 percent) and consists mostly of ash and limestone particles, which must be below five millimeters in size for effective fluidization. Stones, because of high density, can be separated in the washing process. This reduces the transport cost and lowers the amount of ash to be disposed of. Washed coal of commercial grade could be burned by simply feeding, as supplied, to the surface of the fluidized bed.

It is extraordinary that the British engineers were first in arriving at the fluid combustion idea, for British coal is low in sulfur and they therefore lack the powerful antipollution incentive present in the United States and in Germany, both of which are cursed with an abundance of high-sulfur coal.

In order to lessen the anguish of acid rain, the United States government is considering an early retirement for old power generating stations. In connection with this step, EPA is considering mandatory washing of coal used in new utility boilers. Douglas Costle of the EPA admits that such washings could have some adverse effects such as the sudden appearance of large amounts of coal waste gunk and some increase in particulate emission in the vicinity of coal-cleaning plants. But so powerful is the general incentive for fluidized combustion that these are considered small geographical misfortunes. The main thing is to keep the sulfur oxides in locked-up form, where they are a pain in the neck only to Ohioans, rather than spreading them to the immense wind which guarantees delivery to the whole northeast seaboard.

Fugitive Emissions

One explanation of why so much expenditure of money and effort has resulted in so little improvement in the quality of the atmosphere is the concept of fugitive emissions. These are pollutants that escape controls—leak through them or just prove too expensive to dominate. This is especially true of particles, smokes, matter so finely divided that it behaves like a gas. *Point-source emissions* is a term for sources of pollutions that are controllable. John Cooper at the highly regarded Oregon Graduate Center estimates that only 40 million tons of the 400 million tons of particles emitted in the United States each year are from point sources.

The most hopeless generating places for these fugitive emissions are probably unpaved roads. Other major sources of non-point emissions are harvesting, animal feedlots, coal mines, mill tailings, ponds, and unplanted farmland.

There is nothing that can be done in general about fugitive emissions. If they are found to be on the whole carcinogenic, it would probably be cheaper to make everyone everywhere wear a gas mask—inside the house as well as out, even in the shower, during dinner, and while making love. Sooner or later the species would be born with natural gas masks or cancerproof lungs. Luckily, it appears likely that most fugitive emissions are *not* carcinogenic. In fact, paving a road with asphalt is more likely to increase the carcinogenicity of dislodged road particles.

Coal Gasification

The production of relatively low-energy gas (mixtures of hydrogen, carbon monoxide, carbon dioxide, and nitrogen) is so easy that it has been done for several generations. Although a tremendous loss of total available energy is always involved, partly burning coal reacting with steam will produce coal gas varying in Btu content from 90 to 300 per cubic foot, depending on circumstances. Such plants are great expensive beasts and are not getting cheaper. An example is the proposal by the Great Plains Gasification Associates (a consortium of natural gas companies) to build a plant for making synthetic material gas from liquids in North Dakota. The plant was estimated in December 1975 at $1.2 billion, but inflation will wash it up on the shore at over $5 billion. The Federal Energy Regulatory Commission will allow an average of $8 per thousand cubic feet of the output of 125 million cubic feet per day into the group's standard gas shipments. Eight dollars a thousand for junky gas of this type is actually about eight times what it is realistically worth.

Since the supply of real natural gas—averaging 1,200 Btu per cubic foot and costing around $4 per thousand—is now at a record high because of the new deep-well discoveries, it is doubtful that monstrous boondoggles such as the North Dakota scheme will actually go anywhere.

If reasonable prices for intermediate-Btu gas can be arrived at, however, there is a vast market waiting. The largest market is the Houston area which consumed more than 600 trillion Btu of energy in 1976. Next are the Chicago–Gary–Hammond region with 318 trillion Btu and Port Arthur with 305. Memphis industries bought 93.5 trillion. The total projected demand in 1990 in eighty markets (but not at the North Dakota project's brigand price of $8 per thousand) is seven quads (quadrillion) Btu.

The proposed Memphis plant is a typical example. Using the U-gas process developed by the Institute of Gas Technology, it incorporates a single-stage, fluid-bed coal gasifier, the reactant gases being steam and oxygen. Economic estimates suggest the gas will be sold at $3 to $4 per million Btu. This begins to make sense. At present the industry is buying natural gas for $2.65 per million Btu and fuel oil for $3.70. By the mid-1980s the Memphis plant probably could produce fuel at a competitive price.

The coal gasification process with which the world has the most experience is the Lurgi system, developed in Germany to produce "synthesis gas," a mixture of hydrogen and carbon monoxide of a precise ratio. By the use of the Fischer–Tropsch process they can be recombined to give liquid hydrocarbon fuels or chemicals such as methanol, if preferred. South Africa has gone overboard for Fischer–Tropsch and has huge facilities (Sasol) to which it continues to add.

Some rather fantastic variations on the gasification scheme have recently made the front pages. Mobil Oil Company, for example, has a catalytic process for making gasoline out of methanol. Since methanol can be made from coal, this is a somewhat tortuous but workable way to make gasoline out of coal W. R. Grace is enamored of this sequence and plans a 50,000-barrel-a-day plant at Baskett, Kentucky, starting up in 1986. On the other hand, Occidental Petroleum is planning 59,000 barrels per day of gasoline by the Fischer–Tropsch route. Oxy is asking for partners in this $4 billion project.

As far as "synthetic" liquid or gaseous fuels (synfuels) from coal or shale oil are concerned, the big push is on but the whole concept of synfuels has been oversimplified by congressional law. The United States Synthetic Fuels Corporation was set up through passage of the Energy Security Act, signed June 30, 1980. Some experienced and bullet-creased veterans of the energy wars, such as Carl M. Mueller of Bankers Trust, are afraid that the whole synfuels picture is going to blow up in a cloud of million dollar bills. His concern is the kind of cost overrun encountered when a plant, built to imaginative design specifications, simply does not work. This is really a "make-it-run" cost rather than an overrun and can drain the treasury quickly and indefinitely.

Mueller points out that the new act requires the United States Synthetic Fuels Corporation to consider completion guarantees in the comprehensive strategy study it must deliver to Congress within four years. But such completion guarantees are science fiction.

A hint of the enormous sums involved in synfuels can be garnered from the frank admissions of Johannes Stegman, Managing Director of Sasol Ltd., the coal gasification and liquid fuel producing complex in South Africa. Although the core of the plant is the Fischer–Tropsch process, thoroughly tested in Germany during World War II, what Stegman calls "end-of-the-job" investments (original estimates plus overruns or make-it-runs) would translate into the United States economy for a similar but scaled-up complex at about $600 billion in 1980 dollars!

The peculiar enormity of American synfuel costs in a sense is a corollary to the rapacity of United States railroads. Why, for example, put a huge lignite gasification plant in North Dakota? Because that's where the lignite is. Since lignite contains 40 percent water, it is impractical to ship it somewhere else by rail at the present incredible freight rates. The answer, a perfect one in the case of lignite, is to slurry it in water and pump it through pipelines. This method, which can use dirty water (about 250 gallons per ton of coal dust) would make available nationwide at a reasonable price the vast reservoir of low-sulfur western coal, tar, and shale oil. Because pipelines are capital-intensive rather than labor-intensive, like the railroads, they should be less affected by future inflation.

The railroad lobby has defeated eminent domain legislation for coal-slurry pipelines for the past eighteen years. Long ago the railroads reluctantly accepted oil and natural gas pipelines, but then they were up against an industry (petroleum) much stronger than themselves.

Some large utilities actually find it cheaper to buy coal from Poland or South Africa than to pay the absurd railroad freight rates from Montana or Wyoming.

Underground Synthetic Gas

The expensive part—the "nut"—at the heart of all these gasification and liquefaction processes for transforming coal is the enormous cost of surface hardware. By producing the synthesis gas by partly burning coal underground, you are home free from a lot of heat-and-chemical-resistant steel and waste disposal problems. The earth is not only your heat-resistant reactor; it is your endless garbage can.

Partial combustion of hard-to-mine fossil fuels, such as tar sands and oil shale, has been regarded as possibly the only really practical way of handling these elusive enormities. Something in the human psyche is prejudiced against burning fuel in order to recover fuel for burning, but in the case of deep-lying coal deposits, it may be economically a sensible answer. Are you going to let it lie down there, representing zero energy, or burn part of it, perhaps one-half, recovering large amounts of low-quality gaseous energy?

For fifteen years in the Donets Basin, working on coal seams 0.5 to 1.0 meters thick and 60 to 200 meters deep, the Asgrenskay has been turning out gas of 96 Btu per cubic foot. At Yazhro–Abinskaya partial combustion has been proceeding for twenty-three years, yielding gas of 110 Btu per cubic foot. The combustion products from such synthetic gas contain no particulates. Nitrogen oxides are low.

In this country the most ambitious underground coal gasification program has been one directed by the Lawrence Livermore Laboratory, sponsored by the Department of Energy and the Gas Research Institute, at Hoe Creek in northeast Wyoming. In parallel experiments, this project used air in one series and steam plus oxygen in another. The air-burned product came out at 114 Btu per cubic foot compared with 217 Btu for the steam/oxygen burn. On the basis of a computerized analysis, the Lawrence Livermore scientists estimate that substitute natural gas costs of $4 per million Btu could be realized. This is in the right ballpark.

One trouble with the underground burning process is that it leaves empty, unribbed caverns down there which the earth is inclined to wipe out by shrugging its shoulders. The result is "subsidence." Out in Wyoming some dark night the kitchen stove starts walking toward the liquor cabinet; the beams fall down, and one kisses another old house goodbye —perhaps along with its owners. One method of avoiding subsidence is the so-called Uniwell process, in which concentric pipes are drilled, the inner one to the bottom of the coal seam and the outer one to its top. Air or steam/oxygen is injected in the center, while product gases come up the annulus between the two pipes. This localizes burn cavity formation. One ends up with a collection of small caverns not important enough for the earth to shrug at.

In any method of injecting energy (steam, for instance) there is some degree of pollution involved. In the heavy oil fields near Bakersfield, California, very hot steam is injected to get the turgid oil to move toward a pump. But in the generation of the steam, you burn a considerable proportion of the heavy oil (which is high in sulfur) and thus have a battery of little sulfur dioxide producers. Definitely these are going to be attached to scrubbers.

In his desire for more coal production, more coal burning, but less acid rain, President Carter created some typical dilemmas. Congress completed the confusion by legislation bordering on insanity. The Environmental Protection Agency, in an effort to placate the industry and at the same time preserve a modicum of public health, has become almost paranoid. Recent medical discoveries have not helped quiet the confusion.

For example, Milton Lear and his associates at Brigham Young University, have found dimethyl and monomethyl sulfate in coal fly ash and in the air-borne particulates of a power plant that burns low-sulfur, western coal. The concentrations run as high as 830 parts per million. Dimethy sulfate is a viciously active mutagen and causes cancer in rats. Apparently the compounds form in the flue gas after combustion by reaction of sulfur dioxide with carbon monoxide and water.

In the meantime, EPA had decided to exclude fly ash from the hazard list. The power companies themselves will be responsible for determining if this waste is hazardous. At about the same time the National Research Council's Committee came to the conclusion, in reviewing the prospects for 1985 to 2010, that if one takes all health effects into account, coal appears to be a lot more risky than nuclear energy, and a lot of the risk is from the heavy metals and radioactivity in the fly ash. Moreover, W. A. Korfmacher at the University of Illinois has found that polycyclic hydrocarbons adsorbed on coal fly ash are stabilized against photochemical decomposition. Some powerful carcinogens, such as benzo (a)-pyrene on fly ash are very slowly decomposed, if at all.

Because of the congressional action cited above, since June 1979 all *new* coal-burning facilities, except those burning the rare low-sulfur *anthracite* coal, must install scrubbers to remove what is in some cases nonexistent sulfur dioxide. The new regulations, seemingly designed to cut off the profits of the western surface miners who produce inherently low sulfur coal, also give a push to *dry scrubbing,* which uses either a powder such as soda ash to absorb the sulfur dioxide or a wet slurry which is delivered as a spray so that the water is evaporated by the hot gas.

Environmentalists have been sore in the thumb since early 1980 when President Carter sent to Congress a request for $10 billion in grants for paying utilities to convert to coal, with only $400 million for pollution equipment to control sulfur dioxide emissions. The EPA complained that the net effect would be a 20 percent increase in sulfur dioxide and acid rain in New England. If indeed there are any fish left in the Adirondacks, they won't be there long.

9

The Future of Transportation

Transportation rears her ugly head
—Winston Churchill

God doesn't like the internal combustion engine, or, in fact, the heat engine. This is shown by his stipulation of the Carnot Cycle—the law that limits the efficiency of engines operating between heat sources and heat sinks (the place where heat ends up; for example, cooling water). The Carnot Cycle does not apply to electric motors as a means of motive power.

Much to the chagrin, no doubt, of John DeLorean, author of *On a Clear Day You Can See General Motors,* it is General Motors that has taken up the challenge of the electric car and envisions them gliding through the urban streets by the year 1990. Since the electric car has been my favorite, ideal vehicle as long as I can remember, I am going to pour a good deal of cream on this dish, but first we must look at a lot of other possibilities, threats, and occasions.

171

Stratified Charge and the Lean Burn

The invention of the carburetor by which air and gasoline are premixed, then exploded in a movable cylinder, seemed an idea of positive genius. Actually, if the carburetor had never been thought of, we might be a cleaner and better planet today, and we would have much more economical vehicles. (I wrote the previous sentence before a clap of thunder shook my study and several ravens flew in to tell me about the problem of micro-soot—about which, more later.)

The explosion of carbureted mixtures needed supplements to combat combustion knock. They are largely tetraethyl lead, which contributes to our overall decline and fall. Moreover, the engines could not be operated at low enough fuel-/air ratios—until the diesel engine came along to get good mileage.

Increasing the gasoline mileage of a car is a very tricky process, simply from the standpoint of arithmetic. The point one forgets is that the pay-off is not really miles per gallon but gallons per mile. And this makes a very large practical difference. For example, increasing the mileage from 15 to 16 miles per gallon involves the saving of 1.75 times as much fuel as increasing the mileage from 20 to 21 miles per gallon. I implore you to try this out on your pocket calculator. It is one of the pleasures of life that what appear to be innocent statements of arithmetic are full of subtle crevasses and unexplored caverns.

On the subject of mileage, one must also cock a steadily skeptical eye at the numbers claimed now and for the future. The famous 27.5 miles per gallon mandated for 1985 actually may be closer to 19.5 miles per gallon, because the mileage stickers on new car windows usually overstate the actual figures by 30 percent. The imaginary mileage is compiled from prototype cars tailored and tuned for the test. Moreover, the tests are run on chassis dynamometers under perfect wind and temperature conditions, that is to say, unearthly conditions. Douglas Costle of EPA intimates that as long as *all* the figures on all the cars are for the Land of Oz, nobody except the customer is being fooled.

Instead of the consecutive explosions of the typical carburetor engine, we can use a stratified charge system and save fuel, because this method of burning relies primarily on ignition of lean mixtures by free radicals rather than by a spark discharge.

The Honda is a good example of the stratified charge, designed specifically to lower nitrogen oxides, carbon monoxide, and unburned hydrocarbons in the exhaust. In general, a stratified charge engine operates first by conventional spark explosion of a fuel-rich portion of the cylinder contents; the larger fuel-lean portion is then exploded at a slower rate. The fuel-lean region catches fire from free radicals shooting in from the small rich chamber. Since free radicals start fuel-lean fires better than electric sparks, the fuel-air mixture burns more efficiently and reliably than in a conventional central-spark engine. The Ford Proco and the Texaco Combustion System are variant ways of applying the same basic principle. However, only where there is no carburetion at all (that is, no premixing of fuel and air) do the requirements of octane number and (for diesels) cetane number disappear. These performance characterizations do not mean anything when a fuel is injected continuously rather than periodically.

In the Honda, the Japanese researchers discovered that hydrocarbon and nitrogen oxide emissions could be further decreased by a sort of internal exhaust gas recirculation. Known as the *branched conduit system,* it permits burnt and unburnt gases to circulate from the main chamber into the torch chamber and then to recirculate back into the main chamber for a second try at combustion. The recirculation of unburnt gases sustains combustion for a relatively long period without raising the maximum temperature; therefore, the formation of nitrogen oxides is reduced.

In the lean-burn Toyota, a turbulence-generating pot has been added, resulting in lower nitrogen oxide emissions. This prechamber is charged from the homogeneous mixture in the main chamber during the compression strokes. The spark plug is located in the orifice to improve the ignition of the air/fuel mixture by scavenging around the electrodes.

The turbulence pots cut down nitrogen oxide emissions because (1) jet flow from the prechamber causes gas motion in the postflame region, which leads to a decrease in temperature of the burnt gas, and (2) the jet flow motion increases the heat loss to the chamber wall and lowers gas temperature.

However, the fancy, new, efficient stratified-charge engines seem to be doomed, along with the diesel and all direct injection engines, except possibly gas turbines, because of the smoke problem. This statement is made in the full knowledge that my neck is stuck far out.

The fact is that delayed cancer caused by soot or smoke has been found *to overshadow by far the other miscellaneous pollutants which surely do us no good but pose a much less certain threat of cancer.*

Lung cancer is the dominating pollution threat of the present and foreseeable future. Any propulsion device that emits smoke or soot, and all smokes and soots are guilty, unless proved innocent by twenty-year tests, is simply too dangerous to tolerate. Inherently combustion without carburetion emits submicron particles.

It may be that a realization of this was the compelling reason why both General Motors and Ford have suddenly turned to intensive research on electric vehicles.

General Motors has other reasons to regret its sudden splurge into diesel-powered automobiles. It is now shouldering huge repair bills. For a time in 1980, it couldn't sell diesel cars in California because the test cars kept breaking down before they completed the state's pollution control tests. In June GM notified the owners of 485,000 diesels—nearly every diesel car it has made—of a multimillion dollar program to modify troublesome fuel systems and to extend warranty on certain parts to five years or 50,000 miles.

A typical clinical case is the following: a 1979 diesel Oldsmobile station wagon was okay for 30,000 miles. Then the fun began: sputtering; smoking; blown head gaskets; three fuel-injector pump overhauls; and engine-related transmission problems. Then one night a big bang left the car with a snapped crankshaft and cracked engine block. Present status: unsalable junk.

But the biggest problem is the extraordinary susceptibility of the engine to small amounts of water, which is more common in diesel fuel than in gasoline. Critics contend that General Motors tried to economize by using a lightweight, converted gasoline engine. Diesels are crabby, demanding tender loving care. They are fussy about fuel quality and require more frequent lube oil changes.

Some Alternate Systems

The so-called Otto-cycle engine, which drives 90 percent of our cars, is not the only or even the most efficient internal combustion system invented. Engineers at Caltech's Jet Propulsion Laboratory (JPL) periodically review the status of various types of new engines for road vehicle use. Recent data show that both the Stirling and gas turbine should meet the emission goal of 0.4 grams per mile of nitrogen oxide, while giving performance equivalent to the Otto engine in both small and full-size cars. In the Stirling engine a cylinder containing hydrogen or some other appropriate gas is alternately heated by burning any convenient fuel, and cooled by performing work against the transmission system. The Jet Propulsion Laboratory group concludes firmly that continued diesel engine use in other than small cars is out of the picture and even in small vehicles it is highly questionable because of the nitrogen oxide soot problem.

Cost premiums for gas turbine car or bus plants may be acceptable but the Stirling's higher costs could delay its introduction indefinitely. Yet the projected fuel economy of Stirling-powered vehicles is up to 40 percent better than the 1985 baseline (27.5 miles per gallon).

The projected economics of the Brayton powered vehicle (gas turbine) are up to 30 percent better than the projected 1985 baseline for full-sized vehicles, but offer little advantage in small-sized ones. Ceramic turbine blades, permitting very high temperatures are needed to show any significant fuel economy advantage for Brayton cars.

The JPL engineers are especially gloomy about big diesel engines. Here the catalytic elimination of pollutants cannot be applied, because of low exhaust temperature. The presence of particulates in the exhaust would chew the steel off the exhaust gas recirculation equipment. (They do not mention chewing the tissue out of lungs of people driving behind them.)

Reducing nitrogen oxide emissions in a stratified-charge or diesel engine which operates very lean (low fuel/air ratio) requires increased recirculation of exhaust gas. This results in fuel economy penalties. For those engines then, fuel economy penalties associated with nitrogen oxide emissions below 1.0 grams per mile are likely to be tough for cars heavier than 3,000 pounds.

Limited emissions data for cars with Stirling engines indicate that there should be little difficulty meeting standards. A Stirling-powered car showed its ability to meet the most stringent Japanese or California requirements. On paper, Stirling engines should have the cleanest exhaust of combustion-based engines, because the burning is a gentle, steady, low-pressure process. However, a limit on the temperature of the heater head may be imposed to limit nitrogen oxide formation—possibly limiting the achievable fuel economy for a Stirling constructed of ceramic.

The combination of a diesel and a Stirling is a rather attractive bastard. The diesel part of the assembly is *adiabatic,* that is, all the heat it generates is transferred to the exhaust stream rather than being scattered around. The exhaust of the adiabatic diesel should be hot enough for the hydrogen-charged Stirling's needs under all operating conditions.

Steady-state emissions from the gas-turbine engines are very low but transient effects have shown bursts of high emissions. Careful studies at the University of Michigan have, however, underlined an exceedingly important point. Although the usual snakes of pollution (nitrogen oxide, carbon monoxide, hydrocarbons) were about the same in a heavy-duty gas turbine as for high-power gasoline and diesel engines, outfitted with platinum exhaust catalysts and exhaust gas recirculation, *the smoke or particulate matter from the gas turbine was practically nil.* It ran clean all the time, while under certain conditions both the gasoline and diesel engines practically filled the engine laboratory with smoke.

Since the danger of lung cancer has made this particular emission behavior by far the most crucial, I think the gas turbine is still very much in the running for ground transportation. If the fuel economy could be significantly improved, it could take the place of the diesel, especially for buses and heavy trucks.

In a timely and fortunate move, the government has awarded General Motors a $65 million contract to develop a "super" gas turbine auto engine by 1985. A team including General Motor's Detroit Diesel Allison Division and the Carborundum Corporation will aim to produce a gas turbine for a 1985 model Pontiac capable of achieving 42.5 miles per gallon on diesel fuel. The injection of Carborundum into the team will obviously further development of a ceramic material to withstand the high temperatures required for stipulated efficiency.

According to Jet Propulsion Laboratory, odor is the most difficult of the unregulated emissions to describe or to control. Although one would have guessed the opposite, odor occurs primarily from very lean combustion and is likely to be a problem with diesel gas turbines, Proco, and other lean-burn engines.

The Flywheel as a Pollution-Free Prime Mover

Although flywheels are conventionally considered simply methods of storing energy or smoothing its delivery from engine to axle, a flywheel can run a car in the same sense that a battery can with periodic recharging. Encased in a vacuum or in helium where friction is nil, the flywheel is recharged by revving it up with an engine, which can be located on the curb or in the garage. Buses with only flywheels as motive power have been used in Switzerland. Such vehicles, of course, present no air pollution problem whatever. They don't even emit water.

With support from the Department of Energy and Department of Transportation, General Electric is developing a pollution-free bus using a 3000-pound flywheel. The wheel, fabricated from a stack of steel discs, will spin at 10,000 revolutions per minute and could power a 28,000-pound bus with full payload for 3.5 miles in stop-and-go driving. The flywheel would be re-energized at curbside charging stations in ninety seconds. Energy is taken off the flywheel by a special alternator developed by General Electric. Storage is in low-pressure helium to reduce frictional and windage losses.*

There are other lines of flywheel research. Two of the main goals are to increase the practicality of battery-powered cars and to find a way to recover some of the energy lost in stop-and-go (city) driving.

When standard friction brakes are used to stop a car, all the energy from acceleration is converted into heat and literally thrown away. Through a suitable system of gearing, a flywheel car can recapture much of that lost energy. In the braking process the flywheel is engaged and its drag slows the vehicle. The wheel picks up and stores energy in the process and is then disengaged in idle.

The flywheel can provide all the power, as in the Swiss buses made by the Oerlicon Company, or can be hooked up to a small, inoffensive motor for continuous "charging." According to Arthur Raynard, a flywheel expert with the Garrett Corporation, the imaginary need for quick acceleration is the curse of the automobile. It means that most vehicle manufacturers use engines four times more powerful than required for cruising. The flywheel could eliminate the need for oversize engines.

Engineers at General Electric have calculated that a flywheel could save 47 percent of the fuel consumed by a diesel bus in typical city driving conditions. Even when all the auxiliary power demands—air-conditioning and lighting,

---

*Low-friction flywheels of this sort, with no load to draw, show an exhilarating property. You can leave your flywheel car home turning over while you spend a summer abroad, and on your return your faithful wheel will immediately go into action. It will take you to the grocery store and back.

for example—are included, the potential fuel savings are an estimated 26 percent.

A sort of City of the Blessed (no pollution, no noise) traveling in electric flywheel vehicles would eliminate the need for liquid fuel, drawing on electricity from nonpolluting nuclear power sources. Such a sensible method of transportation (for everything except airplanes) doesn't fit normal human politics and therefore is probably too good to be true.

Standard electric (battery-driven) cars accelerate sluggishly because electrons simply can't come out of the battery fast enough. By adding a special flywheel, power can be tapped quickly and the range increased, since leveling the drain on the batteries increases the total amount of energy that can be extracted. An experimental flywheel electric car developed by Garrett doubled (to ninety-six miles) the urban driving range of a conventional electric car.

The Department of Energy estimates that if 15 percent of all United States cars were powered by flywheel-hybrids (where the recharging device for the flywheel is any kind of simple motor) by the year 2000, a savings of at least 300 million barrels of fuel could be realized.

Hydrogen as Fuel

A few years ago there was a sudden frenzy to use hydrogen as automotive and even aeronautic fuel. Aside from nitrogen oxides fixed by the high flame temperature of the gas, the only pollutant is, of course, the only combustion product: water. Since there is no carbon in the exhaust, hydrogen poses no cancer threat. As in the case of gas turbine engines, which seemed played out before the full impact of the cancer figures crashed upon us, there is now a renewal of interest in hydrogen.

The major problem is that hydrogen can be produced

economically only from natural gas or, in very impure form, from the gasification of coal. Production from water by catalytic decomposition or by electrolysis makes pretty stories with cute pictures but in fact these schemes accumulate more dollar signs every time one's back is turned. A lovely dream —still in the tremulous stage—is the *photochemical* decomposition of water into hydrogen and oxygen. This indeed would be a clear knockout victory for solar energy.

The Department of Energy, the Department of Transportation, Los Alamos Scientific Laboratory, the New Mexico Energy Institute, and the Deutsche Forschung und Versuchsanstalt für Luft und Raumfahrt are participating in a cooperative effort to study problems involved in fueling autos with liquid hydrogen. Although considered by viewers who saw newsreels of the explosion of the Graf Zeppelin as about equivalent to liquid nitroglycerine, liquid hydrogen is regarded by members of this elite team as making feasible the lightest engines with the most packaged power. Because of their small engine size, such cars are well suited for higher engine performance.

For preliminary testing, a 1979 Buick Century with a 3.8 liter turbocharged V-6 engine was selected. The hydrogen tank was installed in the trunk. The gasoline carburetor and the emission control equipment were deleted. A special carburetor and new spark plugs were installed, together with a change in ignition timing. Operation was at a constant very lean fuel-air ratio in order to stay below the threshold temperature for nitrogen oxide production by reaction of nitrogen and oxygen in the air. This was also below the flashback zone. A minimum fuel economy of 5.6 miles per gallon, equivalent in terms of gasoline to aabout 20 miles per gallon, was attained.

The cost of liquefaction must be added to normal production costs from natural gas. An estimate of the cost of liquid hydrogen as delivered to a car is $10 per million Btu, which is equivalent to gasoline at $1.13 per gallon. On a large scale a hydrogen engine is estimated to cost only $300, with an additional $250 for the fuel tank.

Loss of the insulating vacuum surrounding the liquefied hydrogen tank is a major worry. Although there are staunch defenders of the liquid hydrogen concept, I personally believe that riding around with a large tank full of material with the widest explosion limits and the highest known flame speed is just plain dangerous. Visions of the fiery end of the Graf Zeppelin persist.

A well-explored alternative to carting around a vacuum-insulated tank of hydrogen is the use of metallic hydrides—loose compounds of hydrogen and metals. From a fundamental, chemical standpoint, hydrogen is unique. It can behave either as an alkali metal, such as sodium, or a halogen, such as chlorine; that is, in forming a chemical bond it may either donate or accept an electron. That is why it readily forms hydrides. Moreover, it is possible to pack more hydrogen into a metal hydride than into the same volume of liquid hydrogen.

When gaseous hydrogen contacts a metal that forms a hydride, hydrogen is just adsorbed on the surface. Some of the adsorbed molecules dissociate into hydrogen atoms which then enter the crystal lattice of the metal and occupy open sites among the metal atoms. As the pressure of gas is increased, some of the hydrogen atoms are forced into the crystal. At some critical concentration and pressure the metal becomes saturated with hydrogen and goes into a new material—the metal hydride form. At further pressure ultimately all the original hydrogen-saturated metal material will be converted into metal hydride.

The heat of formation—the heat given off when the hydride is formed—is identical to the heat of decomposition, that is, the amount of engine heat necessary to retrieve hydrogen from the hydride for engine use.

Hydrides must have certain qualities to replace hydrogen in a tank. Hydrides that don't decompose at fairly low temperatures (say, below 300° C.) can be eliminated from consideration. Yet the hydride must not be so unstable that an impractically high hydrogen pressure is needed to form it. These criteria, strangely, eliminate all *binary* (two-component) hydrides, except perhaps the hydride of magnesium, but this is not as limiting as it sounds, since hydrogen reacts as readily with metal alloys.

So far, the compounds showing the most promise are based on iron titanium hydrides, which have a cost-advantage over the lanthanum nickel hydrides.

Hydrides are very skittish. If a virgin alloy is to be made into a hydride for storing hydrogen, it must first be activated —prepared for marriage by hydriding for the first time. Pure iron-titanium alloy is difficult to hydride because of a surface barrier that must first be eliminated. This can be broken down by heating it in the presence of pure low-pressure hydrogen to about 400° C. and then cooling it to room temperature. Eventually the alloy is entirely converted to hydride. Many cracks and fissures develop in the process; fortunately this greatly increases the surface-to-volume ratio and speeds up the release of hydrogen to the engine.

The hydriding process may be poisoned by contaminants in the hydrogen such as air, carbon monoxide, and carbon dioxide. In automotive applications this has not so far been a critical factor. The most recent advance in the art is to develop dual-bed storage systems with one bed containing iron titanium and the other a lighter hydride based on magnesium-nickel, which heats up faster. A dual-bed hydride Daimler-Benz bus has been demonstrated in Germany.

An experimental vehicle that can run on either hydrogen

or gasoline has been tried out, as well as one burning hydrogen and gasoline simultaneously. The oxidation of hydrogen greatly increases the thermal efficiency of the gasoline. Experiments carried out by the Billings Energy Corporation and the Denver Research Institute show that hydrides are not only safer than stored liquid or gaseous hydrogen but are also safer than gasoline.

If you want to get into an explosive argument about the relative merits of hydrogen and battery power for the future automobiles, don't interview the experts at General Motors or Daimler-Benz, but talk to Ronal Wooley, the fiery technological boss of the Billings Energy Corporation of Provo, Utah. The mileage range with hydrogen is at least five times greater than with battery-powered structures. A hydride tank can be replenished in half an hour. The hydride tanks are less expensive than batteries and have unlimited life compared to about two years for batteries. But for these blessings you pay rather steeply: $15,000 for the car; another $15,000 for the electrolyzer that converts water to hydrogen.

Back to the Electric Car

A case can be made for the electric car on the simplest of terms. So simple, in fact, that even Congress was persuaded in 1976 to pass the Electric and Hybrid Vehicle Act. But Detroit wasn't listening very hard.

The Germans have done the most practical economic thinking on the electric automobile. On the other hand, Fritz R. Kabhammor of the Electric Power Research Institute is the most brutal critic of the battery-run car. He is thinking in terms of Paradise Lost.

What makes the replacement of the combustion engine vehicle such a task, he emphasizes, is simply the high density of energy storage possible with gasoline. A twenty-two-gallon tank with a volume of three cubic feet can store three million Btu in the form of chemical energy. In that volume lead-acid batteries can store only about six kilowatt-hours, equivalent to 20,500 Btu. But here we are making the classic boner of comparing apples and avocados. Energy storage problems are not so serious, because electricity represents a higher grade of energy than fuel. About 40 percent of the energy stored in a battery is available at the driving axle compared with about 10 percent of the energy stored in liquid fuel.

Urban electric vehicles of the near future should be able to get two miles per kilowatt-hour, or about fifty miles on a dollar's worth of electricity (assuming, somewhat optimistically I fear, a typical residential rate of four cents per kilowatt-hour). A conventional vehicle is likely to go only half that distance in urban traffic on a dollar's worth of gasoline. The experience of the United States Postal Service with its fleet of limited production electric vehicles shows that overall economics can favor electric vehicles even today.

A careful study on the relative costs of using electric vehicles as efficient coal burners (that is, using the electricity generated by coal-burning power plants to drive cars) has been made by Dr. Ing. H. G. Mueller of the GES Gesellschaft für Elektrischen Strassenverkehr and Dr. Victor Wouk of Victor Wouk Associates. Their data indicate that coal can be used more efficiently to generate power for electrical vehicles than to produce synthetic fuel for internal combustion engines. The learned doctors, reflecting the recently acquired tastes of the West German society, suggest that perhaps it may be practical to have an electrical vehicle as a first car and one powered by an internal-combustion engine for occasional longer trips on the autobahn.

The differences cited here are not puny. The use of coal to generate power for use in electrical vehicles is about twice as efficient as the conversion of coal into fuels for powering internal-combustion engines. As far as pollution is concerned, the exhaust from several powerplant stacks is more readily controlled than that from myriads of automobile tailpipes.*

The authors emphasize a very crucial point that is seldom made. The number of additional power stations required for the extra electricity used in electric cars would be very small —less than 5 percent if all vehicles were electrically powered. The authors are confident that electric cars run on electricity from nuclear power plants would show an even greater advantage, unless the price of uranium skyrockets again. This sort of economy would leave synthetic fuels where only liquid fuels will serve, i.e., airplanes, long-haul buses and trucks, and petrochemicals.

There is also an obvious savings in capital. Electric vehicles which can travel 135 kilometers per day with *biberonnage* (a European term for charging batteries when the vehicle is not in use) will require less investment for the biberonnage outlets than a reasonably sized synthetic fuel plant. An estimate of $150 per biberonnage outlet has been made. Ten million electric vehicles could be provided with such outlets for the $15 billion mentioned as the cost for a large synthetic fuels plant.

Who is going to take over the electric car business? (Rather ominously, the Japanese have been little heard from —not even any of the slick SAE papers.)

In late 1979 the E T V-1, an advanced expansion of the electric passenger car unveiled in Washington, D. C. in the

---

*This is a German notion and superficially a reasonable one. In this country the attempt to control the emissions from plants with big stacks has been about as easy as was the enforcement of the Volstead Act. It is now easier to control the auto manufacturers ("control" being used here in its purely bureaucratic, not pragmatic sense.)

summer, was put through performance tests at the Chrysler Chelsea proving-grounds. With a two-passenger load the tests showed the vehicle range to be about 120 miles at a constant speed of 35 miles per hour. During stop-and-go driving the range falls to 75 miles. The top speed is over 65 miles per hour. It is powered by high-energy lead-acid batteries with a new plate design that supplies a uniform current density. The projected battery life is 500 cycles or 30,000 to 50,000 miles. This design is a joint development of the Department of Energy, General Electric, Chrysler, Jet Propulsion Laboratory, and Globe Union, Inc. It is designed for mass production in 1980s at a cost of about $6400 in 1979 dollars.

General Motors, following the rather succinct statement from President Estes that they were tossing their hat in the ring (an announcement that must have startled John DeLorean), gave out routine bulletins on the consolidation of electric-car research, preparing for a market debut by 1985. A control project would be established at the technical center in Warren, Michigan, to put together work done by several divisions. Development work on electric-powered vans will continue separately at the Pontiac, Michigan, Coach and Truck Division, which already had delivered twenty vans with a forty-mile range, powered by conventional lead-acid batteries, to the Pacific Telephone Company in Culver City, California. The new venture involves an unspecified breakthrough in the technology of nickel-zinc batteries and a target range of one hundred miles between charges at a top speed of 50 miles per hour.

In the meantime, Gulf and Western Industries announced a clear breakthrough in battery design with the zinc chlorine system. The real inventions that made a zinc chlorine battery practical were (1) the storage of the chlorine in cold water, (2) the use of a special polyvinyl chloride resin to contain the horribly corrosive electrolyte, and (3) the use for electrodes of graphite plates, coated with zinc. The chemically passive graphite allows an infinite number of charges, meaning an indefinite battery lifetime. Immortality had been achieved! This is regarded as the greatest advantage over the General Motors nickel zinc system, and General Motors admitted it might offer to buy a giant chunk of Gulf and Western.*

Ford is working on a sodium sulfur battery for commercialization hopefully in 1982. Perhaps the biggest stimulus for Detroit comes from a little-known rider attached to the Chrysler bail-out bill passed by Congress in December 1979. The measure, sponsored by Idaho Senator James A. McClure, allows automakers to include electrics in meeting the federally mandated 1985 corporate fleet average of 27.5 miles per gallon. Since the electrics use no gasoline at all, manufacturers with a good sale of these vehicles, could relax and luxuriate. They could even go back to turning out some gas guzzlers.

The Department of Energy is probably right in its belief that people will buy electrics, if the price is reasonable. Figures show that 90 percent of all car trips in America are for twenty miles or less.

In a sense the field is, or should be, wide open. There are scores of little fellows and they all seem to have squawks. For example, Pat Jacobs, president of JMJ Electronic Corporation of Atlantic City, criticizes the Department of Energy's "no action attitude" on the electric car. He is convinced that someone high-up in the department wants to see the electric

---

*On October 2, 1980, the *Wall Street Journal* released information so damaging to the claims of Gulf and Western Industries that it raises eyebrows about the whole zinc chlorine battery program. The battery, it seems, "developed less than 65 percent of its expected power output in some tests and was so difficult to service that it could be recharged only by 'highly trained personnel.' " Not surprisingly, General Motors appears to have lost interest.

car fail. He has talked with six other electric car manufacturers in the United States. They all complain.

JMJ is turning out one car per week and, according to Pat Jacobs, should be producing one hundred cars a day. But lack of encouragement from the government (presumably lack of special credits or fast write-offs) hold him down.

According to Predicasts, Inc., a Cleveland market research firm, and a conservative one, electric vehicles will account for about 30 percent of all cars produced in the United States by the end of the 1980s. That means that by 1990 some 1.6 million vehicles will be battery-powered. The end of the century may imitate its beginning. In 1900, 40 percent of all cars were electric.

Fuel Cells

One particular angle on battery power should not get lost in the perspective: the fuel cell. I shall have a particular reason to go into this subject later in connection with alcohol fuels, but I should like to give the reader a little hint of the power and subtlety of this gadget and its obvious advantages over the ordinary storage battery.

In the first place, a fuel cell is a storage battery only in the same sense that a tank of gasoline is a storage battery. A fuel cell produces electricity by the reaction of liquid or gaseous materials—usually the oxidation of a gas, such as hydrogen, by oxygen. At one electrode of a cell the hydrogen loses electrons and goes into solution as a hydrogen ion. At the opposite electrode the oxygen accepts electrons and goes into solution as a negative ion. In the meantime the lost electrons during the operation complete a metallic circuit and, as an electric current, can perform the same work that a standard chemical battery can.

The earlier goal of fuel cell technologists was to design

cells that would work on simple hydrocarbon fractions, such as butane or methane. After much agonizing, however, it was found that even with powerful electrode catalysts containing platinum it was impossible to convert hydrocarbons to carbon dioxide and water, or in other words, to parallel the combustion reaction, and at the same time get electric current. First the hydrocarbons had to be "reformed" by converting them into mixtures of hydrogen and carbon monoxide. Thus as a preliminary step to using a hydrocarbon as a direct source of electricity, a sort of catalytic steam cracking reaction had to be performed on the hydrocarbon.

Various agencies, including those as diverse as the Pratt and Whitney Division of United Technologies, Los Alamos Laboratory, and the University of Arizona have worked on the problem, and the efficiency of steam-reformer units for hydrocarbon fuel cells has increased from about 60 percent in 1967 to as high as 85 percent in early 1980. Since the basic thermal efficiency of a fuel cell is directly linked (as things now stand) to that of the reformer, this represents a healthy improvement.

The fuel cell now is most popularly considered in connection with an auxiliary battery. The fuel cells are paralleled by batteries and used for cruising power and for recharging the batteries, while the batteries focus on acceleration and starting. As mentioned earlier in this chapter, a vacuum flywheel can also play a lively role in such combinations.

It is estimated that in 1990, a fuel cell bus running on methanol would save 1.56 cents per mile in fuel costs. A fuel-cell-powered Volkswagen Rabbit was used as a baseline comparison with spark-ignition and diesel-engine versions. It looked very good indeed.

Fuel cells not only reduce the number of batteries required to achieve a given range but also maintain the voltage, preventing deep discharge.

Fuel cells have the great virtue of being independent of size for efficiency. They can be hidden under the sofa or can occupy a ten-story building. On the large scale the Tennessee Valley Authority has just launched the $25-million first phase of a program to develop stationary fuel cells for power generation, a 2550-kilowatt pilot plant in Muscle Shoals, Alabama. The plant will use phosphoric acid as electrolyte and will be powered by hydrogen-rich gases produced by a TVA coal gasifier under construction. If the results from the pilot plant look good, they plan to spend over $50 million to build a two-megawatt-fuel-cell demonstration version.

The very great advantages fuel cells offer for residential use will be described in the last chapter.

Mass Transit

The cost of owning and operating a 1980 six-cylinder Chevrolet Malibu is about twenty-five cents per mile. This is a modest car with no overweening compulsion to gulp gasoline. A few years ago this figure would have seemed ridiculous. Today it is essentially the reason why mass transportation and a complete revolution in the automobile landscape are what we face during the decade.

The automobile business is in for several tough years, and it seems doubtful that any but General Motors with its vast immovable dealerships can get through these tough years without the humiliation of government hand-outs, direct as cash or indirect as import restrictions. It will take the United States automakers until 1985 at least to expand their four-cylinder-engine capacity to 40 percent of the output, while something like 70 percent is really needed. Nearly all imports are now powered by fours. With a waiting list as long as six months, the import share of the skimpy 1980 market was about 30 percent.

The consumers, aware that Detroit must make more fuel-efficient cars, will to a large extent hold on to what they have. A similar balking by consumers was responsible for the 1974–75 slump in auto sales and on a vastly larger scale may have triggered off the Great Depression of the 1930s.

In addition to the front-wheel-drive X-car of compact size, General Motors is planning another front-wheel-drive, the J-car. It will give Chevrolet and Pontiac each a subcompact to go with the briskly selling Citation and Phoenix compacts.

On the *larger scale* introduction of the ultra modern, front-wheel-drive subcompacts, General Motors will beat Ford and Chrysler to the dealer showrooms by one to three years. As one Ford dealer complained, "GM is going to eat everybody's lunch." Maybe not *everybody's*. What General Motors has most to fear for the next few years is probably competition from the only Japanese company to build cars in this country. Honda is spending $200 million on a plant in Marysville, Ohio. Honda's Ohio motorcycle plant, opened in the fall of 1979, is turning out products of the same quality as those made in Japan.

Honda has distinctive ideas about its United States auto line, made up entirely of subcompact, front-wheel-drive cars, and hence potentially in direct competition with GM's 1981 J-car.

The first phase of change—eliminating the really big car —resulted in an average weight reduction of 800 pounds. That helped boost car fuel economy by six miles per gallon to the present average of 20 miles per gallon. This eliminating process, minimal as it was, cost the industry $30 billion. But merely slicing weight will no longer work. To preserve more passenger room automakers must scrap front-engine, rear-drive designs and switch entirely to front-wheel-drive configurations. That hump down the middle of the passenger space floor has become obscene. However, such changes cost about $3 billion each.

The three-year lead time in tooling orders means that most companies are still locked into spending for engines, transmissions, and other parts that were ordered in the late 1970s to preserve full-size cars. But the interest in full-size cars seems dead. Their percentage of United States sales has fallen from thirty percent in 1977 to less than ten percent today. However, Nissan is considering the broadening of its United States line to larger cars, including the deluxe Cedric and Gloria models sold to rich people in Japan. Microprocessors are everywhere on these disdainful beauties. One computer system cuts fuel consumption by 10 percent; another automatically prevents the car from skidding; another activates a gentle simulated woman's voice, "Please turn off your lights."

Aside from the lung cancer panic, this change in demand could mean premature write-off for the V-8 diesel capacity that has built up in the last two years for the large cars, because the front-wheel-drive versions due in 1983 and 1984 will require smaller power plants. And it promises sheer disaster for Ford which at this writing seems to be following Chrysler into bankruptcy, because of the overnight obsolescence of its 313 million automatic transmissions built in Livonia, Michigan. They were designed solely to extend the market life of the Ford V-8 engine. Basically, anything spent on rear-wheel-drive in the past five years is a write-off.

There is one unexpected bonus in the midst of all these grim tidings: *an improvement in productivity.*

An extraordinary experiment in comparing Japanese and American productivity was carried out in the manufacture of Savin, a Xerox-like copier process. Two plants in California used American craftsmen, but in one case the manager and foremen were Japanese and in the other case they were Americans bossing Americans. A third plant had 100 percent Japanese craftsmen as well as bosses. All were located in comparable environments in southern California.

Head and shoulders above the other two in productivity was the plant manned by American craftsmen and Japanese bosses. Similarly, Sony's plant in San Diego holds the Sony world record for consistently high quality. It was Japanese management with United States workers. Whatever the psychological clue, it is evident that we have already learned and will learn more from the Japanese on productivity in the auto industry.

There is also the need for plant modernization. General Motors plans to build two new assembly plants that together will be able to produce 150 cars per hour with no more manpower than it took to build 115 per hour at the sixty-year-old plants they will replace at St. Louis and Pontiac. With the price of a compact nosing toward $10,000, there is a reduction in the variety of model sizes, engines, and other mechanical options. The cost of capacity has, of course, soared. The longtime General Motors policy of building enough plants to meet peak demand without requiring heavy overtime is a thing of the past.

Another losing ploy has been the "import fighter". In fact, every time Detroit has brought out an import fighter, such as the Vega, it has failed. (John DeLorean's account is somewhat different. What the Vega finally represented, he indicates, was a top-heavy, expensive monstrosity that had no hint of import fighting in it. It was a typical fourteenth-floor camel originally intended to be a horse.)

It is seldom realized that the average mileage of United States cars declined from 15.4 miles per gallon in 1936 to 13.6 miles per gallon in 1972. Although the automatic transmission was largely responsible for this, there is blame to be scattered right and left. The overdrive on the 1935 cars, long forgotten, was only recently revived. "Aerodynamic styling" was the exact opposite of what it pretended to be. Pretty curves were devised but they had more to do with sexual grace than with true aerodynamics. The Volkswagen bug was greatly superior to the Porsche in reducing air drag.

The X-cars from General Motors have been successful, with 300,000 Chevrolet Citations sold in the first year. But the Citation flopped as an import fighter. General Motors concedes that the car is appealing largely to former big-car buyers. Very few foreign-car owners have switched to it.

One reason we have no good import fighters is that the American public is no longer sure we know how to build quality cars. Japanese cars are scrupulously reliable. The doors don't fall off or hang crooked. Ford's plant at Mahwah, New Jersey was a typical example of poor quality assembly practices. One inspector saw an angry worker slam a door shut by smashing his fist into the side of it. He kicked the next door shut with his foot. In late 1974 Ford began producing the Granada sedan at Mahwah. But the front end of the auto was so far out of alignment that Ford had to set up circus tents in parking lots to repair hundreds of new cars.

I hesitate to say this, since I am an exuberant feminist, but a sudden influx of women workers in 1976–77 almost ruined Ford. Many women, quite sensibly, weren't up to assembly-line work. They quit, creating a high turnover that hurt quality control badly. The notion that women are as strong as men is all right, as long as you don't bet any money on it. For example, windshields on Ford trucks were pounded into place with an instrument so heavy that women couldn't handle it properly. They kept cracking windshields.

A frank but anonymous supervisor blames the increasing complexity of American cars, as compared to foreign ones. On Fords you can have power windows, power seats, power locks, automatic speed controls. "We've optioned ourselves to death . . . and right now there's a whole bunch of scared people running Ford."

Quality should be the only game in town. Ford dealers complain about gaps in window moldings, roofs that buckle, automatic transmissions that go bad right after the warranty runs out, driveshaft belts in Fairmonts that come loose, air-conditioner drains in Pintos that leak water into the interior, etc., etc. The Japanese have built a reputation for quality by producing a few basic models with relatively few options and infrequent model changes.

The importance of simplicity is proved dramatically by the Volkswagen, U.S.A., experiment. Ever since it opened its Westmoreland, Pennsylvania plant in 1976, the company has routinely torn down models built in the United States and compared them with German-made Volkswagens. For a long time, the American VW's came out ahead, a result probably due to newer equipment. Then in the fall of 1978 the American made VW's turned sour. There was an epidemic of lemons. At the same time the line, which had started out with only the two-door Rabbit now included new models and options—a four-door model, two types of transmissions, two grades of trim. Moreover, it started producing diesel engines and pickup trucks. The lesson is obvious. If you want quality, keep your line simple.

I am a limited optimist. I think the American auto industry has learned its lesson and will have a few more years with the internal combustion principle. Not only will General Motors, Ford, and Chrysler concentrate on a few models but they are going overnight to front wheel drive, four-cylinder engines, and a minimum of options. Already, in California, the big, clunky American cars left over from the early 1970s, look utterly absurd taking up freeway space beside the neat little Datsuns, Toyotas, and Hondas. Now the picture is changing. Compared with a new generation of space-efficient, front-wheel-drive cars, the rear-wheel-drive Japanese cars looked cramped and old-fashioned. The price barrier is the only thing that can hold the rejuvenation of the American car back.

It is significant that American teen-agers are again scratching through the junk yards to retrieve parts to rebuild Volkswagen bugs. There is not much cash around for the generation that literally lives in a car and, in many cases, was conceived in one.

The truth is that the industry has been dealing with a market that it no longer understands. This may therefore be the bugle call for either a complete reinvention of the automobile (the electric car?) or a monumental shift to mass transportation.

Is mass transportation ready?

The Taxicab Mess

If you want to allow a bit of semantic leeway, taxicabs are a kind of mass transportation. And it is the one form of this kind of transit that is, in America at least, a complete failure.

In 1979 the Department of Transportation sponsored a large test of the taxicab industry in New York. The diesel cabs got 50 percent better mileage (14.7 miles per gallon.) Taxicabs using regular gasoline managed to achieve only 9.7 miles per gallon. Although these figures for the diesel cabs seem low, one must remember that fleet cabs in New York are driven two shifts a day (twenty hours) and seven days a week. With 90 percent utilization and covering a hundred miles a shift, they average about 73,000 miles a year. The average speed of the test fleet during a normal ten-hour shift was eleven miles per hour. The engines are seldom turned off during a shift, so eleven miles per hour was about the true average speed.

The chief data of interest were the exhaust emissions. The

amount of hydrocarbons, carbon monoxide, and nitrogen oxides were not only much lower for the diesels, but the emission control of the diesels degraded much more slowly. Through 80,000 miles the photochemically important emissions produced by the diesel cabs were well below the federal standards of 1976. Through 5000 miles, the gasoline engines exceeded the standard for carbon monoxide, then by 80,000 miles they were over the mark for all three pollutants, and very substantially so.

But now the expected bad news. The diesel engine exhausts tested recorded below the arbitrary smoke standard up to 55,000 miles of use, but by 110,000 miles the smoke was at least double the standards. In other words, diesels cannot avoid emitting lung carcinogens at ages that are too tender, if the cab company is going to make its accustomed and possibly necessary profit.

The Mass Transit Dilemma

Whether underground rapid transit costs less per passenger mile than cabs or private cars is—strange to relate—still unknown. Lobbyists on all sides cite reams of statistics, depending on their bias.

In late 1977 the Congressional Budget Office, that myriad-legged nuisance machine, made a study that bitterly attacked new heavy rail transit systems, such as the Washington Metro and San Francisco's BART, because such systems "actually waste energy rather than save it." Quoting further: "When such factors as construction energy, energy used to get to and from stations, and the roundaboutness rail travel involved are considered, the energy per passenger mile computed from door to door for rail rapid transit is greater than that for any other public mode except dial-a-ride."

That feisty study succeeded in uniting the transit lobby all over the country. It buried Congress in technical rebuttals, including an emphasis on the fact that rail transit can be run on coal.

In the course of this hassle, some intercity recriminations were more or less settled by the following tabulation from ITT Research Institute:

GASOLINE PURCHASES IN GALLONS PER WEEK PER LICENSED DRIVER

Chicago	6.80
New York City	
all boroughs	9.76
Manhattan	4.43
Washington	8.19
San Francisco	12.17
Los Angeles	13.97
Houston	16.17
Bridgeport, Connecticut	17.84

The only sense I can make of these figures is that cities with good rapid transit (New York, Chicago, Washington) buy less gasoline. San Francisco is disappointing, in view of its compactness and the presence of BART. One concludes on the other hand that the surprisingly good performance of Los Angeles is that, in spite of its enormous freeway mileages, its bus system, contrary to popular impression, is working rather well.

The Congressional Budget Office said, "It is assumed in the analysis . . . that homes, jobs, and businesses don't move because of changes in transit programs."

This assumption is ludicrous. Homes, jobs, and businesses *do* move because of changes in transportation programs. The evidence is available in the Washington area itself.

The new Capitol Office Building was completed in 1964,

and in the same decade Washington moved to the suburbs. Now, however, with only half the Metro system in operation, developers are fighting over downtown parcels of land they wouldn't touch two years ago. The Federal City Council released a study in 1979 showing that over $970 million worth of private development has taken place near the Metro subway stations and another $5 billion is contemplated if the entire 101-mile system is completed.

Transit has also encouraged downtown office development, not necessarily to save energy but to improve mobility in congested areas. Energy savings result, however, not only because people are encouraged to avoid driving downtown, but also because people will be encouraged to live closer to major transportation facilities that make it easy to get to work. Much of that close-to-downtown construction must be high-density apartments, row houses, or townhouses.

Row houses or apartment buildings share walls and need less heating or cooling than the stand-alone ramblers. Under Department of Energy standards, a new gas-heated single-family row house in the District of Columbia should use no more than 23,000 Btu per square foot per year for heating and cooling. A detached home, however, would be permitted to use 31,000 Btu, a third more.

Actually the Washington Metro is an extravaganza which will cost as much as an artificial rainbow from Jupiter to Mars. It is bigger than necessary by a very large factor and the nominal $7.2 billion price tag will be higher than the combined cost of all five of the other new subway systems in the United States. Together with downtown merchants, the most visible beneficiaries are commuters from two of the nation's most affluent suburban counties, Maryland's Montgomery and Virginia's Fairfax.

"We keep parading these pretentious systems as a means of helping the poor, when in fact they only help the rich," says Martin Wohl, Professor of Transportation Planning at

Carnegie–Mellon University in Pittsburgh. Wohl's views reflected a clear swing of the pendulum against rapid rail systems among experts on urban mass transit. Professors John F. Kain and John R. Meyer of Harvard, MIT's Alan Altshuler, along with an original backer of rapid rail systems, Melvin M. Webber of the University of California, Berkeley, have decided there are far more effective approaches to mass transit. Washington would be better and more cheaply served by an innovative mix of express busways and private car pooling, plus stiff penalties for commuting alone in private automobiles.

NEW RAPID MASS TRANSIT SYSTEMS

Location	Miles	Total Cost, billions	Cost per mile, millions
Atlanta	53	3.0*	56.6
Baltimore	8.5	.748*	88.0
Buffalo	6.4	.440*	68.8
Miami	21	.867*	41.2
San Francisco	71	1.6	22.5
Washington	101	7.2*	71.3

*Projection. (The Washington cost estimate is now believed to be incredibly low and actually may hit over $20 billion.)

Some of the older subway systems are strapped. The most remarkable thing, however, is that a few of the systems are in good shape.

Boston: The system ran a $166 million deficit in 1979, despite nearly 4 percent increase in ridership. In 1978 it carried 160 million passengers.

San Francisco: Ridership has grown but BART has struggled through the worst year since 1972. The rail system was shut down for three months after a train fire in 1979. More recently there was a second fire. Both are suspected to be arson. It has also been closed by labor disputes.

Washington: Though the system is only half complete, the ridership had increased to 270,000 per day by the end of 1979.

Philadelphia: The fifty-five-year-old subway system had a 5 percent increase in ridership last year but a deficit of $40 million. On the whole, it's still keeping its head above water.

Chicago: With a 3.8 percent jump in ridership in 1979, the current rate is 526,000 per day, but the deficit is expected to reach $242 million in 1981. No cutbacks are expected in the 191-mile subway system. In fact, plans have been made to extend the system to O'Hare Airport by 1982. On the whole, Chicago is doing about as well in mass transit as in nuclear power, where it leads the world.

New York: Aside from labor union crunch and recently a record number of break-downs, this subway system is holding up well. It celebrated its seventy-fifth anniversary with a 3.6 percent boost in ridership. 461.5 million passengers per year.

Atlanta: First phase of 13.7 miles has been completed and ridership has reached 28,000 per day. Atlanta is a case of typical, and unnecessary, overoptimism on cost estimates. Under the original 1971 schedule the Atlanta system was supposed to be finished in 1979 at a cost of $1.3 billion. Completion is now forecast by 1989 at a cost of $4 billion (read realistically: at least $10 billion).

Cleveland: This is a relative bright spot. The ridership in 1979 had pulled far ahead of the 1978 total of 14.9 million.

Will Trolleys Come Back?

The trolleys, or so-called light-rail systems, may make a comeback against the heavy rail rapid transit system. Light rail systems in Edmonton and Calgary are outstandingly attractive and efficient. Edmonton built a 4.5 mile trolley line for about $14.5 million per mile (compare the table above).

Calgary has estimated $17.6 million per mile, and Portland, Oregon, hopes to get 15 miles for $61 million, or less than $11 million a mile.

General Motors under the saintly Alfred Sloan methodically wrecked the American streetcar in every city of the country, with the exception of San Francisco if you want to count those little toy cable cars as trolleys. The motive was simple: with its two-stroke diesel, General Motors had a virtual monopoly of the motorbus industry, having knocked off Ford, International Harvester, Studebaker, Twin Coach, and Chrysler (Dodge). So buses must prevail over trolleys.

The first step was the formation in 1938 of National City Lines which, in addition to General Motors, included Standard Oil of California, Firestone Rubber Company, Phillips Petroleum Company, and Mack Truck. Subsidiaries, often more pitiless than the mother company, were formed for specific jobs. For example, Pacific City Lines operated in Los Angeles and started the monopoly campaign by buying up the Pacific Electric Company (the "big red cars") in southern California and the Key System in the San Francisco Bay area. As early as 1940 the Pacific City Lines began to acquire and to scrap immediately the magnificent $100-million big-red-car system, including its crucial rail lines from Los Angeles to Burbank, Glendale, Pasadena, Santa Ana, and San Bernardino. In 1951 the last big red car ran through Watts to Long Beach and might as well have continued right into the convenient oblivion of the Pacific Ocean, for along with hundreds of brothers it would be stripped and burned. The unparalleled 1164 miles of broad-gauge track was torn up and sold as scrap steel.*

In 1944 another affiliate—American City Lines—was financed by General Motors and Standard Oil of California

---

*The only existing functional analogy for the dear old big red cars that I know of is the Green Line buses that carry one into the English countryside from London.

to motorize downtown Los Angeles. Unlike the Pacific Electric tragedy, which had involved a nearly unique pattern of transportation and one which had, so to speak, made Los Angeles what it was, the dismantling of the yellow car downtown system had now become standard practice throughout the country. The Los Angeles Railway Company was purchased, its power transmission lines torn down, the tracks uprooted and General Motors diesel buses proceeded to fill the Los Angeles streets with their singular body odor.

National City Lines accomplished the same ends in fifty-six other previously well-served cities throughout the land, yet a peculiar and fateful phenomenon must be noted. Although the trolleys and the electric interurban train systems disappeared, they were not replaced by a corresponding number of General Motors buses or by any buses at all (since General Motors has a bus monopoly). What they were chiefly replaced by was an unprecedented swarm of automobiles.

The reason is easy to see. One bus can eliminate thirty-five automobiles. One streetcar, subway car, or rapid transit vehicle can supplant fifty passenger cars. The train can displace a thousand cars or a fleet of cargo-laden motor trucks. The arithmetic has the simplicity of the guillotine. Gross revenues at General Motors are ten times greater if it sells cars and trucks than buses, and twenty-five to thirty-five times greater if it sells cars and trucks rather than train locomotives. General Motors can maximize its profits by wrecking the rail and trolley systems of America or any other country. It has succeeded in doing so only in the United States.

Amtrak's Golden Chance

Amtrak had a chance to highball. But will the apparently bottomless lethargy and left-handed-old-man ditheriness of the railroad spirit be up to the glorious opportunity? American railroad people are apparently born with an instinctive aversion to carrying human passengers. Coal? OK. Cattle? OK, if they don't need private toilets. People? For heaven's sake, keep them off the rails.

Although Amtrak's ridership did jump dramatically during the gasoline crisis—by 24.6 percent, or two million passengers, in June 1979—the company itself gloomily projects that 75 percent of these new riders will disappear as gasoline continues to be in oversupply.

In early 1978 the administration had proposed killing all three trains that go through West Virginia, a small state populated by senior congressmen. It is the home state of Harley Staggers, Chairman of the House Commerce Committee, Jennings Randolph, Chairman of the Senate Public Works Committee, and of former Senate Majority Leader, Robert C. Byrd. Congress kept all these trains.

Amtrak still operates aging equipment not likely to be replaced in three years. The late deliveries of new orders and the disappearance of domestic railcars and component suppliers mean that Amtrak will not be able to provide much in the way of attractive service (oh, for the bedrooms and roomettes and damask tablecloths of my youth!).

The present system badly needs about 1300 cars. Amtrak has 2000 but at any given time 400 are being repaired. Some are so old that you have the feeling walking up the aisle that your foot is going to crash through a rotten board. To meet additional passenger demands in the summer of 1979, Amtrak had to use about a hundred coaches (Lazarus cars) that it had planned to dump because they had no heating system.

The State of California has sued the Department of Transportation and Amtrak to prevent cutbacks. California's transportation director, Adriano Giantureo says Washington is making a mistake by cutting back, especially in California where ridership is climbing. For instance, the San

Joaquin run (Oakland–Bakersfield) increased in August by 45 percent over the previous year. According to Giantureo, "I'm always asked why we don't pay for it if we think the train service is so great. The fact is we *are* paying for it."

California has decided to pay 20 percent of the operating expenses of the San Joaquin, rising to 50 percent in two years. Six other states are subsidizing sixteen Amtrak trains, or will do so soon. A cost-sharing provision was included in the Amtrak authorization law, specifically to let states pay for trains not considered to be in the national interest.

Congress decided that any long-distance train that recorded fewer than 150 passenger miles per train mile and lost over seven cents per passenger mile must have its throat cut. However, (to save West Virginia) provisions were added to the law ordering trains kept for "regional balance"—at least one train for each quadrant of the country.

In elegance and speed the French are now the leaders in fast passenger trains. The right-of-way (and a very straight right-of-way it is) for the Train de Grande Vitesse at 180 miles per hour has been signed up for traffic between Paris and Lyons (two hours) to start October 1981; Paris to Dijon (one hour). By 1983 Marseilles (now seven hours from Paris) will be four and a half hours; Geneva, three and a half.

The fares fall somewhere between air rates and those on special luxury trains already in service, such as the Mistral and the Aquitaine. Meals will be served at the passenger seats, exactly as in an airplane. These are not monsters; they are elegant speedsters. A full eight-car train will take only 111 passengers, first class; 275, second class. This is fewer than the B-747 Jumbojet airplane.

We sometimes forget that in many ways we were an advanced transportation culture ninety years ago. American trains pulled by steam locomotives regularly exceeded one hundred miles per hour on good tracks. Trains such as the

Aquitaine, or the Bordeaux to Paris run, routinely exceed one hundred miles per hour. The great block to successful high-speed railroading has been right-of-way. There have been too many curves. The French have solved this by building new tracks on pitilessly commandeered right-of-way.

Their motive power is blameless from the standpoint of pollution. Although originally the prototype was the gas turbine, electric rails were found more practical and actually less costly.

In the United States the only real hope is in creative mergers. Union Pacific, a company rich in petroleum and coal, wants to merge with Missouri–Pacific. This would make the routes from the energy-rich Rockies to the Sun Belt very profitable. The chances are that if these deals fall through, we will see government-owned freight railroads to supplement Amtrak—or rather to make up for Amtrak's losses.

Will long-distance fast-rail travel continue on expensive diesels? There seems some doubt. The electric streetcar may come back in an unexpected flow of circumstances. If the theory that small-particle pollution causes lung cancer holds up, the diesel will certainly fade out of the picture. Moreover, in the long run the electricity will cost less than diesel fuel.

An interesting experiment now underway is the so-called Tijuana Trolley—a sixteen-mile structure between downtown San Diego and the Mexican border. This is the first new United States streetcar system in decades. It is privately financed and expects to make money.

Amtrak actually is already making money—or at least not losing it very fast. Its revenue-to-cost ratio exceeds that of most urban transit systems, *as well as that of many passenger rail systems in other countries.* In Japan, fares on the nationalized rail passenger network cover only 87 percent of costs. Because Japan is much more densely populated than the United States, it is better able to support rail service.

But even so, Fremio Takagi, president of the Japanese National Railways, says the rail share of land passenger travel in Japan has dropped from 50 percent fifteen years ago to 28 percent today, as more people use cars. "In the long run there will be a continued trend away from railroad traffic to auto traffic in Japan," he says.

This seems incredible, as the air pollution problem begins to envelope Japan in its cruel stranglehold. I can see this trend taking place at the same time as the United States is trending in the opposite direction only if Japan has in the meantime gone to the electric car—or to the alcohol car.

10

The Alcohol System

Sip delicately at the bottle like effete bees.
—Steinbeck

The almost instantaneous general success of the gasohol concept* points to the fact that the American people distrust not only the validity of the petroleum companies' profits, but distrust their propaganda. Because of its surly and know-nothing attitude toward gasohol, Exxon, for example, (the nation's largest corporation) not only does not sell a gasohol brand but refuses to allow its credit cards to be used for buying gasohol. At the other end of the spectrum Texaco (which normally spends only a fraction of the money Exxon lays out for self-glorification) has leaped on the gasohol bandwagon. It not only sells the stuff; it is preparing in conjunction with the CRC Company to make ethyl alcohol (ethanol) for use in blending gasohol. Television advertise-

---

*"Gasohol" is a word owned by the State of Nebraska. It refers to a mixture of 10 percent grain-produced ethyl alcohol and 90 percent gasoline.

ments with Bob Hope holding up an ear of golden corn and announcing "We have a lot of hungry cars to feed out there" are among the most popular plugs ever devised. Gasohol will pay off for Texaco, even if it never makes a dime manufacturing and selling the fuel.

This book is not going to have an inordinate amount to say about gasohol, because the subject is air pollution and gasohol does not solve that problem. The emissions from the exhausts of cars powered by gasohol run about the same as the emissions from cars running on straight gasoline, with one possible exception: since gasohol has a good octane number without lead, very few gasohol blends contain this toxic material.

What we really want to consider is the use of straight alcohol for which emissions are so low that the universal adoption of alcohol in place of gasoline would solve the Los Angeles problem overnight.*

Using ethanol as a fuel would be almost equivalent, as far as pollution is concerned, to the electric car. And one of the unexpected and unpublicized bonuses of alcohol is that it can be used as part of an electric car. Either methyl or ethyl alcohol smoothly undergo the fuel-cell reaction with little or no "reforming." Unlike gasoline or any other hydrocarbon fuel, they don't require elaborate and indeed dangerous precracking to give off electrons to oxygen.

An electric car running on alcohol! Isn't this what God had in mind?

One caveat must be plainly expressed. Neither ethanol nor methanol are satisfactory diesel fuels. Brazilian experiments with pure alcohol in diesels showed an alarming 70 percent increase in fuel consumption. We are not too concerned

---

*Some ignorant scare stories attribute to alcohol the production of deadly formaldehyde. There is no truth at all in the rumor.

about this in the long run because, as noted in the last chapter, we believe the diesel is doomed to extinction for health reasons.

Early Days of Alcohol Fuels

It was, at least, what Henry Ford had in mind when he was tinkering with the prototype of the Model T Ford automobile. Indeed, he designed the Model T specifically to run on alcohol, gasoline, or "any mixture in between." Alexander Graham Bell in 1922 called alcohol a "beautifully clean and efficient fuel which can be produced from vegetable matter —waste products of our farms and cities." Although not as specific as a chemist would be, Bell clearly is referring to the possibility—now a proven fact—that alcohol does not have to be made from grain or from sugar; it can be made from waste *cellulose,* the woodlike carbohydrate that exists in greater abundance than any single organic material on earth.*

In the 1930s when things were tough all over, the farmers (who also endured the agonies of the Great Depression) got together, especially in Illinois and Iowa, to make *agrol,* a mixture of ethanol and gasoline identical in all practical respects to the present gasohol. Agrol came in at a most inopportune time. Instead of competing with petroleum at $35 per barrel, or whatever the latest OPEC rate is, agrol was confronting the greatest flood of petroleum ever seen before

*Since there seems to be a special educational block in regard to the difference between cellulose and the grain carbohydrates, such as starch, I am trying in the earliest stage of this chapter to make clear that *cellulose is not edible.* By using cellulose as a source of alcohol, you are not therefore snatching food from the starving Calcuttans or Cambodians or San Franciscans. Cattle can digest cellulose, in the form of grass or even as newspapers, and so can certain insects, such as termites. But human beings can use the New York *Times* only for reading or burning. They cannot eat it, even the gastronomic section.

or since—the uncontrolled and absolutely enormous East Texas Field. At one time this high quality oil was selling for five cents a barrel. Needless to say, agrol was hardly a runaway box-office hit.

Early in racing-car technology methanol (methyl or wood alcohol) became popular, mainly because of the very cool flame which enabled an engine to stagger through 500 hours of full-throttle operation. Sometimes nitromethane ("pop") was added to give the fuel a little more zip. There was always a rather drastic way to tell whether the racing car was running on methanol or not. If it turned over and burst into flame, the flame would be colorless in the case of methanol. This is because the redness or yellowness of a flame is caused by the burning of carbon particles formed by the decomposition of fuels that have more than one carbon atom per molecule. Methanol's single carbon atom does not go through the charring reaction necessary to form carbon particles. Hence the flame is colorless, like that of hydrogen and very pure natural gas (methane).

The Standard Beefs About Gasohol

Only a couple of years ago, when James Schlesinger was Secretary of the Department of Energy, he was asked by an insistent correspondent why he was not paying more attention to gasohol as a means of reducing, at lease modestly, this country's dependence on OPEC oil. The gasohol notion, like an irresistible Populist movement had already caught fire in the Middle West, especially Nebraska. Schlesinger had one of his assistants look up the subject, since he was not even sure what gasohol was. The assistant formulated the answer that was sent back to the insistent correspondent: ethyl alcohol has a Btu content of 76,000 per gallon, while gasoline runs about 110,000 Btu per gallon. A tankful of gasoline will therefore take you almost twice as far as a tankful of alcohol. Adding alcohol to gasoline is simply a way to reduce your fuel economy.

Then why, insisted the correspondent, did the two-million-mile roadtest conducted by the state of Nebraska on a variety of automobiles show that gasohol slightly *increased* the fuel economy? The tests were haywire, answered Schlesinger. And the books were closed on the subject. But not for long. The farmers had an irresistible issue and a new way to sell excess grain.

The question of the calorific value of gasoline versus alcohol is an interesting technical subject, since it opens up for discussion again the whole philosophy of the internal combustion engine. The energy content (Btu per gallon) of a fuel is determined in a calorimeter—a precision piece of laboratory apparatus which carefully measures the exact amount of heat given off when the fuel is completely and reproducibly burned.

But an automobile engine is not a calorimeter. It is a complex arrangement whereby chemical energy is converted into motive energy, and the overall efficiency of this conversion is almost ludicrously low—in the neighborhood of 10 percent. Thus, admitting that the calorimetric energy content of the fuel should have some effect, it is not necessarily a *crucial* effect. A fuel of lower Btu value, which burns efficiently (i.e., loses less heat to the cylinder liners and to the coolant, or burns well at low fuel/air ratios) may give as good or better mileage than a fuel of higher Btu content, which does not behave so well in the peculiar environment of an internal combustion engine. This is true of gasohol. Its calorimetric value does not predict its car performance.

This is not true all the way along the line or with all cars. In Brazil, for example, billions of test miles on straight alcohol and all conceivable alcohol-gasoline blends show its Btu deficit in comparison with straight gasoline or diesel fuel. The calorimetric disadvantage begins to show up in most cars in equal blends of ethanol and gasoline. But also at about this time the superiority of ethanol in reducing noxious pollutants begins to be obvious.

The calorie deficit is really not serious enough to halt the march not only to gasohol but to straight alcohol. As Continental Oil Company says, "After all, they're *our* calories, not OPEC's."

Another beef against gasohol has somewhat more substance, though not much more. It is usually assumed that the ethanol you add in gasohol must be anhydrous, that is, 200 proof, which is much more expensive to make than the so-called azeotrope, which contains about 4 percent water. The reason for being so finicky about the water content of the ethanol is that below about $-10°F$. the wet alcohol will often separate out.

The economics of production of anhydrous ethanol, however, are not the reason for the prejudice. It is the economics of keeping the pipeline system and the gas station tanks and pumps scrupulously free of moisture so the gasohol does not pick up enough water to form a separate glob.

It seems to me that this is a very labored attempt to build a fire with toothpicks. Water in motor fuel is easy to keep dispersed with a very small amount of emulsifying agent. This will prevent separation even at low temperatures. What is more, there is a possible benefit in fuel containing water— a benefit realized during World War II by Cleveland inventor Norman E. Waag while he was working for Thompson Products (now TRW). His water injection device was especially useful for getting more bursts of temporary power from the P-47 fighter plane.

Lorne Cannon, Jr. is marketing in Florida a modern version of this gadget which he calls the Waag Water-Alcohol Injection System. It is designed to make car engines run more efficiently by injecting equal amounts of water and alcohol into the combustion chamber. An "improved gasohol" called Hydro Fuel is marketed by a company (United Industrial Reward, Inc.) of Hauppauge, New York. This contains water but is stabilized against separating out by a special additive Hydrolate.

Some of the antigasohol oil companies and their lackeys have now dropped the water beef from their act, not because it was so illogical, but because most of the oil companies have decided to market gasohol. In an almost dreamlike switch from the antialcohol atmosphere among United States oil companies three or four years ago, we now have agricultural entrepreneurs distilling corn who complain the oil companies won't sell them unleaded gasoline for independent production of gasohol, because the oil companies themselves want to monopolize the gasohol market.

It is interesting to note the following combinations:

As mentioned before, Texaco is by far the most active, finding an alcohol-experienced partner in CPC International, a large diversified food company of Englewood Cliffs, New Jersey. The joint venture is to produce sixty million gallons of fuel-grade ethanol from corn at CPC's wet-milling plant at Pekin, Illinois. Production could start in 1981. The Pekin plant alone would put out almost triple the United States production of fuel grade ethanol from the small current total of thirty-six million gallons per year estimated by the Department of Agriculture. More was actually manufactured during World War II in connection with the synthetic rubber program. The Department singled out corn wet-milling as interesting to investors in ethanol. Corn wet-milling is a means of separating corn kernels into their components— starchy corn oil, gluten, and fiber. The Pekin site has another advantage since the plant burns coal for boiler fuel.

It has been many, many years since any oil refinery flared gas containing ethylene. It is true that ethanol could, was, and could again be made by hydrating ethylene. Until recently this was the major source of ethanol, but in the past four decades much has happened in the field of ethylene. It is now an exceedingly valuable raw material for making perhaps the single most versatile and salable plastic known —polyethylene. Not only is every single ounce of ethylene recovered from gasoline cracking units but very large separate petrochemical plants are continually being built to produce ethylene as a sole product by splitting ethane and other hydrocarbons, including naphtha. The price of ethylene has skyrocketed from about three cents a pound in the 1950s to over twenty-eight cents a pound on the present market— much too expensive for making ethanol. It is in fact worth more per pound than ethanol.

There is another rebuttal to the use of petroleum or even coal as sources of ethanol. If we go back to an energy balance criterion, the route to ethanol via ethylene produced in cracking processes of any kind is wasteful. Such ethanol invariably costs more energy than it contains, because the cracking process demands very high temperatures attained only by burning a lot of fuel. In the old days we did not think of energy balance because energy was regarded as practically free, like air.

Thus ethanol from petroleum and from coal fails to compete with ethanol from biomass (grains or cellulose) because of a cost and energy waste.

Energy Balance

Is more energy used in making ethanol from corn than can be recovered in the alcohol product? One has to list an extraordinary number of energy inputs: cost of land, cost of fertilizer, cost of fuel for farm machinery, cost of farm labor, cost of transportation from the farm to the distillery, and above all, the cost of fuel used in the fermentation and distillation processes.

The last item, not surprisingly, is far and away the most crucial. If you use petroleum fuel to distill alcohol, you are immediately out of energy balance. You will find that you are putting in more energy than you are getting out, both in Btu terms and in real dollars. Even if you use coal as process fuel, you are about neck and neck. In this case, though, one might distinguish between a technical and a political energy balance. It is not as bad to use domestic coal, since one is not adding to the dismal import total; and coal is not usable in running a present-day automobile.) In the present case of excess natural gas from deep domestic wells, that might be at least a temporary answer, although the price is so unreliable that the alcoholmaker might better stick to faggots for fuel.

One of the many technical arguments about gasohol revolves around the use of grain by-products (corn husks, cobs, and stalks) as boiler fuel for the distillery. Sugarcane is an economically attractive source for alcohol because the bagasse, automatically harvested along with the cane, usually provides more than enough energy to run the distillery boilers. For this reason the Brazilians, by far the most experienced alcohol fuel technologists in the world, prefer sugarcane to tubers, such as manioc. In crops like manioc one is forced to use part of the alcohol product as boiler fuel. But the suggestion that we can get enough energy out of corn husks or stalks to run a distillery absolutely infuriates some agricultural professors. They insist that this roughage is necessary to revive and stabilize the soil, which would blow or wash away without such a decaying binder.

A good many fistfights take place on issues like this at the University of Nebraska, but on the whole the farmers themselves are strongly pro-gasohol, and the politicians realize the votes are there. In depression years, something new and smelling of the soil may constitute a Populist boom all by itself.

The Political Balance

In February 1980, in strict contradiction of its attitude two years before when the Secretary of Department of Energy wasn't sure just how to spell gasohol, the department chartered the Office of Alcohol Fuels.

Helping the administration to a rational outlook, a large number of farmers, also in February 1980 descended on the Washington Mall in a mood contrasting with the 1979 tractorcade that brought commuter traffic to a halt. The farmers, demonstrating equipment that runs on alcohol, made it plain they did not want alcohol production to be dominated by large corporations or oil companies. Tim Apple of Belleville, Arkansas, showed off his yellow Ford pickup truck which he converted to run on 100 percent methanol fuel made from wood. The conversion, he claimed, cost him $100 in equipment.

Granville Maitland of Petersburg, Virginia, displayed a nine-foot asbestos-coated column and pipes—a portion of a still in the back of his truck. He complained of federal red tape and a six-month delay in getting federal permits to produce alcohol fuel. He said that farmers could fuel their stills on methane from manure or wastes such as peanut hulls.

The gasohol program, largely symbolic until now, may get rolling after all, if the depression continues. The United States has set a goal of increasing alcohol fuel capacity by 610 percent by 1982. But except for a fairly modest construction-ban proposal the current program contains few initiatives that haven't been included in pending legislation. The plan calls for boosting alcohol fuel capacity to 320 million gallons per year in 1980 and 500 million gallons in 1984. This proposal is scaled down from earlier suggestions by Charles Duncan, then Secretary of the Department of Energy, that the United States might be able to achieve a capacity of 500 million gallons by 1980. The only new proposal in the plan is a ten-year, $300-million-a-year program to provide loans and loan guarantees for the construction of small and medium sized production equipment on farms.

The existing exemption of gasohol from the federal tax (four cents a gallon) may be extended to the year 2000. (It otherwise expires in 1984). The Senate has proposed that a tax credit of forty cents a gallon be granted producers of alcohol used directly as fuel without being mixed with gasoline and that $1 billion from the proposed synthetic fuels corporation be used to encourage the production of alcohol from sources other than grain, such as garbage.

The various incentives now add up to federal subsidies of nearly fifty cents per gallon for alcohol production. Depending on the rate of production, the administration estimates that direct loans and loan guarantees could range from $8.5 billion to $13 billion over the decade. The Office of Technology Assessment has estimated that a new distillery takes at least two years to come on stream. (In the farmer's backyard it is more like two weeks—at least before the first explosion.) Not unexpectedly, the gasoholiest state in the union is probably Georgia. Most active there is probably the Pryor Oil Company, which uses wood waste as boiler fuel.

Under new Department of Energy rules refiners may recover the extra cost of gasohol production through price increases in *all* the gasoline they produce. The department has also made gasohol producers eligible for *entitlements* of about five cents per gallon. Entitlements are paid by refiners using low priced, controlled oil to refiners buying high priced, uncontrolled oil, in an effort to balance refinery costs. The incorporation of gasohol producers into the entitlement program is an attempt to provide economic incentive sooner than that which would eventually be provided by complete crude oil decontrol.

Gasohol has one deadly enemy—one so used to having its own way that it regards anyone representing a different interest as nothing but a hound dog. Highway interests are fighting the extension of the gasohol tax exemption in Congress and in various states, some of which have rather recklessly proposed to sacrifice their own motor fuel taxes where the motor fuel is gasohol.

In the *Country Journal,* Scott Splar (Acting Director of Research and Development at the National Center for Appropriate Technology) has reported his experience with alcohol rather than gasohol. He has run his own 1964 Rambler Classic for eight weeks on 180-proof* ethanol without major problems. Older cars with higher compression run better on ethanol than newer models. (Ethanol has a very high octane number.) The conversion is simple: install a manual choke ($8 kit); drill the carburetor jets 0.75 times wider; replace the plastic carburetor float with a metal one, and add a cold-start system ($10).

Splar contrasts the costs of ethanol production with that of synthetic fuels. A big ethanol plant costs between $35 and $40 million. A coal liquefaction plant costs $2 to $3 billion. Splar believes that alcohol manufacture should be widespread rather than centralized. The idea of dispersing energy production in terms of employment, national security, and transportation makes more sense to him than vulnerable, centralized, large-scale systems.

---

*Water content (in this case 10 percent) is less frowned upon in alcohol fuel than in gasohol. Obviously there is no separation problem. In this sense "straight" alcohol is cheaper to make than alcohol for gasohol.

Ancel Crombie and *Mother Earth News* have developed two varieties of still; others are on the drawing boards and are about to be introduced by the National Center for Appropriate Technology.

In Brazil one project under way at the Institute of Technology at Sao Paulo aims at developing a method of small-scale ethanol production to supply the fuel needs in remote areas. These miniplants are designed to produce 50,000 to 150,000 liters of ethanol during six months of the year—enough for the needs of a small farm having one tractor, one truck, and an electric generator. The miniplants are designed for operation by unskilled farm laborers and require low capacity investment. Local materials are used, such as wood staves for distillation columns and bamboo for column packing, and a do-it-yourself construction, operation, and maintenance manual has been prepared.

I would suggest one condition to Splar's emphasis on wide distribution of alcohol production—"a still in every farmyard." Because of certain providential advances in the production of anhydrous alcohol, which invoke rather technical specialization and which will be described later in this chapter, it might make sense to encourage farmers to send relatively low-proof distillate (50 to 70 percent ethanol) to research centers where they could be further concentrated. Recent experience shows that production of anhydrous ethanol on a farm is difficult.

A brisk Tulsa firm, the Union Development Company, is selling plants which produce about 400,000 gallons of ethanol per year. It claims a remarkable energy balance, and the boilers can be refired with wheat straw. The plants are specifically designed to work with corn but can handle any grain. Union already has sold five of its plants in Oklahoma, Texas, and Mississippi, and expects to market them nationwide. The cost of installation, judging by the Waurika, Oklahoma plant, is $500,000. It takes only six months to construct one.

Governor George Nigh of Oklahoma is seeking federal funds to create an information clearing house for the construction of alcohol stills based on Oklahoma wheat. In the Oklahoma legislature there is a movement to encourage alcohol production on small farms by reducing the licensing fee. At present a farmer has to pay the same distiller's fee of $3125 as a brewer who makes whiskey.

It is interesting to note that the first really modern, farm-style alcohol plant in the United States came into being, as set forth by Scott Splar, as the result of a grain contamination problem. Southwestern Alabama saw its grain crops year after year afflicted with aflatoxin, a highly carcinogenic mold. The Department of Agriculture ordered the crops burned to keep them from being sold on the black market and to keep the toxin from leaching into ground water. With the aid of the Office of Minority Business Enterprise Albert Turner of the Southwest Alabama Farm Cooperative Association and other black farmers built a fine modern alcohol plant to use up the tainted grain.

Mapco, Inc., is building a $1 million plant to make ethanol from milo in Moore County, Texas. The plant is coal-fired but still the economics are very close to the break-even point. Mapco figures that what puts it definitely over the hump is the "distillers grain" protein by-product. The plant is close to a giant cattle feed lot in Moore County. The company chose milo grain because there is a lot of it in Moore County and because the price is lower and more stable than that of wheat or corn.

Old Grandpa Stills for Gasohol

Although newly developed processes look very good for the freshman ethanol entrepreneur, there is one caveat on the horizon that threatens all energy plans that involve construction. A new sort of Parkinson's Law decrees that whenever the price of petroleum goes up, the cost of any alternative energy source goes up by a little more. Thus if OPEC oil costs $37 per barrel, suddenly the production of shale oil costs $45 per barrel. This particular example is vivid to me, since I was once on the research fringes of oil shale. In 1969 partly refined shale oil, equivalent to the best low-sulfur, high-gravity petroleum crude, could be produced at $5 per barrel. In this dreadful decade, inflation in steel goods, such as pumps, valves, and gauges has far exceeded the inflation of even southern California real estate. A rock pump, for instance, costs 3,300 percent of its 1971 quotation.

These escalations are absolutely ruinous. If there is any excuse at all for government control of the alternative energy program, it is to spot and nab these damnable hardware rip-off artists. They are everywhere.

It is because of the gnawing fear of still worse inflation that gasohol plants and other alternative energy projects are being planned at such a pitch of fever. Prospective gasohol producers are looking at old liquor distilleries in which depreciation costs at least are low because the facilities have already been depreciated off the books. Examples include the Hiram Walker distillery complex at Peoria. Early in 1979 the company said it would close what was once the world's largest distilling plant because of high operating costs and the need for massive pollution control outlays. Now a parade of prospective buyers tour the facilities with gasohol in mind. In the meantime Publicker Industries is cranking up its long idle alcohol plant in Philadelphia. During World War II it made over 100 million gallons per year of aviation fuel. Other grandpas are Grain Processing Corporation of Muscatine, Iowa; Midwest Solvents of Atchison, Kansas; and Archer-Daniels-Midland

Company in Decatur, Illinois.

Most of these large, already-paid-for distilleries share the fatal disadvantage of relying on natural gas or petroleum fuel oil for their furnaces. Thus a very large increase in throughput in these ancient boilers might actually increase the imports of OPEC petroleum. Only if they can convert to wood, trash, or at least to coal will they be able to compete with a modern plant using cellulose wastes and the like.

Unless you have taken a recent trip through gasohol country, you cannot imagine the furor out there. It has taken on the frenzy of a gold rush. Everybody is either building a still, telling somebody how to build a still, or getting drunk on his own production line.

Indeed one of the serious problems of the independent fuel-alcohol producer is that he must add denaturant to his alcohol so it *won't* be drunk. The Treasury Department's Bureau of Alcohol, Tobacco, and Firearms has set up a new formula for "completely denatured alcohol," that allows the use of less costly denaturants. It would, in fact, allow the use of gasoline as a denaturant.

There may be something peculiar involved here, for I am taken back in memory to a time when I was a very young research director for a southern California oil company. The research laboratory was at that time connected with the refinery test rooms through which all manner of products, raw and refined, were analyzed. I remember a big Swede who was in charge of analyzing casing head gasoline, which is a very volatile but pure natural product that comes to the inspection laboratory in one-liter "bombs." My friend would enter one of the cubicles, depressure a bomb of natural gasoline, shake it up with a few ounces of milk, and drink it down. It was, he claimed, better than Schnapps. Although he went around smelling somewhat like a newly discovered oil well, I never say him fall to the floor and his health seemed excellent. Later I found out that the taste for unleaded (white) gasoline was quite common in the area. Service stations had to be careful to lock up their white gasoline pumps at night. In these declining years of the century I have a suspicion that drinking gasohol itself may become a very sporty habit. It will start in California and whatever happens there is automatically chic and becomes a national, if not an international, craze.

Speaking of California, gasohol in that state has been, in effect, prohibited except during the winter, because of a law regulating the evaporation rate of motor fuels. Because of the formation of low-boiling azeotropes, gasohol evaporates faster than straight gasoline. A new law permits the year-around sale of gasohol for a three-year test period beginning January 1, 1981.

Let me list in random fashion some of the features of the gasohol boom. The first sizable alcohol producer has already gone broke. Highway Oil Company of Topeka, Kansas, the first to market gasohol in that state, has announced it's getting out of the business, because the alcohol price is too high. It had risen from $1.49 per gallon to $1.88 in eleven months. This move affects fifty-five cooperative service stations in Kansas and another thirty-eight independents in Kansas City and southern Missouri.

Archer-Daniels-Midland, Highway's top supplier, is blamed for the inflationary alcohol price, but they blame it all on the price of corn, which should stay at $2.50 a bushel but has a habit of wandering up and down the scale.

There is a raft of small companies making single-farm stills and all of them are up to their neck in orders. For example, Paul H. Archerd, who owns J. F. Thermal Products, introduced newly designed ethanol distillation units which will retail at $8000, aimed at farmers and small businesses. It will handle up to 300 gallons per day of alcohol. Archerd prefers molasses to grain as feed stock because of its availability, low cost, and little need for by-product disposal.* After a unit begins production, the boiler will be fueled with a portion of the alcohol it produces. This is a losing game and Archerd is riding for a fall unless he gets away from this cannibalistic habit.

Archerd runs his own car on a mix of 95 percent alcohol and 5 percent gasoline (in effect, simply denatured alcohol). "It cost me $3.80 to change jets in my carburetor." The fuel lines and hoses should be checked. "Ethanol is a great solvent, so all that gum left by the gasoline gets washed away and can clog up your fuel filters."

Jack White describes his recent Arkansas operations in the *Country Journal.* His plant is located along the Arkansas River adjoining the 420-acre, corn spread of the Farmers Cooperative. White invested $3 million in a plant that will turn out daily close to 100,000 gallons of gasohol (9000 gallons of 200-proof alcohol), which is blended on the spot with gasoline and sold to Farmer's Cooperative. Arkansas has exempted its seven-cents-per-gallon state tax in the case of gasohol, while neighboring Oklahoma voted a 6.5-cents exemption.

Jack White uses biomass (corn stalks and hay from weeds) to fuel the plant. He also has an arrangement with the city of Van Buren to burn city garbage.

"We use high-moisture corn. Ordinarily corn must have a moisture content below 14 percent to move in normal market channels. We can use corn as high as 20 percent. All that is necessary is for it to be dry enough to *crack.* Besides, we have to add thirty gallons of water to each bushel of corn."

Production begins by cracking the corn into *chops,* making

---

*When starting with a full grain, the final step leaves a still residue called *distiller's grain,* which consists of the protein part of the virginal stock. This makes excellent cattlefeed when fresh, but unless it is well dried (which costs money) the rate of spoilage is very high.

a slurry with water, and adjusting the pH to 6.0–7.0 by adding acid or alkali. As primary enzyme, to turn the starch into fermentable sugars, alpha amylase is added. The mash is then boiled, the pH adjusted to just on the acid side, and a second enzyme, glucoamylase is mixed in. The mash is finally inoculated with brewer's yeast and allowed to ferment. The distiller's grain is filtered out, leaving *beer* for the final step.

The beer is run through the seventy-foot-tall distillation column at near-boiling temperature. The alcohol vaporizes at 173°F., while water boils at 212°F., the alcohol will rise through the refluxing tower into a cooling tank, then to the *dryers* to wring out the last bits of moisture. Final drying may be redistillation with benzene. Benzene forms an azeotrope with water which boils at a lower temperature than the alcohol. Drying may also consist of filtering through a desiccant powder such as calcium chloride or silica gel.

Also in Arkansas is the *Korn Likker Times* of Fayetteville which demonstrates and offers free information on how to set up your own still.

There is a private distillery across the line at Waurika, Oklahoma, completely financed by Aaron Wood and his brother-in-law, Philip F. Brown. They produce 50,000 gallons of gasohol a day from corn, milo, or wheat, whichever is the cheapest. The plant uses wheat straw as boiler fuel. The alcohol is blended with gasoline from refineries at Duncan and Ardmore, and the gasohol is distributed by the Eaglewood Oil Company of Waurika. In explaining why he used his own money instead of grants, Wood says, "The feds are all talk and no go."

In January 1980 a gasohol seminar was sponsored by the Georgia Institute of Technology. It was expected to draw perhaps 50 or 60 people, but more than 250 persons paid $250 each to attend.

Colby Community College in northwest Kansas has become the first institution of higher learning to offer a course in the art of moonshining (the distilling of ethanol). The project was started by Dr. Paul Middeaugh, a still designer from South Dakota. Scores of farmers, chemists, engineers, and businessmen from as far away as Oregon, Florida, and even Italy are coming to the tiny campus. The Department of Energy is finally moving to encourage farmyard distillation by providing grants to other community colleges for alcohol fuel courses like Colby's.

From my own experience as a working chemist I could give a course on one of the worst curses in the art of distillation—what chemists have always called *puking*. Suddenly for no apparent reason the whole mixture in the flask or pot boils over in one liquid eruption. Fires are often started this way. When fresh out of college and in my first job, I was put in the same laboratory with an eccentric character who held conversations with his own hardware. In preparing a flask for distillation, he would warn in a deep voice, "Now don't you dare puke, you little son of a bitch!" Then in a squeaky voice, he would answer back, "I'll puke if I want to, you old bastard!"

Crooks and Crazies

Now just as the con men and the whores went along in the California and Klondike gold rushes, so in the great gasohol boom, many unwelcome creatures have crawled out of the woodwork to make here and there a dishonest buck or a million bucks. I have myself been the victim of some Florida crooks, although it was my pride rather than my pocketbook that was most sorely wounded. I was ostensibly hired as a consultant on a gasohol deal and asked to send in my bill along with advice. I sent the bill in promptly along with the advice but have never seen the color of the checks they write.

The trouble, says the *Wall Street Journal* (from which I

get all my epistemology) is that fuel-grade alcohol is more difficult to produce than bathtub gin.* The Kansas attorney general is investigating the extravagant advertising claims of twenty concerns selling alcohol plant equipment, including one that offers a small kitchen still supposed to operate on potato peel, lemon rinds, and other leftovers. This is very advanced, if true. As we shall see, these cellulose materials are fundamentally the most appropriate sources of alcohol. Federal postal inspectors and the Wisconsin attorney general are looking into complaints about a mail-order pitchman in Orlando, Florida, who offers alcohol-fuel plans ranging from an instruction manual at $10 to a full set of blueprints at $50. Ready made plants are available, including a widely promoted model called the "OPEC Killer," and dubbed the "world's only portable distillery" by its maker, United International of Buena Vista, Georgia.

Stanley McKinley of Hooker, Oklahoma recently placed a "Wanted to buy" ad in *Gasohol, USA,* the Kansas City-based bible of gasohol enthusiasts. The ad sought a small, efficient, mechanized, farm alcohol plant. It got no response. "I really didn't expect any," Mr. McKinley says, "I was asking for something whose time hasn't quite come."

If that is true, I am willing to certify that the time now is at hand.

Improvements in Ethanol Production

Before a flood of recent technical improvements made the future of ethanol suddenly overwhelmingly attractive, the Department of Energy had to undergo an expected attack from the rear. This came in the form of a memorandum to the Energy Secretary from a special "Advisory Board" con-

---

*Yet in some parts of the country moonshining has been a cottage industry for generations. A moonshiner should have no trouble in the gasohol business. It is, in effect, his golden chance to go straight and get rich, simultaneously.

sisting of very suspicious characters indeed. The report says ethanol from coal may be marginally acceptable, on the basis of economy, but alcohol from grain and other biomass is just plain silly. The chairman of this antifermentation group was Professor David Pimental of Cornell University, a well-known antigasoholist. Another prominent member was Paul Weisz, Mobil's research director, a man dedicated to his company's process for making gasoline catalytically out of coal-derived methanol. Luckily, Duncan, then Energy Secretary, apparently did not take the memorandum seriously, although it nearly broke the backs of the Alcohol Fuels Office.

The central worry about the cost of distilling ethanol (the "thirty pounds of steam per gallon" doctrine) has been knocked off the map by some extraordinarily creative chemical engineering at Purdue University, reported on recently by Dr. Michael Ladisch and Dr. Karen Dykes. In order to understand what Purdue has done, we need to review what a distillation column is like. In making any separation of consequence via the boiling route, one works with a column tall enough to accommodate as many as forty real or imaginary *plates.* These are stages where one can calculate what is happening, specifically to determine the effect of *reflux ratio.* This is the ratio of condensing vapor to uncondensed vapor at any stage along the column. The purer the final product desired, the higher the reflux ratio and the more energy required to reboil the reflux.

Now the Purdue engineers took advantage of a remarkable fact about distilling alcohol from water: very little reflux and hence only modest external energy are needed to produce alcohol of about 80-percent purity. Going from 80 percent to the azeotrope at 95.6 percent and to pure anhydrous alcohol, your steam bill escalates very swiftly. Since separation by distillation from 80 percent to gasohol-grade alcohol is so expensive, why not try some other method of removing the stubborn 20 percent water? How about an adsorption agent that would selectively adsorb water vapor but not alcohol? Purdue tried this expedient, in most cases inserting the adsorbent as pellets in a distillation column containing actual plates. This worked with elegant charm, especially with powdered starch, powdered cellulose, or plain cornmeal as the absorbents. They sucked up all the water in the column and didn't touch the alcohol. They could easily be regenerated by brief heating and could then be recycled indefinitely. The savings in distillation energy are incredible, especially since the product, with cellulose as adsorbent, is 99.8 percent pure. We have gasohol-grade ethanol in one simple distillation column. *Ten times more energy is obtained as alcohol than the distillery furnace burns up in fuel.*

These economic facts are revolutionary, but the process appears to be as old as World War II, when the Germans had to rely on alcohol to run their tanks in the last months of the war. They used lime to get a water-free product, but with the return of cheap petroleum, alcohol was forgotten as a fuel, and the plants were closed down by 1958.

From the standpoint of the United States economy a natural two-stage system emerges from the Purdue rediscovery of adsorptive distillation. Let the farmers and housewives make the 80-percent ethanol (or even lower), then transport it from its individual sources to a few, very large, specialized plants where the final adsorption step to produce high purity alcohol takes place.* The scale factor (efficiency as affected by the size of plant) is important in processes such as adsorption.

*In most cases the farmer is interested in producing enough alcohol to take care of his own fuel needs, including heating. But with very simple stills he can produce 80-percent ethanol which can be burned without trouble, as long as he doesn't have to mix it with gasoline.

Moreover, I think we have enough information already to show that the average farmer is going to have a very tough time making a forty-plate still behave so that he comes out with nearly anhydrous alcohol. Making 80-percent ethanol should be as easy as making booze—easier, in fact, since the extraordinarily finicky senses of smell and taste are not involved.

Another point: the transportation savings on delivery of watery alcohol rather than grain to large, central finishing plants is very large indeed.

Iowa State University has built up a fascinating project based on selective adsorption of alcohol rather than water. The adsorbent that looks best is a highly active silica gel. The Iowa goal is to dispense with distillation entirely. Since the fermented mash contains only about 6 percent alcohol, why spend all those Btu in heating and distilling water, which requires more than any other substance of its boiling point both for heat and for evaporation (It has the highest specific heat and heat of evaporation)? Why not dip in and take out the alcohol from the "beer?" Iowa State claims the energy costs with silica gel are less than any other process or combination of processes using distillation. The energy costs are less because stripping alcohol from the adsorbent will involve less material and trouble than distilling the fermented beer. Hardware costs should be less and the equipment easier to operate.

Another dewatering technique has been studied by Bernard Miller of the Textile Research Institute in Princeton. He finds that textile yarns such as rayon retard the movement of water vapor but allow alcohol vapors to travel freely. Miller and his associates have developed a continuous process based on this principle. One endless loop of yarn fibers is pulled slowly through a tube into which alcohol and water vapors are introduced. The water is removed by the yarn (which is then dried by heating) and pure alcohol vapor is recovered at the other end of the tube. The energy requirements are modest.

Alcohol dissolves readily in some liquids that don't mix with water to any great extent. Richard de Felippi of Arthur D. Little unexpectedly found this to be true of liquid carbon dioxide. At fifty to eighty times atmospheric pressure carbon dioxide becomes a critical fluid and can be used to extract alcohol from fermentation beer that has been filtered to remove solids. De Felippi estimates the energy cost of the whole extraction process at 40 to 60 percent of the alcohol fuel value. One advantage is that carbon dioxide, a byproduct of the fermentation process, is cheaply at hand.

Several other laboratories have different solvent extraction schemes under development. For example, the University of Pennsylvania and General Electric are working together on a process using butyl phthalate—a water-immiscible solvent for alcohol. Harry Gregor of Columbia University is optimistic that membranes, without additional solvents, can be used for alcohol purification. He calculates that with membranes the energy and cost of recovering 100-percent alcohol from fermentation beer could be reduced to about 60 percent of the alcohol fuel value. Zeolites ("molecular sieves") absorb molecules smaller than a certain size. Garry Baughman of the Colorado School of Mines Research Institute finds a promising candidate in clinoptilolite, a naturally occurring zeolite with holes that water, but not alcohol, can fit into. The relative abundance of clinoptilolite makes it attractive. According to Joseph Gelo of Union Carbide, researchers there are also exploring the use of *artificial* zeolites.

Although traditional beverage distillation technology requires almost ten times more energy than the Purdue drying technique, a number of commercial modifications have been developed that improve the energy efficiency of distillation.

Engineers at Raphael Katzen Associates International have designed plants that incorporate heat-recouping schemes and use a total of about 65 percent of the fuel value in producing a given amount of alcohol. Only about 22 percent of the fuel value is needed for the distillation steps. One of the tricks is to run two separate distillation stages at different pressures so that the waste heat from the higher-pressure distillation can be used again in the lower-pressure unit.

Conventional distillation technology requires a separate column to recover 100-percent alcohol. Traditionally benzene is used as an entraining agent to break up the water-containing azeotrope. But in fuel alcohol plants made by the ACR Process Corporation in Champaign, Illinois, gasoline is substituted for benzene. Since the alcohol is intended for use in gasohol, there is not need to remove the gasoline that remains in the end product, so one step is eliminated. ACR says that the total energy of this process is equivalent to about 53 percent of the alcohol fuel value, but this doesn't include the cost of drying the distiller's grain.

Several laboratories have been working on vacuum distillation to remove alcohol from mashes that are still fermenting. While this requires a fair energy investment, it produces only slightly concentrated alcohol (17–18 percent would be obtained from 6–7 percent beer in one scheme). But when the alcohol is removed, the yeast or bacteria can produce alcohol much faster than it could in a normal beer.

A huge amount of research work is being done on new methods of fermentation, on new enzymes, and even on processes that produce alcohol *without* fermentation. A good deal of the work fits in with the new industry, awakening like some gigantic Mount St. Helens,—the DNA recombinant or genetic engineering technology. It seems possible, for example, to the Cetus Corporation of Berkeley, now working with National Distillers on better ways to gasohol, that bacteria can be synthesized by the DNA recombinant technique which will ferment so fast that the whole process of making alcohol can be made rapid enough to be continuous. But, says Cetus, "They're all looking over their shoulders at the Japanese," because the Japanese have built up a matchlessly strong and modern fermentation industry.*

One need not look very far for natural bacteria that may stand the alcohol industry on its head. For example, there are the organisms in the hot springs of Yellowstone National Park. The strain, tentatively named *Thermoanaerobacter ethanolicus,* converts sugars to ethanol in a process without oxygen. It is extremely efficient and operates at temperatures higher than the fermentation by yeasts (78°C. versus 37°C.). Because of the great chemical voracity of this bug, its use might make continuous fermentation feasible. One should also point to the wonderful anaerobic (working without oxygen) bacteria recently discovered a mile deep in the "forests" surrounding gigantic marine hot springs off Galapagos and off Baja California. Under unimaginable pressures and local temperatures so high that the ocean water becomes a reducing agent (converting sulfates to sulfides, for example) these little organisms have made the marine springs along the rift that circles some 30,000 miles around the world's oceans into blooming metropolises of life in an otherwise lightless, aqueous desert.

They make possible the growth not only of plants but of enormous red worms, along with clams, mussels, and who knows what other presently inconceivable living creatures? Our real aliens may be down there, rather than in outer space. Perhaps Darth Vader's uncle lives down there. Compared with the Yellowstone bacteria, certain strains of the

---

*Much work is being done on *Zymonas mobilis,* a high-temperature fast-fermentation bacterium that has been used for many decades in the manufacture of tequila.

roughly similar deep marine microorganisms may be as fiercely superior in chemical and enzymatic activity as in their maximum temperature tolerance. Their exploitation, however, is for the future of my son and grandchildren, not for me.

Cellulose Takes Over

Of course by far the most important improvement in making alcohol starts not with edible grains and sugars, but with cellulose. We cannot eat cellulose, although it is certainly the most plentiful plant product on earth. Luckily, practically everything we have been saying about ethanol from the fermentation of corn starch or natural sugar is true of the conversion of cellulose to alcohol. There are a few additional tricks that must be used to get cellulose to convert at a reasonable rate and at a reasonable yield to ethanol.

In civilized countries cellulose means one of three important things: (1) paper, (2) cotton, and (3) rayon. The cellulose in rayon and in most cotton is very pure, while that in paper depends on what you're willing to pay. If you can tolerate a lot of wood splinters and poor ink retention (most newspapers and wrappings), it may be edible by a goat but not by a cow, at least by a cow with dignity.

Paper, of course, comes from wood which is a combination of cellulose, hemicellulose, and lignin. The papermaking process consists essentially of isolating the cellulose from the other two. This is also one way of making a cellulose that is readily converted to the sugar (glucose) and then by fermentation to alcohol.

Grass and indeed all nonwoody vegetation, including marine plants, are predominantly cellulose. We burn millions of tons of cellulose every summer when we surrender our grass cuttings to the trash collector. The manure from cellulose-eating animals, such as cattle, is very high itself in cellulose (about 80 percent). One estimate puts the amount of ethanol potentially available from processing 70 percent of all the cattle manure recoverable from feeding lots at 170 billion gallons a year. (Our present use of motor gasoline in the United States is in the neighborhood of 100 billion gallons a year, a decline from 110 billion gallons in 1978.)

The amount of cellulose in the average garbage can is remarkably high and most of it is nonwoody, in the form of paper, orange peel, potato peel, etc. Even in households which save old newspapers for the Boy Scouts or the Knights of Columbus, there is still a huge amount of paper thrown out, as for example used Kleenex.

Every estimate I have seen puts the amount of readily collectible cellulose in this country at at least five and nearer to ten times the amount needed to make a complete substitution of cellulose-derived alcohol for petroleum-derived fuel. One of the big question marks is the cost of collection, and we shall suggest an answer later in the chapter.

Actually the idea of making alcohol out of cellulose is not of 1980 vintage. It was first seriously tried during World War I, but the yields were poor, and people in the next decade were much more interested in drinking alcohol than in burning it.*

In the 1960s and 1970s a powerful entity, Gulf Oil Chemical Company, found itself researching ways to convert cellulose wastes (including by-product paperpulp, lumbermill residues, corn husks, excess or low-grade cotton, and garbage) into motor-grade alcohol. They used a special enzyme or material produced by a mutant species of microorganism (apparently *Trichodema reesei*) obtained, according to one

---

*I have come across a persistent rumor, never verified, that Al Capone had control over all the garbage in the city of Chicago and used it to make booze.

account, simply by exposing the bacterial emulsion to sunlight. Gulf was prepared to put up a supersophisticated, full-scale ethanol plant in Kansas in 1979.

Suddenly they abandoned their plans and turned the whole project over to the University of Arkansas: patents, know-how, pilot equipment, even research personnel, including the project director, Dr. George H. Emert. I am prompt in admitting my mystification. The mind of Gulf's top management is more inscrutable than the mind of an oriental empress. I can guess that Gulf thought it was getting out on a limb—too far away from the other old boys, especially too far ahead of the fearsome shadow of Exxon, which at that time at least frowned upon gasohol. Or maybe Gulf was afraid that gasohol would infuriate the supersensitive and superarrogant rulers of Nigeria, which produces the sweetest crude oil in the world, a lot of it going to Gulf.*

The fact remains that Gulf's process, or something like it, based on the vast resources of waste cellulose, embellished by some engineering shortcuts by Purdue University and other nimble agencies, will in the near future unquestionably lower the price of anhydrous ethanol from $1.88 per gallon to around sixty cents per gallon, or indeed to whatever lower price the intense impending competition drives it.

Purdue has also come up with another method of converting cellulose in high yield to glucose before or during fermentation of the latter. Natural cellulose and most waste cellulose materials are much more complicated in structure than starch, although both can be regarded as polymers of the simple sugar glucose (also known as dextrose). This is because the cellulose molecules are commonly protected by layers of unreactive lignin and hemicellulose. Purdue has

*Gulf is now bragging, however, of a process that converts coal into methyl alcohol, then transforms this catalytically into a mixture of ethanol and methyl acetate which they call ethylfluid.

discovered two solvents which the project director, Dr. George Tsao, refused for the present to identify (patents pending).* The first solvent selectively dissolves hemicellulose, leaving a mixture of lignin and cellulose. The second solvent is selective for the cellulose which can be later precipitated by adding water. In this form the cellulose is extraordinarily reactive, yielding with simple enzymes 100 percent glucose. The glucose is, of course, readily fermented to ethanol.

It now becomes clear that the function of the mutant microorganisms developed by the United States Army at Natick, Massachusetts, and by Gulf Oil Chemical Company in Kansas was primarily to destroy the chemical protection of cellulose by its structural armor, hemicellulose and lignin.

Provided that the handling of the solvents and their redistillation do not involve serious energy expenditures, the Purdue solvent process immediately disposes of the glucose yield problem which had been worrying all workers with cellulose as an alcohol fuel source. If Dr. Tsao is right, yields have immediately climbed from about 50 percent to 100 percent. In its susceptible form cellulose is a piece of cake, like starch.

In order to get the attention of the farmers who don't understand cellulose-to-alcohol very well, Dr. Tsao pointed out in testimony before the House Appropriations Committee that, not even counting the huge adsorptive distillation savings, preliminary solvent treatment of corn stalks, bought from the farmer at $30 per ton, would yield ethanol at 78 cents per gallon. (My private calculator tells me that with adsorptive distillation this would convert to about 37 cents per gallon.) The corn stalks would also be used as process fuel, although the arbitrary price is higher than coal.

*The Purdue team has described the use of a special cellulose solvent (cadarsen), consisting of 5–7 percent cadmium oxide in 29 percent ethylene diamine. This, however, although described in the rayon literature, is probably impractical in alcohol technology because of the toxicity of the cadmium.

Cocking his eye at the corn farmer, Dr. Tsao predicts a glowing picture which may be a realistic one. For each acre of cornfield there is a yield of two or three tons of cellulosic residue per year (stalks, leaves, and cobs). Saving a portion of the residue for soil conditioning, on the average one can harvest about one ton of crop residue per acre per year. This ton of residue will yield an extra gross income of $30 per acre per year, which is not to be sneezed at.

The government's "land-set-aside" program costs the taxpayers large sums of money. The acreage can be used for growing cellulosic crops. Dr. Tsao's farmer friends tell him that on one acre of set-aside land, alfalfa could yield about seven tons of dry cellulose per year. At $30 per ton this can give them a better income than planting corn. And there is feed by-product—the wet, freshly harvested alfalfa on pressing yields a juice containing high-grade protein.

The goal of better yield and faster production of alcohol from cellulose is by no means being left to Purdue University. The University of Southern Mississippi, under a Department of Energy grant, is working on technology for converting such raw cellulose sources as corn husks, rice hulls, and pine trees into ethanol. It requires no fermentation and uses free energy from nuclear power plant wastes. The principal investigator is Dr. Angela O. Badenbaugh.

The first step is turning the biomass—whatever it is—into furfural. This dates back to 1922 when the Quaker Oats Company first developed a process for converting oat hulls into furfural by treatment with sulfuric acid. The next step is to convert the furfural to ethanol. Dr. Badenbaugh thinks this can be done most cheaply by gamma radiation, such as that from cobalt-60 or cerium-137.

As to solvent processes along the lines of Purdue's approach, I should like to make a point: because the nearly one hundred-year-old rayon industry is based on solutions of cellulose, there is a vast amount of technical and patent literature on the subject. Thus the chances are very good that, if Purdue's solvents don't work out, somebody else's will. There are so many somebody-elses. Dimethyl sulfoxide, a kind of wonder child as a therapeutic agent, is an excellent cellulose solvent at high enough temperatures. It may be a favorite in the race.

New York University is making progress on a continuous way of converting waste cellulose into sugars that will ferment to ethanol. The key is an extruder—a twin-screw device —that converts sawdust and chopped newspapers into a product that is more accessible to the weak sulfuric acid used to convert the cellulose to glucose. The EPA is rooting for this process and is seeking funds for a large pilot plant. EPA thinks glucose can be produced in the extruder for three to four cents per pound and that alcohol can be made for about eighty cents a gallon.

Even in Brazil, where alcohol from sugar cane is economically acceptable, and where the chances are that the taxi that picks you up at the Sao Paulo Airport is placarded "Movida a alcool," there is talk of using cellulose sources, such as eucalyptus and bamboo. Here the big argument, however, is whether to use Amazon Basin wood as a source of ethanol or of methanol (wood alcohol). We will face up to more such questions in the next chapter.

How to Collect Waste Cellulose

Until recently I was very gloomy about the cellulose collection problem, because my impression of waste collection is that it is—wasteful. New York garbage collectors ply their noisy trade at salaries higher than professional engineers and have an ingenious habit of disappearing down large hidey-holes for beer and pool for several hours every working day. I never will forget that several years ago the state of Michigan gave up collecting beer cans along its highways, because they had estimated that, without free Girl Scout labor, the collection was costing 30 cents a can.

Since those days of pessimism, I have arrived at a conclusion: collecting stuff is only expensive if done by amateurs, of which the most amateurish are government employees, whether federal, state, or municipal. And I have acquainted myself as to what can be done if professionals (people who make a profit on collecting trash) are given the job.

The most notable outfit of this type, in my opinion, is *Waste Management, Inc.* of Oak Brook, Illinois.* Since it went public in 1971, it has grown at a compounded average rate of 48 percent. Last year it earned $37 million on sales of $382 million. Its return on stockholder's equity is 20.5 percent.

This company learned at the start to pare costs to the bone with highly efficient equipment, minimal but sophisticated crews, and precise route scheduling. Because of its productivity, its costs are about 30 percent lower than that of even the best municipal collectors. Waste Management, Inc. operates not only nationwide, with trash collections in some 140 communities from Wisconsin to Florida, but also abroad. Under contract it collects refuse and sweeps the streets of Riyadh, capital of Saudi Arabia, and has a similar ten-year contract with Buenos Aires. Its newest business is the disposal of chemicals and hazardous wastes, suddenly a big police problem because of the tough regulations of the 1977 Resource Construction and Recovery Act that went into effect in 1980.

Waste Management was the first to develop a commercial waste-shredding system, using equipment it bought from Britain and modified. The processing center at Pompano

*Others doing a good job are Browning-Ferris Industries of Houston, and SEA Services of Boston.

Beach, Florida, transforms garbage into a relatively dry and odor-free mass and is the only practical alternative to costly incineration in areas like coastal Florida, where the water table is too near the surface to permit conventional landfill. Five years ago the company won a multimillion dollar federal contract to build and operate a demonstration plant for converting garbage to methane gas.

Waste Management generally sticks to well proven techniques. Many companies, including Monsanto, have come to grief trying to perfect promising but complex methods for getting energy out of refuse. Waste Management is marketing a Danish process called System Volund—one of several European garbage-to-energy conversion processes with proven track records.

The availability of such fast-moving, efficient and highly motivated organizations as Waste Management makes a giant project, like collecting enough waste cellulose to make over a hundred billion gallons of motor fuel ethanol a year, eminently practical. Suddenly we see the light; it reveals the shape of the greatest chemical conservation program ever conceived.

11

Alcohols Triumphant

In ourselves are triumph and defeat.
—Longfellow

As long as the country has large amounts of coal at reasonable prices, it will probably be cheaper to make methanol (methyl alcohol) than ethanol. In the long run, with perfection of the various processes of producing ethanol from waste cellulose, ethanol will probably be the preferred liquid fuel —at least for internal combustion engines. This may not be the case if the electric car progresses along the line of the fuel cell battery referred to in a previous chapter.

In Saudi Arabia until recently about five billion cubic feet a day of natural gas were being flared—simply burned to get rid of it. The amount of flaring worldwide (simply throwing it up into the sky every day as carbon dioxide, water vapor, and wayward heat) is deeply shocking to conservationists but it is also very tantalizing to energy merchants.

By expensive compressive and cryogenic equipment you can store the methane in liquid form, ship it in special tankers designed like floating thermos bottles, and sell it in natural-gas-hungry countries. This is a dangerous traffic and insurance rates are out of sight. Even Lloyd's of London gets a sinking feeling when contemplating these risks.

There is another thing you can do with the orphaned methane. You can convert it to methanol, either by direct oxidation or by first reforming the methane into mixtures of carbon monoxide and hydrogen, then catalytically reacting this mixture to form methanol. Methanol is a good clean fuel but even lower than ethanol in energy content. Since it burns without any noxious pollutants it would be well suited as a fuel for gas turbines. Factories that now use natural gas in operations requiring a very clean flame (baking and glass annealing, for instance) could switch to methanol by substituting pumps and nozzles for burners.

Methanol from coal involves more or less the same sort of chemistry as its production from natural gas. The coal is first reacted with steam to form carbon monoxide and hydrogen, then these gases are made to react catalytically to form methyl alcohol. This looks better over the medium run than natural gas as a source, when there is no chance of pipe-lining the gas, in which case its conversion to methanol and transportation as a liquid is a good option.*

During the several remaining centuries of access to coal, can we see methanol as a motor fuel? Testing by Exxon Research and Engineering, by the Department of Energy, and by the Continental Oil seems to point to a somewhat muddled consensus. Methanol by itself with a special carburetor and with a tank large enough to make up for its low energy content per unit volume, is a very satisfactory fuel. It solves the exhaust air pollution problem, in fact better than

---

*This has been considered in the disposal of natural gas from Prudhoe Bay in northern Alaska.

hydrogen, since it burns very cool. Peak flame temperatures that occur with hydrogen and are responsible for nitrogen oxide formation are eliminated. Thus, if it were at a price advantage, and available now in sufficient volume, it could take on the job of substituting for gasoline in fleets of cars and trucks, and take it over with little argument.

In the meantime, how much of it could be blended with gasoline? What kind of fuel would metho-gasohol be?

Here the fist-fighting starts. It looked pretty good at MIT and other places with cars of the vintage of 1967 or older, and the reason seems to be that the older generation of cars generally ran with rather rich-set carburetors (high fuel/air ratio). It didn't look so good in the leaner carburetor engines from 1973 on. What the addition of ten parts of methanol to gasoline did was automatically make the mixture leaner. Since the methanol contains oxygen in its molecule, its addition is chemically equivalent to burning the same amount of gasoline with an extra amount of air. In the rich-running older cars the effect is to improve both economy and emissions. In the lean-running newer cars the effect on economy or emissions is either harmful or hardly perceptible, except for an anomalously low nitrogen oxides figure, which may be due to the effect of methanol in lowering flame temperature. On the 1975 and later exhaust-catalyst cars the effect is intermediate, but the improvement, if any, is minuscule.

However, Exxon and Continental both concluded that the blends are unsalable, but for unforeseen reasons. Methanol is so unlike gasoline that it is not entirely miscible with it, and just a few drops of water (with which methanol is completely miscible) causes the alcohol to separate as a bottom layer— a phenomenal extrapolation of the same tendency in ethanol. Conceivably, as mentioned in connection with ethanol, a powerful and otherwise harmless emulsifying additive could inhibit the separation of the wet methanol, but methanol and gasoline do not like each other well enough to guarantee this form of marriage counseling.

Again, because methanol in gasoline finds itself in alien company, it has a very strange effect on the evaporating behavior of the hydrocarbons. Even 1 or 2 percent methanol greatly increases the vapor pressure and alters the distillation performance. This is because methanol forms with individual hydrocarbons in the gasoline loose couplings (azeotropes) which boil at lower temperatures than the boiling points of the hydrocarbons or the methanol by itself.* An excess of low-boiling constituents, even though artifically present as azeotropes, will give vapor lock in an automobile engine— a condition in which the engine misses or simply refuses to fire, because the cylinders have too much fuel vapor and not enough air.

In order to avoid vapor lock, the gasoline must be stripped of its lighter components—butanes and pentanes—before mixing with methanol. This defeats the purpose of the whole exercise, since the loss of energy in the form of butanes and pentanes more than counterbalances the gain in the form of methanol. What do you do with the discarded butanes and pentanes? One might suggest that you use them as bottled domestic fuel. A much better alternative is to use the methanol as bottled fuel and continue to burn the butane and pentanes in the gasoline.

Even when, by cutting out butanes and pentanes and substituting methanol we have prevented vapor lock, we have a mixed fuel that is unpleasing from the standpoint of acceleration and other driving features that the car-savvy public has become used to. In particular, the blended fuel shows with newer cars what Detroit calls "stretchiness". This is an exas-

---

*This tendency has recently shown up in stationary storage. Gasoline-alcohol mixtures lose more fuel from a refinery tank than gasoline itself.

perating hesitation in responding to your foot on the accelerator. It is probably connected with the fact that modern cars operate on the ragged edge of the lean limit of fuel-to-air ratio and the additional leaning effect of the oxygen-containing methanol may carry the carburetor mixture over the ragged edge.

It should be emphasized that these troubles are peculiar to *blends*. Pure methanol motor fuel is much more practical. Because it takes more energy to vaporize methanol than gasohol, the fuel entering the carburetor may have to be heated. Volkswagen has experimentally adapted test cars to run on 100-percent methanol by heating the intake manifold with exhaust gases. A small amount of gasoline is also injected to get the engine started.

As set forth in papers published by the Society of Automotive Engineers, Volkswagen's research workers, Holger Menrad, et al., show a positively unteutonic euphoria about straight methanol as a motor fuel. Their work included single-cylinder and four-cylinder engines, driving tests, emission tests, and durability tests.

They find that the greatest advantage of methanol is its very high octane number, allowing compression ratios as high as 13/1 (almost in the diesel-engine range). Using the same engine with the same compression ratio in tests with gasoline and pure methanol showed better thermal efficiency, lower emission rates, and better power output with methanol. The lean limit was farther extended with methanol, as well.

The very substantial savings in fuel consumption through high compression ratios do not, of course, erase the crippling disadvantage of the very low heat content of methanol. The Bank of America has for some time been testing a fleet of cars on methanol. They find it takes one and a half gallons of methanol to take the car the same distance as it would travel on one gallon of gasoline. They paid 88 cents a gallon for the methanol and $1.30 a gallon for the gasoline. But the bank's studies indicate that the price of methanol is going to come down, so that it is just a matter of time before methanol is the more economical. The Bank has been using twelve methanol-powered cars now for several months and has ordered another fifty. It has also installed two 10,000-gallon storage tanks because "we'll probably convert the entire fleet of one thousand."

In the Volkswagen tests, the very spectacular difference between the diesel and the methanol-powered cars in exhaust emissions is unfortunately played down, possibly on orders from above. It is this difference that is going to put the diesel out of business and put either the alcohol engine or the electric battery in its place.

There is No Soot at All from the Methanol Engine

As we have mentioned before, since it contains no carbon-carbon bonds, methanol cannot form any unoxidized carbon particles or precursors to soot. This is an immense health advantage. It is also an internal advantage in vehicle engineering of whatever kind, since less energy is lost by radiation to the cylinder liners and coolant. It is a bit of a disadvantage in boilers, however, where one wants all the heat transfer one can get. Soot or carbon formed in an engine running on gasoline or diesel fuel is quickly dissolved or burned out when a switch is made to methanol. (Incidentally, this is a good way to get an old car to stop "dieseling" —running with the ignition turned off. The dieseling is caused by carbon deposits that continue to glow and act like tiny spark plugs at top dead center in the cycle.)

Methanol is not good to drink, as wood alcoholics have found out. It is not safe to breathe it very long, either. It is dangerous at concentrations lower than one can smell it. The upper tolerance in factories that use methanol is 200 parts per million for a single shift on a forty-hour week, about 10 percent of the level at which you can smell the vapor.

One other precaution is important. Air saturated with gasoline will not explode: it is too rich to be within the explosive limits. However, air saturated with methanol *will* explode.

It is obvious that methanol, either as a straight automotive fuel or as a blending agent with gasoline, is not all that the doctor ordered—especially if the doctor is interested in keeping you healthy and in one piece.

There is a very cunning trick, however, that enables you to erase immediately some of methanol's worst failings. Before burning, catalytically decompose it into a mixture of carbon monoxide and hydrogen. The Solar Energy Institute of the Department of Energy at Golden, Colorado, figures that this will not only eliminate the toxicity problem but will give methanol a mileage equivalent to that of gasoline. The energy content of a mixture of hydrogen and carbon monoxide, at a 2/1 ratio, is higher than that of methanol because, using engine heat to carry out the catalytic decomposition, you have automatically converted thermal into chemical energy; moreover, you have added it in the form of energy that would otherwise have gone into the air at the radiator.

This concept was to be tested with a 1980 Chevrolet Citation. The Department of Energy is confident that this vehicle, which has an EPA city driving rating of twenty-four miles per gallon with a conventional gasoline engine, will be able to get the same mileage with methanol.

The compression ratio will be increased from a normal 8/1 to about 14/1. Meanwhile the Jet Propulsion Laboratory is developing an attachment that uses a platinum-palladium catalyst coated on ceramic pellets to decompose the methanol. Connected to it will be a tubular heat exchanger to recycle the engine heat.

The boost in efficiency over methanol is caused by a combination of (1) higher energy content, (2) higher compression ratio, and (3) use of very lean mixtures. The one fly in the soup is the fact that while the mixture of hydrogen and carbon monoxide has a higher energy content, it also gives a higher flame temperature due to the hydrogen. Therefore it will generate more nitrogen oxides. As far as air pollution is concerned, we have jumped out of the crude toxicity of methanol back into square one of the endless dilemma of photochemical smog.*

Datsun, General Motors and Ford are said, nevertheless, to be interested in this kind of methanol engine.

Some Peculiar Virtues of Methanol as Turbine Fuel

The new, more efficient power plants consist of so-called combination cycle units. What this means is that the fuel is burned first to drive a gas turbine, and the still hot exhaust gases are then run to a boiler to generate steam for a conventional steam turbine. Because the unusually large proportion of water vapors given off per unit of fuel when methanol is burned, the combination turbine power output is raised to 105,400 kilowatts compared with 95,700 kilowatts from fuel oil in the same plant. That water vapor goes on to give steam turbine outputs of 51,500 kilowatts for methanol as against 49,200 kilowatts with oil.

The requirements can be lowered by such tricks as using the heat of combustion to vaporize the methanol before it enters the combustion turbine; reforming the methanol to hydrogen and carbon monoxide before burning; raising the turbine inlet temperature to about 2300°F.; lowering the stack gas temperature below 280°F.; and preheating feed

---

*This is one of the most powerful reasons for looking at methanol as a fuel for an electric fuel cell. The electric car runs away from all these pollution dilemmas.

water and combustion air.

Methanol as a powerplant fuel has some pollution advantages that show up in stack gases perhaps more crucially than in vehicle exhausts. In a turbine at the Florida Power Corporation, which had been running on No. 2 fuel oil, emissions of nitrogen oxide dropped 74 percent when methanol was substituted. This is noteworthy because existing turbines are unable to meet the federal government's proposed emission standards even with natural gas.

The inlet temperatures of today's gas turbines are deliberately held several hundred degrees below optimum to minimize the damage to turbine blades from trace material in the fuel oil.

Methanol from Biomass

Methanol got its nickname *wood alcohol* for the very good reason that it was customarily produced by the dry distillation or cooking of wood. Over the range of outlooks that we have become accustomed to, therefore, methanol is available from renewable biomass sources in the same sense as ethanol. They are contemporaries in the race for eternal availability. Ethanol seems older because it is present so amiably in one of the oldest of human foods—wine; and people with alcohol in their blood will be around when the sun explodes or turns cold or whatever it is going to do.

Methanol can be made from forest and farm wastes—a fact that commended it to the editors of *The Last Whole Earth Catalogue.* In Maine a group of industrial and land development companies and the Maine Wood Fuel Corporation are studying the production of gas or methanol from wood chips and from branches and brush left behind by timber cutting. Methanol can also be produced from garbage. The City of Seattle was considering building a $200 million plant to make methanol from the municipal refuse that now must be hauled to distant landfills.

In considering the conversion of biomass to methanol, what is the difference between the way we go about it, compared to converting biomass to ethanol? Essentially, the microorganisms are batting on our team in the ethanol conversion. Without enzymes and yeast, ethanol would hardly live on the same street as methanol. With complex and subtle enzymes and living molecules one teases biomass to transform itself to ethanol. To get methanol from the same biomass we resort to brutish torture—like dry distillation, which is roasting to death.

Efforts to tap Brazil's huge forests are bogged down in a debate over whether the wood should be used to produce ethanol by fermentation or methanol by gasification. For the time being, ethanol is the official alcohol fuel of the government program, although tests have shown that either alcohol can be used alone or mixed in the same engine. Proponents of ethanol from wood say the process is simpler and cheaper ("Simpler" obviously refers to the human problem, not the chemical process, since nobody has the slightest idea of how enzymes really work.) Supporters of methanol-from-wood say the process requires only one-third the amount of wood to produce the same volume of alcohol.

In late 1978 a Brazilian government-controlled company was set up by the State Forestry Development Institute (IBDF) to begin commercial production of ethanol from pine and quince trees. According to the typically eloquent IBDF president, Carlos Nevea Galluf, the venture can help turn Brazil into the "OPEC of wood," selling "green petroleum."

An alternative wood-resource project being developed by the Sao Paulo State Energy Co. (CESP) could become equally big for methanol. The state was considering building a $350 million project for a 2000 metric-ton-a-day methanol unit that would use eucalyptus from forests already owned by CESP.

Although the Brazilian straight-alcohol car was started in earnest in the summer of 1980, there had been what seemed to the chatos an interminable delay. Car stickers began to appear marked "Powered by alcohol—only the driver."

CESP is now investing about $100 million in a test program to compare three processes for wood gasification. CESP itself developed one of the test processes, involving an electrothermal technique that passes an electric current through wood charcoal in a retort. Steam reacting with the charcoal gives a very clean synthesis gas consisting of carbon monoxide plus hydrogen. This process takes 60 percent more electricity than a conventional methanol plant but needs only half as much hard wood and no oxygen plant, so the capital investment is low.

West Germany has the new Ohde high-pressure, high-temperature technique. One or more of the processes under advanced development in Brazil will be chosen to begin industrial-scale methanol production in 1982. The output, equivalent to petroleum at about $25 a barrel, probably will be used in the transportation sector, in thermal power plants, and for industries that require large amounts of process heat.

Brazil can without exaggeration take the crown as alcohol-fuel king of the world. It exports alcohol-distillery equipment to other South American countries, to the Philippines, and to India. And it is exporting alcohol in large quantities to the United States.

Other Conversions of Biomass

The thermal conversion of solid wastes and biomass into standard fuels of various kinds is receiving attention all over the world. A symposium on the subject in late 1979 in Washington drew scientists from Indonesia, the Philippines, Japan, and Western Europe. For countries with lots of land

and few people, like Canada and Brazil, conversion of biomass to alcohol and other fuels receives the most attention. For crowded countries, the cellulose-containing urban wastes are a more intriguing source.

The United States biomass effort focuses on fourteen conversion projects managed by the Department of Energy's Northwest Laboratory in Richland, Washington. There are four broad categories: direct combustion, direct liquefaction, gasification, and indirect liquefaction from synthetic gas (carbon monoxide plus hydrogen).

Direct combustion is already practiced and has been discussed in a previous chapter.

Government funded gasification research aims primarily at medium-Btu gas production. Here biomass has two potential advantages over coal. It is renewable and is more reactive, which means that it can be converted at lower temperatures without the addition of pure oxygen. Transportation costs, however, are higher than with coal because of the water content.

The Department of Energy's direct liquefaction work centers on a demonstration project managed by the Lawrence Berkeley Laboratory at Albany, Oregon. This is a brand new concept in which a slurry of hydrolyzed wood chips (that is, wood chips partly digested in acid) is converted directly to oil over a very curious catalyst consisting essentially of sodium carbonate. The oil has a heating value of 15,500 Btu per pound.

Indirect liquefaction work is being done at Arizona State University. Gasification of wood takes place in a dual fluidized bed in which one bed serves as a thermal decomposition reactor and the other as a combustor to heat a solid flux that is continuously transferred between the two vessels. The unseparated gas—composed mostly of hydrogen, ethylene, carbon monoxide, methane, ethane, water, and carbon dioxide—is fed into a modified Fischer-Tropsch reactor containing a cobalt-aluminum oxide catalyst. Heating yields a low-octane hydrocarbon probably suitable as diesel fuel.

Another industrial liquefaction process, designed especially for municipal solid wastes, is being developed at the Navy Weapons Center, China Lake, California. The process centers on olefin production* in the gasification step, compressing and purifying the olefins and polymerizing them noncatalytically to a kind of gasoline.

Very finely divided cellulose waste is rapidly heated to 700 °C. In this process free radicals are formed that quickly react to form the main product. If the system is relatively dilute and the residence time short, olefins are the dominant product rather than aromatic tars or alcohols. After the gasification step, the olefins are purified. The principal product actually is ethylene, which can be polymerized to gasoline by a noncatalytic process developed in the 1930s.

Canada is busy on a number of hybrid energy systems. On the whole these have lower capital costs and better utilize the biomass carbon. A system to produce first synthetic gas and then methanol, for example, is being designed both for a methane-biomass mixture and for biomass only. The University of Toronto is specializing on the liquefaction and gasification of shredded wood.

Japanese law has required the incineration of solid wastes since 1963 in order to reduce the volume of gunk being dumped in landfills. It was only after the 1973 oil embargo that serious efforts were directed at recovery of energy. During the first phase of a national program which lasted from 1973 to 1976 two thermal decomposition processes were tested in waste treatment. One, developed by Ebara Corpora-

---

*Olefins are hydrocarbons with double bonds; i.e., the links between adjacent carbon atoms are still reactive enough for chemically connecting with each other, as in polymerization.

tion, uses a dual fluidized bed reactor and recovers fuel gases. The other, by Hitodi Ita, is a fluidized bed for oil recovery.

Other decomposition processes are being incorporated into municipal refuse systems in Japan. For example, a cracking and melting procedure worked out by Nippon Steel will be used by Iburaki City to treat forty-five tons per day of garbage. Chichibu City began in 1979 the construction of a plant using the Purox system, first developed by Union Carbide and modified for Japanese waste treatment by Showa Denko Company.

Some attention, especially on the part of Nobel laureate Melvin Calvin at Berkeley, has been devoted to "growing fuel on trees." Brazil's The Copaiba tree *(Copaiflora langslefria)* grows well in most of Brazil. It can be tapped like a maple tree; except, instead of syrup, it yields a hydrocarbon in the diesel fuel range. Calvin roughly estimates that even without improving the strain, single trees could produce 150 liters, or 39 gallons, of oil per year and could be grown at a density of over a hundred trees an acre (15,000 liters, or 3900 gallons, per year per acre).

The North American gopherweed *(Euphoria lathyras)* looks like an oleander, is related to the poinsettia, and grows wild in Arizona, Texas, and New Mexico. At full growth of about four feet, it yields a milky-white latexlike oil, which has also attracted Melvin Calvin's attention. Studies of the plant are largely funded privately, although Texas A. & M. University is seeking a grant from the Department of Energy. Calvin says the gopherweed could yield oil at ten barrels an acre right now, but believes this can be improved to thirty barrels an acre. He estimates future net production costs at $15 per barrel.

The cattail may become an energy crop and as important to Minnesota as oil is to Texas. The cellulose fiber would be a good source of alcohol. Cattails grow at the rate of 10,000 to 35,000 per acre. Even the lower number is twice as productive as corn, our fastest-growing crop.

An even more subtle and chemically desirous plant is the fungus *Cyatheus stacoreus* known as the "fairy goblet," which degrades lignin in plant materials to liberate cellulose. Donald T. Wicker of the Peoria station of the Department of Agriculture claims this is the best grass lignin remover he has come across. The fungus can digest half the lignin in wheat straw and thereby expose most of the cellulose.

One obvious but neglected way to use trees is to feed them to cattle. Since cattle are not equipped like elephants to make an instant meal out of a tree, State Technology, Ltd. in Ottawa has learned how to feed birch and poplar to cattle. "Trees are really only tall grass" is their motto. Poplar trees in their entirety are cut, made into chips and fed into a processing machine. There the chips are cooked for several minutes in high-pressure steam. The product—soft, sweet-smelling, and dark brown—shoots out in cloudbursts of vapor.

Aside from such curiosities as have been touched on above, biomass in the United States is in what can only be described as a hell of a mess. This is because such a large percentage of the forests are owned by the federal government and congress has passed so many ill-considered laws. The United States commercial forest is producing only about one quarter of the timber it is capable of growing. Some is rotting and much is covered with what foresters call *green junk*—a tangle of scrubby growth that strangles potentially valuable trees before they can mature.

The nation's forests are currently being cut at the rate of about 14 billion cubic feet per year. But they are growing at the rate of about 22 billion cubic feet per year. Some economists calculate that the forests could yield 60 billion cubic feet per year, without sacrificing future supply.

The artificial limitation on supply has helped push prices up so fast that lumber now costs five and a half times as much as it did a dozen years ago. Yet the United States trade deficit in forest products has tripled in the 1970s. In 1979 it reached a record of $2.9 billion, 7.8 percent of the nation's $39 billion trade deficit.

Congress encourages this legal stagnation by limiting the export of logs (for example, to Japan) because of the interminable protests of sawmill owners, who don't want to see unfinished lumber, grown in this country and processed abroad, coming back to lower the present, absolutely unheard of price of building an American home.

Methanol and Gasoline

What seems to me a rather perverted process has now become popular enough worldwide to begin talking to itself in the language of megabucks. This is the Mobil Oil catalytic method, previously referred to, for converting methanol to gasoline. This uses a so-called shape-selective catalyst of the artificial zeolite type. The catalyst will also work on a good many vegetable oils, including rubber latex, corn oil, and peanut oil, in every case the product being suitable as diesel fuel or gasoline. Ecologically, or one might say *theologically,* this is a strange, almost revolting sort of conversion of Dr. Jekyll to Mr. Hyde. One starts with a biomass product and ages it half a billion years, so to speak, in a few milliseconds. One creates an artificial fossil fuel from a natural biomass fuel.

In case we start with coal instead of biomass, we have a complete cycle of the eons: fossil fuel to alcohol to fossil fuel. At present this is the popular form of the perversion. W. R. Grace, for example, intends to gasify 20,000 tons per day of high-sulfur coal to synthesis gas (hydrogen plus carbon monoxide); convert that into methanol; then convert the methanol into 50,000 barrels a day of high-octane gasoline, using the Mobil catalyst. The plant is proposed for Baskett,

Kentucky, and will cost over $3 billion.

A somewhat less ambitious methanol-to-gasoline plant, mainly in the nature of a demonstration unit, will be built in Wesseling, West Germany, with the support of the United States Department of Energy, the German government, and German industrial interests. At the time the project was announced, Mobil had actually operated its own four-barrel-a-day pilot plant for only five months. There is something of a fishy smell about the deal. For one hundred barrels a day of demonstration, the German plant is going to take five years to build, and previously the Department of Energy had okayed the gigantic W. R. Grace installation, which is supposed to be on stream in 1983.

If plans go through, the whole island of New Zealand will run its automobiles on gasoline made from methanol by the Mobil process. The New Zealand government has decided to convert its large natural gas reserves in the Maui field to methanol, thence to gasoline. A 13,000-barrel-per-day plant would meet the little country's motor fuel needs.

Although I have referred above to my theological objections to the Mobil process, I really have only one specific beef. It gets us nowhere. In fact, as far as the control of air pollution is concerned, it takes us back in time, because by turning methanol into gasoline, we are giving up the brilliant prospect of a new kind of pollution-free power—the methanol fuel cell.

Fuel Cells Forever!

There is something mystifying in general concept about the fuel cell. Yet it is the most logical piece of equipment in the world. If our wits had been about us, we would not have needed Robert Millikan to prove with his oil drop experiment the existence of the electron. The functioning of a fuel cell not only proves the existence of electrons, it proves to us that the chemical processes we know as oxidation and reduction are, respectively, the loss and the gain of electrons. Oxygen is the great acceptor of electrons. Under normal conditions, hydrogen and all *burnable* fuels are donors of electrons.

In another sense, the fuel cell shows how combustion takes place. *Only it is simpler than combustion.* It is combustion slowed to a snail's pace. It is combustion reduced to the simple and calm transaction of electrons rather than the frenzied chains of reactions that involve the skirmishes of free radicals, as in "true" combustion.*

The fuel cell involves two electrodes immersed in an electrolyte solution (usually phosphoric acid). At one electrode a fuel such as hydrogen gives up an electron and goes into solution as a hydrogen ion. If the circuit is closed, the rejected electron goes around through a wire, through a "load," which can be simply an electric light bulb but might be the wiring of a motor, and reaches the electrode opposite the one it started from. Here oxygen is accepting electrons and going into solution as negative ion, in which form it reacts with the hydrogen ion. The only product (as in the combustion of hydrogen) is water. But unlike combustion, in which hydrogen reacts with oxygen at such high temperatures that nitrogen fixation in the form of nitrogen oxide takes place, the fuel cell process can be catalyzed to take place at such low temperatures that there is no nitrogen fixation whatever.

For an invention that is 140 years old, curiously little

---

*In the early days of the fuel cell, an interesting if rather horrible demonstration of the parallelism between the fuel cell reaction of hydrogen and oxygen and the combustion reaction of the two, took place. In 1839 the inventor Sir William Grove, a British jurist, allowed the hydrogen accidentally to mix with the oxygen and blew himself and his private laboratory sky high.

commercial development has taken place. And at the present time it is the public utilities that are bearing the brunt of the engineering studies. They hope that fuel cells can be deployed before the 1990s to handle peak loads and for "load following." Peaking generators are started only when the need for a lot of power is insistent, although temporary. Load-following generators are started daily and run most of the time to cope with daily swings in the load; they may be shut down at night and over the week-end.

Because the efficiency of a fuel cell does not vary with load or with size, and there is no air pollution, the fuel cell is ideally suited for private homes or business. One great and abiding fault of an economy based on electric power produced at some remote waterfall or far enough in the country to avoid the cries of wounded lungs exposed constantly to air pollution, is the scaldingly high cost of transmitting power by wire. If some of the power source is in your own cellar or attic in a silent box no bigger than your refrigerator, you can feel that godlike sense of independence and power that man feels is his right; it is, so to speak, his freedom.

Millions upon millions of people have seen fuel cells in action, although they didn't realize it, or they forgot. The fuel cells were on the Apollo flights to and from the moon. In this case the electrolyte was potassium hydroxide, reacting with pure hydrogen and oxygen. This makes a good cell, but it will not tolerate sulfur or even traces of the carbon oxides in either fuel or oxidant. Unfortunately, we live in a world dependent on carbon dioxide to keep life going and such a fuel cell is therefore impractical except in outer space.

The electrolyte may be solid, even a polymer (General Electric), as long as it will conduct ionized species from one electrode to the other. The electrolyte is placed in a thin matrix or blotter between two porous electrodes. Individual cells are piled together to form a "stack" with a voltage output that is simply the product of the voltage of one cell and the number of cells.

The fuel cell, like a battery, gives direct current, which for many purposes is converted to A.C. by a simple alternator.

The selection of phosphoric acid as the most popular electrolyte means that the cell will only work efficiently at temperatures from 150° to 200°C. (302 to 392°F.). Below 150°C. phosphoric acid has poor conductivity and above 200°C. most electrode materials become unstable. Porous carbon electrodes are used, containing catalytic amounts of platinum.

Another popular electrolyte for higher temperatures is molten carbonate. This is in a thin layer sandwiched between two electrodes of porous nickel. At 650°C. the reaction rate with most fuels is so high that no special catalyst is needed. Under operating conditions, nickel oxide forms on the oxygen electrode (cathode) and becomes the active electrode material. Nickel remains the active anode.

The best estimate of the cost of a molten carbonate power plant is $350 (1980 dollars) per kilowatt hour, the same as the cost for a phosphoric acid fuel cell plant.

Fuels other than hydrogen, ammonia, and the alcohols need processing or reforming to give mixtures of hydrogen and carbon monoxide before they will react. Even pure hydrocarbons such as methane simply refuse to give up their electrons and so cannot be used without pretreatment. The answer apparently lies in the fact that nonpolar hydrocarbons won't lie down on the catalytic electrode in such a manner that they can be milked of electrons.

It was this stubborn virginity of single hydrocarbons that caused the great hiatus in commercial development of the fuel cell. Once the reforming stage was added, however, it became feasible to feed the cells anything that, upon reforming, would yield hydrogen.

Methanol and ethanol both work without preliminary reforming. So-called direct methanol cells, where the fuel is dissolved in the electrolyte, have better operating characteristics than when the methanol is contacted as a gas with the anode. Unfortunately, methanol in solution may decide to swim directly toward the cathode without first giving up its electrons, and will then be chemically oxidized with no electron contribution to the outside circuit. To avoid this behavior, it is necessary only to place between the anode and cathode a semipermeable membrane that refuses to let methanol through but is permeable to water ions and to the electrolyte constituents.

The first fuel cell applications for motor vehicles are (and here I am betting in a horse race) likely to be methanol-fueled units, for public utility trucks.

Two major United States programs for stationary fuel cells have been going on for nearly two decades. The first is the construction and operation of a 4.8-megawatt unit which will lead to the manufacture of larger 27-megawatt stations, each sufficient for an urban locality of 20,000 people. This size would cover the generating needs of 80 percent of the municipal and rural electric power producers in the United States. The program is being carried out by United Technologies and nine United States electric utility companies, backed by the Energy Research and Development Administration of the Electric Power Research Institute.

In addition, the so-called TARGET (for Team to Advance Research for Gas Energy Transformation) program aims to perfect on-site generators of 40-kilowatt capacity for residential, commercial, and industrial application. TARGET consists of a number of gas-supply utilities together with United Technologies. This program, which has now been running for over twelve years, has gained experience from the operation of sixty-five unattended 17.5 kilowatt units during the early 1970s in the United States, Canada, and Japan.

Both systems are based on low-temperature phosphoric acid cells, running on impure hydrogen from steam-reformed hydrocarbons. The systems consist of reformers, power plants and "power-conditioners" (changing direct to alternating current.) One major disadvantage of conventional steam or gas turbine generators is that they operate at severely reduced efficiency under part-load conditions. Fuel cells, on the other hand, are efficient over a range of output levels from 25 to 100 percent of rated output. Lowered current flow through the cells results in decreased resistance losses, and in fact the efficiency actually increases at part load.

The future scenario for the electric power industry (in its own eyes) is to use coal or nuclear main plants, with maybe peak power from fuel cells operating on impure hydrogen from the reforming of coal. I hope this is not true, for it takes us back to our same old dilemmas in air pollution.

Furthermore, the reader will have noticed that in the use of reformed hydrocarbon, the proposition is skipped over quite blithely as if the step were as natural as running water downhill. But reforming is not natural. Granted it is the only way of making hydrocarbon fuels behave in fuel cells, but it involves a greedy and costly use of energy. Cracking or reforming anything demands very fast and prodigal pouring on of heat. Where do you get the heat? Presumably by burning part of the fuel you are reforming. What is the energy balance? There is no visible answer.

The better scenario would be to plan on alcohol fuel cells for the whole operation. *Skip the coal, except as a temporary source of methanol.* Use nuclear energy as a supplement for biomass alcohol.

Scenarios with the alcohol obtained from cellulose and used for both electrical transportation and electricity in the home and factory have all the aspects of the triumph ceremony of ganders. We are now ready to think of other things than energy and pollution. We are on a course that scarcely wavers as the great gas and oil fields drop off to nothing and even the magnificent coal deposits are nibbled to death by mice. We have our future guaranteed and constantly renewed by the sun and chlorophyl.

Now we are ready for the conquest of death and the stars.

Index

INDEX